Anne Doughty is the author of *A Few Late Roses*. Born in Armagh, she was educated at Armagh Girls' High School and Queen's University, Belfast. She now lives in Belfast with her husband. This is her second novel.

Acclaim for *A Few Late Roses*:

'An engaging story of opportunities lost and refound'
Express

'Excellent first novel . . . an ability to capture between the pages the tender beauty of the Armagh country-side . . . Ms Doughty writes with insight and humour . . . For a first novel this book makes a powerful impact'
Irish Independent

'An evocative first novel'   *Manchester Evening News*

'This first novel has a strong sense of a life lived, tensions confronted and overcome . . . a novel full of life-affirming power'
Newcastle upon Tyne Evening Chronicle

'An excellent first novel'   *Ulster Star*

'A strong sense of time and place'   *Northern Echo*

Also by Anne Doughty

A Few Late Roses

Stranger In The Place

Anne Doughty

HEADLINE

First published in 1998
by HEADLINE BOOK PUBLISHING

First published in paperback in 1999
by HEADLINE BOOK PUBLISHING

10 9 8 7 6 5 4 3 2 1

ISBN 0 7472 5822 8

Typeset by
Letterpart Limited, Reigate, Surrey

Printed and bound in Great Britain by
Mackays of Chatham PLC, Chatham, Kent

HEADLINE BOOK PUBLISHING
A division of Hodder Headline PLC
338 Euston Road
London NW1 3BH

For Peter

Chapter 1

As the ten o'clock bus to Lisdoonvarna throbbed its way northwards, my spirits rose so sharply I found it almost impossible to sit still. Brilliant light spilled across the rich green fields, whitewashed cottages dazzled against the brilliant sky and whenever we stopped, people in Sunday clothes climbed up the steep steps, greeted the driver by name and settled down to chat with the other passengers.

How incredibly different my train journey from Dublin to Limerick. Under the overcast sky of a rain-sodden evening, we steamed westwards, stopping at innumerable shabby stations with hardly a soul in sight. I caught glimpses of straggling villages and empty twisting lanes, weaving their way between deserted fields. The further we went, the more I felt the heart of Ireland a lonely place. It was so full of a sad desolation that I longed for the familiar busy streets of the red brick city I had left two hundred miles away.

Through the dirt-streaked windows of the rattling bus, I took in every detail of a landscape that delighted me. Flourishing fuchsia hedges, bright with red tassels, leaned over tumbled stone walls. Cats dozed on sunny windowsills. A dog lay asleep in the middle of the road, so that the bus driver had to sound his horn, slow down, and wait until he moved. In the untidy farmyards, littered with bits of old machinery, empty barrels and bales of straw, hens scratched in the dust clucking to themselves, while beyond, in the long lush grass of the large fields, cattle grazed. They looked as if they came straight out of the box which held the model farm I played with at primary school.

Some hillsides were decorated with sheep, scattered like polka dots on a billowing skirt. There were stretches of bog seamed with stony paths, the new, late-summer grass splashed a vivid green against the dark, regular peat stacks and the purple swathes of heather. I imagined myself making a film to show to my family on a long winter's evening but this country had been excluded from their list. An unapproved country, like an unapproved road, I thought suddenly as we stopped in Ennistymon, in a wide street full of small shops liberally interspersed with public houses.

An hour later, in the Square in Lisdoonvarna, it was my turn to weave my way through the crowd of people waiting to meet the bus. A short distance beyond the rusting vans, the ancient taxi and the ponies and traps by the bus stop, abandoned rather than parked, I spotted a row of summer seats under the windows of a large hotel. They were all unoccupied, so I went and sat down. It was such a relief to have a seat that didn't shake and vibrate every time the driver changed gear.

It was now after one o'clock. As I watched, the bus disappeared in a cloud of fumes, followed at intervals by the other vehicles. In a few moments the Square was completely deserted. I looked around me. Directly opposite was a war memorial, set within a solidly built stone enclosure. The walls were hooped with railings and pierced with silver-painted gates, hung between solid pillars. Each sturdy pillar was capped by a large, flat flagstone, white with bird droppings. Within the enclosure, grass grew untidily around young trees and shrubs already touched with the tints of autumn. Dockens pushed their rusty spikes through the locked gates and dropped their seeds among the sweet papers and ice-cream wrappers drifted against the wall.

Except for the clatter of cutlery in the hotel behind me and the running commentary of the sparrows bathing in the dust nearby, all was quiet. Nothing moved except a worn-looking ginger dog of no specific breed. He trotted purposefully across the red and cream frontage of the Greyhound Bar, lifted his leg against a stand of beachballs outside the shop next door, and disappeared into the open doorway of a house with large, staring sash windows. A faded notice propped against an enormous dark-leaved plant in the downstairs window said 'Bed and Breakfast'.

'What do I do now?' I asked myself.

Just at that moment, the ancient taxi I'd seen collecting passengers from the bus came back into the Square. To my surprise, the driver went round the completely deserted space twice before stopping his vehicle almost in front of me. He got out awkwardly, a tall, angular man in a battered soft hat, looked around him furtively and began to move towards me.

I concentrated on the buildings straight ahead of me, a cream and green guest-house called 'Inisfail', a medical hall, a bar, a grocer's, and a road leading out of town, signposted 'Cliffs of Moher' and 'Public Conveniences'. The bar and the grocer's were part of a much larger building that occupied almost all one side of the Square and extended along the road towards the cliffs and conveniences as well. Against the cream and brown of its walls and woodwork, 'Delargy's

Hotel' stood out in large, black letters.

'Good day, miss. It's a fine day after all for your visit.'

He was standing before me, touching his hand to the shapeless item of headgear he'd pushed back on his shiny, pink forehead. The sleeves and legs of his crumpled brown suit were too short for his build and his hands and feet projected as if they were trying to get out. In contrast, the fullness of his trousers had been gathered up with a leather belt and his jacket hung in folds like a short cloak.

'Ye'll be waitin' for the car from the hotel, miss. Shure, bad luck till them, they've kept you waitin',' he said indignantly.

I shook my head. 'No,' I replied. 'I'm not staying at a hotel.'

'Ah no . . . no . . . yer not.'

He nodded wisely to himself as if the fact that I was not staying at a hotel was plain to be seen. He had merely managed to overlook it. He sat himself down at the far end of my summer seat and for some minutes we studied the stonework of the war memorial in front of us as if the manner of its construction were a matter of some importance to us both.

He turned and smiled again. His eyes were a light, watery blue, his teeth irregular and stained with tobacco.

'Have yer friends been delayed d'ye think? Maybe they've had a pumpture,' he suggested.

He seemed quite delighted with himself for having seen the solution to my problem and he waited hopefully for my reply. It had already dawned on me that I wasn't going to go on sitting here in peace if I didn't give him some account of myself.

I knew from experience that country people have a habit of curiosity based on self-preservation. Strangers create unease until they have been labelled and placed. And he couldn't place me. In his world people who travel on buses and have suitcases are to be met. I had a suitcase, I had travelled on a bus, but I had not been met. I glanced at him as he pushed his hat back further and scratched his head.

'I'm just having a rest before my lunch,' I said, hoping to put him out of his misery. 'I'm going on to Lisnasharragh this afternoon,' I explained easily.

'Ah yes, Lisnasharragh.'

Again, he nodded wisely, but the way he pronounced the name produced instant panic. He'd said it as if he had never heard of it before.

'Ye'll be having a holiday there, I suppose?' he said brightly.

I was slow to reply for I was already wondering what on earth I was going to do if Lisnasharragh had disappeared. It had been there in 1929 all right. On the most recent map I'd been able to get hold of, the houses referred to in the 1929 study I'd found were clearly shown, but that didn't mean they were inhabited now in 1960. Lisnasharragh might be one more village where everyone had died, moved away, or emigrated to America. There had been no way of finding out before I left Belfast.

'No, I'm not on holiday,' I began at last. 'I'm going to Lisnasharragh to do a study of the area,' I explained patiently.

All I wanted was for him to go away and leave me in peace to think what I was going to do about this new problem.

'Are ye, bedad?'

His small eyes blinked rapidly and he leaned forward to peer at me more closely.

'And yer going to write about it all, I suppose, eh?'

He laughed good-humouredly as if he had made a little joke at my expense.

'Well . . . yes . . . I suppose I am,' I admitted reluctantly.

He leapt to his feet so quickly he made me jump. Then he grabbed my suitcase, stuck out his free hand towards me and pumped my arm vigorously.

'Michael Feely at your service, miss. There's no one knows more about this place than I do, the hotels, the waters, the scenery, everything. I'll be happy to assist you in your writings.'

He tossed my heavy suitcase into his taxi as if it were an overnight bag and opened the rear door for me with a flourish.

'You'll be wantin' yer lunch now, miss,' he said firmly. 'I'll take you direct to the Mount. The Mount is the finest hotel in Lisdoon, even if it isn't the largest. All the guests are *personally supervised* by the owner and guided tours of both scenery and antiquities are arranged on the premises for both large and small parties, *with no extra charge for booking.*'

'Thank you, Mr Feely,' I said weakly, as he closed the door behind me.

As he'd taken my suitcase, I couldn't see I had much option. I settled back on the worn leather seat, glanced up at the rear-view mirror and saw his pink face wreathed in smiles. He looked exactly like someone who has struck oil in their own back garden.

The Mount was a large, dilapidated house set in an enormous, unkempt garden where clumps of palm trees and a pair of recumbent lions with weather-worn faces suggested a former glory. He parked the taxi at the back of the house between a row of overflowing dustbins and a newish cement mixer, picked up my case, marched me round to the front entrance, across a gloomy hall and into a dining room full of the smell of cabbage and the debris of lunch.

He summoned a pale girl in a skimpy black dress to remove the greasy plates and uneaten vegetables from a table by the window, pulled out my chair for me and left me blinking in the strong sunlight that poured through the tall, uncurtained windows.

Across the uneven terrace the lions stared unseeing at groups of priests who strolled on the lawns or lounged in deckchairs. Against a background of daisies and dandelions or of striped canvas, their formal black suits looked just as out of place as the bamboo thicket and the Japanese pagoda I could see on the far side of the garden.

My soup arrived. I stared at the brightly coloured bits of dehydrated vegetable floating in the tepid liquid and recognised it immediately. Knorr Swiss Spring Vegetable. One of the many packets my mother uses 'for handiness'. But she does mix it with cold water and leaves it to simmer on a low heat while she's downstairs in the shop. My helping had not been so fortunate. It was full of undissolved lumps. I stirred it with my spoon and wondered what the chances were that Feely would return to supervise me personally while I ate it.

Fortunately he didn't. My untouched bowl was removed without comment. I wasn't expecting much of the main course, so I wasn't too disappointed. Underneath a lake of thick gravy, overlooked by alternate rounded domes of mashed potatoes and mashed carrots, I found a layer of metamorphosed beef. It was tough and tasteless just like it is at home, but I did my best with it. The vegetables weren't too bad and my plate with its pile of gristle was safely back in the kitchen without Feely having reappeared.

I looked around the shabby dining room as I tackled the large helping of prunes and custard that followed. There were now two very young girls, dressed identically in skimpy black skirts, crumpled white blouses and ankle socks, beginning to lay the tables from which lunch had just been cleared. Out of the corner of my eye I watched them brush away crumbs and place paper centrepieces over the stiffly starched cloths. The table next to mine was beyond such treatment. Well-anointed with gravy, the heavy fabric was dragged off unceremoniously to reveal underneath a worn and battered surface ringed with the pale marks of innumerable overflowing drinks.

I smiled to myself and thought of Ben, my oldest friend. How many rings had we wiped up from the oak-finish Formica of the Rosetta Lounge Bar in these last two months? He would miss me tomorrow when there was only Keith in the kitchen and no one to help him with the cleaning and the serving. The thought of doing the Rosetta job on my own appalled me. If it hadn't been for Ben the whole episode would have been grim indeed.

'Hi, Lizzie, what are you doing up so early?'

He greeted me as I stood disconsolately at the bus stop outside the Curzon Cinema waiting for a Cregagh bus. It was the first Monday in July, seven-thirty in the morning. I was sleepy and cross, my period had just started, and I was trying to convince myself it wasn't all a horrible mistake.

'Holiday job up in Cregagh.'

He looked me up and down, took in my black skirt, my surviving white school blouse and the black indoor shoes I'd worn at Victoria.

'It wouldn't by any chance be the Rosetta, would it?' he asked, as he squinted down the road at an approaching double decker.

'How did you guess?'

'Read the same advertisement. That's where I'm for too,' he announced, grinning broadly. 'When I get my scooter back, I can give you a lift. Save you a lot in bus fares.'

I could see how delighted he was and the thought of his company was a real tonic, but something was niggling at the back of my mind.

'But weren't you going to Spalding for the peas, Ben?' I asked uneasily. 'It's far better paid.'

'You're right there,' he nodded. 'But Mum's not well again,' he said slowly. 'She won't see a specialist unless I keep on at her. You know what she's like. So I cancelled and the Rosetta was all I could get. It could be worse,' he grinned. 'It could be the conveniences in Shaftesbury Square.'

When the bus came, we climbed the stairs and went right to the front so we could look into the branches of the trees the way we always did when we were little.

Tinker, tailor, soldier, sailor, rich man, poor man, I counted silently, as I scraped up the last of my custard, but before the prune stones had told me who I was to marry, a cup of coffee descended in front of me and my future disappeared before my eyes.

The coffee was real coffee, freshly made Cona with a tiny carton of cream parked in the saucer. I could hardly believe it. I sipped slowly and went on watching the pale, dark-haired girls as they humped battered metal containers full of cutlery from table to table. At least we didn't have that to do at the Rosetta. The restaurant only opened in the evenings, at lunchtime we only served bar food, sandwiches and things in a basket. But there were other jobs just as boring as the endless laying of tables.

Every morning at eight o'clock, we started on the mess the evening staff had to leave so they could run for the last bus from the nearby terminus. Stacks of dishes, glasses and ashtrays from the bar. After that the staircases and loos to sweep and mop before we started on lunches. That first day, the manageress set us to work separately and by four o'clock when we staggered off to the bus stop we were not only bored but absolutely exhausted. Next morning Ben had an idea.

'C'mon, Lizzie, let's do it all together. I've worked out a system.'

'But what'll we say if she catches us?'

'Wait and see,' he grinned.

I knew there was no use pressing him, because he's good at keeping secrets. You could sooner get blood out of a stone.

We were standing under one of the Egyptian kings who provide the decor at the Rosetta with Ben holding a table on its side and me vacuuming under it, when she appeared.

'I thought you were supposed to be doing the washing-up, Ben,' she said crossly.

'Oh, that's all finished,' said Ben cheerily. 'But you were losing money on it.'

'What? What d'you mean?'

She wrinkled up her brow, peered into the kitchen behind the bar, and saw it was all perfectly clean and tidy.

'Time and motion,' he said easily. 'I did you a complete survey yesterday. No charge of course, it's just a hobby of mine, but when I processed the results last night I really was shocked . . .'

He put the table aside, pulled out a chair and motioned to her to sit down.

'You must never stand while talking to employees, it's bad for your veins. Senior staff must safeguard their well-being, it's one of the first principles of efficient management.'

Standing there with the vacuum cleaner in one hand and a clean duster in the other, I had an awful job keeping my face straight. Ben is a medical student, so he does know about veins; it was the time and motion study that really got me.

But it worked a charm. After that, she left us to do the jobs in whatever way we liked. Often, we even enjoyed ourselves.

As I finished my coffee I began to wonder how much my lunch was going to cost. Just because it wasn't very nice didn't mean it couldn't be expensive. Then there would be the taxi fare to Lisnasharragh and a night in a hotel if I'd got it wrong. Suddenly, I felt very much on my own, a solitary figure in an empty dining room. Ben and the Rosetta and the familiar things in my life were all a very long way away. I was painfully aware of being a stranger in a strange place.

It was some time before Feely breezed in. He ignored my unease about not having had the bill, said the car was at the door and he was all ready to take me to Lisnasharragh. Which way did I want to go?

According to my map, there was only one possible way. I took a deep breath and explained carefully that the village lay at least five miles away on the coast road to the Cliffs of Moher. But it might be as much as six.

I might as well not have bothered. As soon as we were out of town, he dropped to a crawl, following the thin, tarmacked strip of road between wide, windswept stretches of bog. Nothing I said had the slightest effect upon him and we continued to crawl along, furlong by furlong, through totally unfamiliar territory. For once in my life, I was more anxious about the distance itself than about the hole this luxurious journey would be making in my small budget. As each mile clicked up on the milometer, I became more agitated. Once it showed seven miles, I would know I'd got it wrong. Either I had misread my map, or worse still, Lisnasharragh no longer existed.

As we approached the five-mile mark, the bog ended abruptly. On my left the land rose sharply and great outcrops

11

of rock dominated the small fields. On the other side of the road, the much larger fields dropped away into broad rolling country with limestone hills in the distance. Bare of any trace of vegetation, the Hills of Burren stood outlined grey-white against the blue of the sky.

We turned a corner and there ahead of us was the sea. Sparkling in the sun across the vast distance to the horizon, it broke in great lazy rollers over a black, rocky island about a mile from the shore. Beyond this island, in the dazzle of light, like the backs of three enormous whales travelling in convoy, were the Aran islands. Inisheer, Inishman and Inishmore.

My heart leapt in sheer delight. For weeks now these names had haunted me with their magic. Now the islands themselves were in front of me. Nothing lay between me and them except the silver space of the sea. As if a window in my mind had been thrown open, I felt I could reach out and touch something that had been shut away from me. My anxieties were forgotten. The islands were an omen. Now I had found them all would be well.

The road began to climb and as it did, I crossed an invisible boundary onto the map I carried in my mind. I knew exactly where I was.

'It's not far now, Mr Feely,' I said quickly, making no attempt to conceal my relief. 'Down the hill and over the stream. There's a clump of trees to the right and then a long pull up. Maybe we could stop at the top.'

'Ah, shure you've been pulling my leg, miss. Aren't you the sly one and you knows Lisara as well as I do.'

Feely turned to me and laughed. He seemed almost as pleased about finding Lisara as I was. Even the idea that I'd played a trick on him didn't appear to bother him.

'Oh no, Mr Feely, I haven't been here before, truly,' I

assured him as I studied the road ahead. I wished he would look at it himself just occasionally.

'Ye haven't?'

'No.' I shook my head emphatically. 'Not at all.'

'Not at all,' he repeated feebly.

To my great relief, he turned away and corrected our wavering course. I stared around me in disbelief.

For the last two weeks of the summer term, I had spent every day in the departmental library copying maps and reading monographs. In the main library I had found reports from the Land Commissioners and the Congested Districts Board. They were so heavy I could barely carry them down from the stack. I had ploughed my way through acres of fine print. Now, it all seemed irrelevant. Nothing I had done had prepared me for the sheer delight that overwhelmed me as I moved into this unknown country on the edge of the world.

Months ago, when the whole question of theses was being discussed, something told me I had to come here. I'd managed to cobble up some good reasons for coming but it had never occurred to me to think how I might feel when I actually arrived.

It wasn't enough to say that it was beautiful, though I thought the prospect of the islands the most wonderful sight I'd ever seen. It was something much less tangible. However hard I struggled, I could find no words to describe what I felt, not even inside my head.

'Mr Feely, could you stop round the next bend. There's a cottage on the left with a lane down the side of it. We could park there while I have a quick look round.'

As we turned the corner and pulled into the lane, my spirits rose yet further. The cottage was not only trim and neat but it had pale patches in the thatch where it had been mended quite recently. Before we had even bumped to a halt, a young woman appeared at the half-door to see who had turned into the lane. I went and asked her if she could help me at all, told her I was looking for somewhere to stay and assured her I would be no trouble.

'And I'm shure you wouldn't, miss.'

She smiled weakly and fingered a straggling lock of dark hair. She looked strained and tired, her face almost haggard as she stood thinking. She couldn't be much older than I was.

'Shure I'd be glad to have you here, miss, but I'm thinkin' you'd not have much peace for yer work with four wee'ans. Is it the Irish yer learnin'?'

As soon as she opened the half-door a chicken made a dive for the house. As she shooed it away it was clear there would soon be another wee'an to care for.

'I'm thinkin', miss, where ye'd be best off. Is it Lisara ye want?'

'Yes, indeed, but anywhere in Lisara will do.'

It was only as I pronounced the word 'Lisara' for the first time that I realised Lisnasharragh no longer existed. Perhaps it never had existed, except as a name some ordnance surveyor had put in the wrong place, or one he'd found that the local people never used. Whatever the story, Lisara was my Lisnasharragh, alive and well, and exactly where it should be.

'Well, I think ye might try Mary O'Dara at the tap o' the hill. She's a good soul an' they've the room now for all her family's gone. Tell her Mary Kane sent ye.'

She leaned against the whitewashed wall of the cottage, weary with the effort of coming out to talk to me.

'I'll do that right away,' I said quickly. 'If she can have me, perhaps I could come down and talk to you about Lisara.'

'Indeed you'd be welcome,' she said warmly. 'We don't have much comp'ny.'

14

I thanked her and turned back towards the car. To my surprise, she followed me into the bumpy lane.

'I'll see ye again, miss, won't I?'

'You will, you will indeed. Goodbye for now.'

Feely was looking gloomy and when I asked him if we could go up the hill to O'Dara's he just nodded and drove off. I wondered if I'd said something I shouldn't have.

O'Dara's cottage was just as trim and neat as Mary Kane's, but there was a small garden in front of it. A huge pink hydrangea was covered with blooms and there were plants in pots and empty food tins on the green-painted sills of the small windows. Sitting outside, smoking a pipe, was a small, wiry little man with blue eyes, a stubbly chin, and the most striking pink and mauve tie I have ever seen.

'Good day, is it Mr O'Dara?' I asked.

'It is indeed, miss, the same.'

For all my flat-heeled shoes and barely reaching five foot three, I found myself looking down at his wrinkled and sunburnt face when he got to his feet.

'I'm sorry to disturb your nice quiet smoke, Mr O'Dara, but I wonder, could I have a word with Mrs O'Dara? Mrs Kane sent me.'

'Ah, Mary-at-the-foot-of-the-hill.'

He turned towards the doorway and raised his voice slightly. 'Mary, there's a young lady to see you.'

Mary O'Dara came to the door slowly. She looked puzzled and distressed. Her face was blotchy and she had a crumpled up hanky in one hand. I wondered if I should go away again but I could hardly do that when I'd just asked to speak to her.

Her eyes were a deep, dark brown, and despite her distress, she looked straight at me as I explained what I wanted. When I finished, she hesitated, fumbled with the handkerchief and blew her nose.

'You'd be welcome, miss, but I'm all through myself. My daughter's away back to Amerikay, this mornin', with the childer an I don' know whin I'll see the poor soul again.'

She rubbed her eyes and looked up at me. 'Shure ye've come a long ways from home yerself, miss.'

'Yes, but not as far as America. It must be awful, saying goodbye when it's so very far away.' I paused, saddened by her distress. 'Perhaps she'll not be long till she's back.'

I heard myself speak the words and wondered where they'd come from. Then I remembered. Uncle Albert, my father's eldest brother. 'Don't be long till you're back, Elizabeth,' was what he always said to me, when he took me to the bus after I'd been to visit him in his cottage outside Keady.

It was also what everyone said to the uncles and aunts and cousins who appeared every summer from Toronto and Calgary and Vancouver, Virginia and Indiana, Sydney and Darwin. Everybody I knew in the Armagh countryside had relatives in America or Australia.

'Indeed she won't, miss. Bridget'll not forget us,' said her husband energetically. 'Come on now, Mary, dry your eyes and don't keep the young lady standin' here.'

But Mary had already dried her eyes.

'Would you drink a cup o' tea, miss?'

'I'd love a cup of tea, Mrs O'Dara, thank you, but Mr Feely is waiting for me. I'll have to go back to Lisdoonvarna, if I can't find anywhere to stay in Lisara.'

'Ah, shure they'd soak ye in Lisdoonvarna in the hotels,' said Mr O'Dara fiercely. He looked meaningfully at his wife.

'That's for shure, Paddy. But the young lady may not be used to backward places like this.'

'Oh yes, I am, Mrs O'Dara. My Uncle Albert's cottage was just like this and I used to be so happy there. Perhaps I'm backward too.'

Maybe there was something in the way I said it, or maybe it was my northern accent, but whatever it was, they both laughed. Mary O'Dara had a most lovely, gentle face once she stopped looking so sad.

'Away and tell Mr Feely ye'll be stayin', miss.'

She crossed the smooth flagstones of the big kitchen and took a blackened kettle from the back of the stove.

'Paddy, help the young lady with her case.'

She bent towards an enamel bucket to fill the kettle so quickly she didn't see Paddy clicking his heels and touching his forelock. He turned to me with a broad grin as we went out.

'God bless you, miss, ye couldn't 'ive come at a better time.'

Feely sprang to life as Paddy lifted my case from the luggage platform.

'Are ye goin' to stay a day or two, miss?'

'I am indeed, Mr Feely. Two or three weeks, actually.'

'Are ye, begob?'

I was sure I'd told him I needed to stay several weeks, but he looked as if the news was a complete surprise to him. Paddy had disappeared into the cottage with my case, so I set about thanking him for his help.

'I don't know what I'd have done without you, Mr Feely,' I ended up, as I pulled my purse from my jacket pocket and hoped I wouldn't have to go to my suitcase for a pound note.

'Ah no, miss, no,' he protested, waving aside my gesture. 'We'll see to that another time. I'll see ye again, won't I?'

He started the engine and looked at me warily.

'Oh yes, I'll be in Lisdoonvarna often, I'm sure. I'll look out for you. I know where to find you, don't I?'

'Oh you do, you do indeed,' he said hastily. 'Many's the thing you know, miss, many's the thing. Goodbye, now.'

He put his foot down, shot off in a cloud of smoke and reappeared only moments later on the distant hillside. I was amazed the taxi could actually move that fast. Before the fumes had stopped swirling round me, Feely had roared across the boundary of my map and was well on his way back to Lisdoonvarna.

Chapter 2

While I'd been talking to Mary Kane, streamers of cloud had blown in from the sea. Now, as I crossed the deserted road to the door of the cottage where Paddy stood waiting for me, a gusty breeze caught the heavy heads of the hydrangea and brought a sudden chill to the warmth of the afternoon.

'Ah come in, miss, do. Shure you're welcome indeed. 'Tis not offen Mary an' I has a stranger in the place.'

Mary waved me to one of the two armchairs parked on either side of the stove and handed me a cup of tea.

'Sit down, miss. Ye must be tired out after yer journey. Shure it's an awful long step from Belfast.'

She glanced up at the clock, moved her lips in some silent calculation and crossed herself.

'Ah, shure they'll be landed by now with the help o' God,' she declared, as she settled herself on a high-backed chair she'd pulled over to the fire. 'It's just the four hours to Boston and the whole family 'ill be there to meet them. Boys, there'll be some party tonight. But poor Bridget'll be tired, all that liftin' and carryin' the wee'ans back and forth to the plane.'

She fell silent and gazed around the large, high-ceilinged room with its well-worn, flagged floor as if her thoughts were very far away. The sky had clouded completely, extinguishing the last glimmers of sunshine. Even with the door open little light seemed to penetrate to the dark corners of the room. What there was sank into the dark stone of the floor or was absorbed by the heavy furniture and the soot-blackened underside of the thatch high above our heads.

I stared at the comforting orange glow beyond the open door of the iron range. One of the rings on top was chipped and a curling wisp of smoke escaped. As I breathed in the long-familiar smell of turf I felt suddenly like a real traveller, one who has crossed wild and inhospitable territory and now, after endless difficulties and feats of courage, sits by the campfire of welcoming people. The sense of well-being that flowed over me was something I hadn't known for many years.

'Is it anyways?'

The note of anxiety in Mary O'Dara's voice cut across my thoughts. For a moment, I hadn't the remotest idea what she was talking about. Then I discovered you had only to look at Mary O'Dara's face to know what she was thinking. All her feelings were reflected in her eyes, or the set of her mouth, or the tensions of her soft, wind-weathered skin.

'It's a lovely cup of tea,' I said quickly. 'But you caught me dreaming. It's the stove's fault,' I explained, as I saw her face relax into a smile. 'Your Modern Mistress is the same as one I used to know. It's ages since I've seen an open fire. And a turf fire is my absolute favourite.'

'Shure it's not what you'd be used to atall, miss.'

'Don't be too sure of that,' I replied, shaking my head. 'I used to be able to bake soda farls and sweep the hearth with a goose's wing. I'm out of practice, but I'd give it a try.'

'Ah shure good for you,' said Paddy warmly.

He put down his china teacup with elaborate care and

turned towards me a mischievous twinkle in his eyes.

'Now coulden' I make a great match for a girl like you?' he began. 'There's very few these days can bake bread. It's all from the baker's cart or the supermarket.'

I thought of the rack of sliced loaves by the door of my parents' shop. Mother's Pride, in shiny, waxed paper. They opened at eight every morning to catch the night workers coming home and the bread was always sold out by nine. 'A pity we haven't the room to stock more,' said my father. 'Or that the bakery won't deliver two or three times a day.'

Bread was a good line. People came for a loaf and ended up with a whole bag of stuff. Very good for trade. And, of course, as my mother always added, the big families of the Other Side ate an awful lot of bread.

'It was my Uncle Albert down in County Armagh taught me to make bread,' I went on, reluctant to let thoughts of the shop creep into my mind. 'He wouldn't eat town bread, as he called it. In fact, he didn't think much of anything that came from the town. Except his pint of Guinness. His "medicine", he used to call that.'

Paddy O'Dara's face lit up. He looked straight at me, his eyes intensely blue.

'Ah, indeed, miss, every man needs a drap of medicine now and again.'

'Divil the drap,' retorted Mary O'Dara. 'I think, miss, it might be two draps or three. Or even more.'

It was true the arithmetic wasn't always that accurate. I could never remember Uncle Albert being drunk, but he certainly livened up after he'd had a few. That was the best time to get him to tell his stories.

'They're all great men when they've had a few,' she said wryly, as she offered us more tea.

'Ah, no, Mary, thank you. Wan cup's enough.' Paddy got

hurriedly to his feet. 'I'll just away an' see to the goose.'

I smiled to myself, as she refilled my cup. Uncle Albert always went to 'see to the hens' when he'd been drinking.

'I'll have to go and see to the goose myself when I finish this,' I said easily.

'Ah, sure you knew we had no bathroom and I was wonderin' how I would put it to ye.'

Her relief was written so plainly across her face that I wondered if she could ever conceal her feelings. I knew what my mother would say about someone like Mary. Only people with no education showed their feelings. Anyone with a bit of wit knew better. You couldn't go round letting everyone see what you felt even if it meant 'passing yourself' or just 'telling a white lie'.

My mother sets great store by saying the right thing. Most of her stories are about how she put so and so in their place, or gave them as good as she got, or just showed them they weren't going to get the better of her.

Whatever my mother might think I knew Mary was no simple soul. She had a wisdom that I recognised. It was wisdom based on awareness of the world, of its joys and sorrows, of how people managed to live with them. I had known the same kindly, clear-eyed perspective on life for eighteen of my twenty-one years. I had lost it when Uncle Albert died and had not found it again. Until this moment.

'Mrs O'Dara,' I said quickly, 'before Mr O'Dara comes back, you must tell me how much I'm to give you for my keep. Would four pounds a week be enough?'

'Four pounds, miss . . . an' the dear save us . . . I couldn't take your money, shure you're welcome to what we have, if it's good enough for you.'

'It's more than good enough. But I must pay my way,' I insisted quietly.

She had taken a basin from under the table that stood against the outside wall of the cottage and was putting the teacups to drip on the well-wiped oilcloth that covered its surface. She looked perplexed.

'Have you a tea-towel, so I can dry up for you?'

'Shure, two pounds would be more than enough, miss. I don't know your right name.'

'Elizabeth, Elizabeth Stewart.'

'Well, two pounds, Miss Stewart, then, if you want to pay me.'

'Oh you mustn't call me that, Mrs O'Dara. I'm only called Miss Stewart when I'm in trouble with my tutor.'

She laughed gently and pushed a wisp of grey hair back from her face. 'Well, indeed, no one calls me Mrs O'Dara either, savin' the doctor and the priest. Nor Paddy either. Paddy woulden' like me takin' your money, miss . . . I mean Elizabeth.'

'But you're not taking my money. It's just grocery money,' I reassured her. 'I'll tell you what. I'll put it in that teapot on the dresser every week, that wee one with the shamrock on it. You can tell him it was the little people. Say three pounds and we'll split the difference.'

I went and took a striped tea-towel from the metal rack over the stove. Long ago, I had learnt to bargain for goods when I knew they were overpriced. I was good at it. This was the first time I had ever had to bargain upwards. I knew that Mary O'Dara would rather go short herself than exploit someone else. What a fool my mother would think she was not to take all she could get and close her hand on it.

I dried the cups and watched her put them away in the cupboard under the open shelves of the dresser. When she came back to the table, she ran the dish-cloth round the basin inside and out, slid it onto the shelf below, wiped the oilcloth and spread both the dish-cloth and the tea-towel to dry above the stove. She moved slowly, with a slight limp and a hunch in her shoulders that spoke of years of heavy work. But there was no resentment in her movements, neither haste, nor hurry, nor twitch of irritation.

I found myself thinking of a novel I'd read at school. The hero believed that all work properly done was an offering to God. His superiors thought he was mad, but his workmates didn't. They were mechanics and the aircraft they serviced flew better than any others and seldom had accidents. The idea of a practical religion that worked on the principle of love really appealed to me, especially since the only one I was familiar with seemed to work entirely on the principle of retribution.

I smiled to myself. After *Round the Bend* I'd read everything Nevil Shute had written and enjoyed it enormously. Then, when my mother finally realised that he wasn't on the A-level syllabus, there was a furious row. 'Filling my head with a lot of old nonsense,' was what she'd said.

Mary straightened up from the potato sack and came towards me. 'Ah, 'twas my good angel that sent ye to my door today, Elizabeth, for I was heartsore. Sometimes our prayers be answered in ways we never thought of. Draw over to the table an' talk to me, while I peel the spuds for the supper?'

'I will indeed, Mary. But first, I really must go and look at the Aran islands.'

She laughed quietly as Paddy came back into the cottage and I went out, crossing the front of the house in the direction from which he had appeared. Somewhere round that side I'd find a well-trodden path to a privy in an outhouse, or the sheltered corner of a field.

The path led up behind the house, so steeply at first that

there were stone steps cut into the bank. I stopped on the topmost one and found myself looking down on the roof. The cottage was set so close to the hillside, I could almost touch it from my vantage point. The thatch was a work of art. Combed so neatly there was not a straw out of place, it had an elaborate pattern of scalloping like the embroidery on a smock, all the way along the roof ridge, a dense weave to hold it firm against winter storms. Beyond the cottage, fields stretched down to the sea. Under the overcast mass of sky it lay calm and grey, but I could hear the crash of breakers where the long swells born in mid-Atlantic pounded the cliffs, a mere two fields away.

I counted the houses. Seven cottages facing west to the sea, each with turf stacks and smoke spiralling from their chimneys. Four more in various stages of dereliction, their roof timbers fallen, the walls tumbled, grass sprouting from the remains of the thatch. There should be another group of cottages facing south to Liscannor Bay, but from this angle they were hidden by high ground. I breathed a sigh of relief; here below me at least was a remnant of the community I had come in search of, a community once more than a hundred strong.

I stood for some time taking in every detail of the quiet, green countryside, the wide, grey sweep of the sea and the now-dark outlines of the islands. I thought of those who had once lived in the tumbled ruins, those who had been forced to go, those who had endured poverty and toil by remaining. Sadness swirled around me with the wind from across the sea. I knew nothing of these people, of their lives here in Lisara, or beyond in America, and yet some part of me felt as if I had known them, and this place, all my life. As I walked up the hillside, the sadness deepened. It was all the harder to bear because try as I might I could find no reason to explain my feelings.

★ ★ ★

By the time we cleared away the supper things the wind had strengthened and the dark clouds hurled flurries of raindrops onto the flags by the open door. Reluctantly, Paddy put down his pipe and went and closed it.

'I may light the lamp, Mary, for it's gone terrible dark. I think we'll have a wet night.'

'Indeed it looks like it, but shure aren't the nights droppin' down again forby.'

Paddy waited for the low flame to heat the wick and mantle, his face illuminated by the soft glow.

'D'ye like coffee, Elizabeth?'

'I do indeed, Mary, but are you making coffee? Don't make it just for me.'

'Oh no, no. Boys, I love the coffee meself, and Paddy too. Bridget always brings a couple of packets whinever she comes.'

Paddy put the globe back on the lamp and turned it up gently. The soft, yellowy light flowed outwards and the dark shadows retreated. I gazed across towards the corner of the kitchen where heavy coats hung on pegs. There the shadows were crouched against the wall. They huddled too beyond the dresser so that in the darkness I could barely distinguish the sack of flour leaning against the settle bed. But here I sat beyond the reach of the shadows in a warm, well-lit space. I leaned back in my chair and let my weariness flow over me, grateful for the moment that nothing was required of me.

Above my head, the lamplight caught the pale dust on the blackened underside of the thatch. The rafters were dark with age and smoke from the fire. A row of crosses pinned to the lowest rough-hewn beam ran the whole length of the seaward wall. Some were carved from bits of wood, others were woven from rushes now faded to a pale straw colour or smoked to a honey gold. A cross for every year? There were a hundred or more of them.

'I'll just get a wee sup of cream from the dairy.'

The lamp flickered and the fire roared as Mary opened the door and the wild wind poured in around us. As she pulled it shut behind her, I found myself gazing up at a tiny red flame that danced in the sudden draught. Beside it, on a metal shelf a china Virgin smiled benignly down upon the freshly wiped table, her hands raised in blessing over three blue and white striped cups and a vacuum pack of Maxwell House.

'Boys, it would blow the hair off a bald man's head out there,' Mary gasped, as she leaned her weight against the door to close it, a small glass jug clutched between her hands.

'That's a lovely expression, Mary. I don't know that one,' I said, laughing. 'I think Uncle Albert would've said, "It would blow the horns off a moily cow." '

She repeated the phrase doubtfully, while Paddy chuckled to himself. 'Ah Mary, shure you know a moily cow.' He prompted her with a phrase in Irish I couldn't catch. 'Shure it's one with no horns atall.'

She laughed and drew the high-backed chair over to the fire. I jumped to my feet.

'Mary, you sit here and let me have that chair.'

'Ah, no, Elizabeth, sit your groun'. I'm all right here.'

I sat my ground as I was bidden. I was sure I could persuade her to sit in her own place eventually, but it wouldn't be tonight. When Mary did come back and sit in her own place, it would say something about change in our relationship. But that moment was for Mary to choose.

I watched Paddy fill his pipe, drawing hard, tapping the bowl and then, satisfied it was properly alight, lean back. The blue smoke curled towards the rafters and we sat silently, all three of us looking into the fire.

It was not the silence of unease that comes upon those who have nothing to say to each other, rather, it was the silence of those who have a great deal to say, but who give thanks for the time and the opportunity to say it.

We must have talked for two or three hours before Mary drew the kettle forward to make the last tea of the day. Paddy had told me about Lisara and the people who lived there, Mary spoke about their family, the nine sons and daughters scattered across Ireland, England, Scotland and the United States. In turn, I had said a little about the work for my degree, mentioned my boyfriend, George, a fellow student away working in England for the summer, and ended up telling them a great deal about my long summers in County Armagh when I went to stay with Uncle Albert.

It was only when Mary rose to make the tea, I realised I'd said almost nothing about Belfast, or my parents, or the flat over the shop on the Ormeau Road that had been my home since I was five years old.

'Boys but it's great to have a bit of company . . . shure it does get lonesome, Elizabeth, in the bad weather. You'd hardly see a neighbour here of an evening.'

I listened to the wind roaring round the house and reminded myself that this was only the beginning of September.

'It must be bad in the January storms,' I said, looking across at Paddy.

'Oh, it is. It is that. You'd need to be watchin' the t'atch or it would be flyin' off to Dublin. Shure now, is it maybe two years ago, the roof of the chapel in Ballyronan lifted clean off one Sunday morning, in the middle of the Mass.'

He looked straight at me, his eyes shining, his hands moving upwards in one expressive gesture.

'And the priest nearly blowed away with it,' he added, as he tapped out his pipe.

'Oh, the Lord save us,' Mary laughed, hastily crossing herself, 'but the poor man had an awful fright and him with his eyes closed, for he was sayin' the prayer for the Elevation of the Host.'

As she looked across at me, I had an absolutely awful moment. Suddenly and quite accidentally, we had touched the one topic that could scatter all our ease and pleasure to the four winds. I could see the question that was shaping in her mind. It was a fair question and one she had every right to ask, but I hadn't the remotest idea how I was going to reply.

'Would ye be a Catholic now yerself, Elizabeth?'

'No, Mary, I'm not. All my family are Presbyterians.'

'Indeed, that's very nice too. They do say that the Presbyterians is the next thing to the Catholics,' she added, as she passed me a cup of tea.

If she had said that the world was flat or that the Pope was now in favour of birth control, I could not have been more amazed. I had a vision of thousands of bowler-hatted Orangemen beating their drums and waving their banners in a frenzy of protest at her words. I could imagine my mother, face red with fury, hands on hips, vehemently recounting her latest story about the shortcomings of the Catholics who made up the best part of the shop's custom. Try telling her that a Presbyterian was the next thing to a Catholic. I looked across at Mary, sitting awkwardly on the high-backed chair, and found myself completely at a loss for words.

''Tis true,' said Paddy, strongly. 'Wasn't Wolfe Tone and Charles Stuart Parnell both Presbyterians, and great men for Ireland they were, God bless them.'

I breathed a sigh of relief and felt an overwhelming gratitude to these two unknown men. The names I had heard, but I certainly couldn't have managed the short-answer question's prescribed five lines on either of them. The history mistress at my Belfast grammar school was a Scotswoman, a follower of Knox and Calvin. She had no time at all for the struggles of the Irish, their disorderly behaviour, their revolts, their failure to recognise the superior values of the British Government.

When she had made her choice from the history syllabus, she chose British history, American history and Commonwealth history. I could probably still describe the make-up of the legislatures of Canada, India or South Africa, and bring to mind the significant figures in the history of each, but I knew almost nothing about a couple of men who were merely 'great men for Ireland'.

Yesterday, when the Hendersons had given me a lift to Dublin they had dropped me by the river within walking distance of the station. Under the trees, I gazed across the brown waters of the Liffey at a city I knew not at all. I had been to Paris and to London with my school, travelled in Europe on a student scholarship, visited Madrid, and Rome, and Vienna, but I had never been to Dublin. My parents had raised more objections to my coming to Clare than to my spending two months travelling in Europe.

It was pleasant under the trees, the hazy sunlight making dappled patterns on the stonework, a tiny drift of shrivelled leaves the first sign of the approaching autumn. I liked what I saw, the tall, old buildings with a mellow, well-used look about them, the dome of some civic building outlined against the sky, the low arches of the bridge I would cross on my way to the station.

'A dirty hole,' I heard my father say. 'Desperate poverty,' added my mother. Neither of them had ever been there.

I sat on my bench for as long as I dared before I set off to catch the last through-train to Limerick. Just as I reached the bridge, I saw the name of the quay where I had been sitting. 'Wolfe Tone Quay,' it said in large letters.

Mary took two candlesticks from the mantelshelf above the stove and I stirred myself. Paddy turned the lamp down and the waiting shadows leapt into the kitchen, swallowing it up, except for the tiny space where the three of us stood beside the newly lighted candles. Paddy blew down the mantle of the lamp to make sure it was properly out.

'Goodnight Elizabeth, astore. Sleep well. I hope you'll be comfortable,' said Mary, handing me my candle.

'Goodnight, Elizabeth. Mind now the pisherogues don't get you and you sleeping in the west room,' said Paddy. 'And you might hear the mice playing baseball in the roof. Pay no attention, you'll not disturb them atall,' he added with a grin.

'Come on, old man, it's time we were all in bed.'

He laughed and followed her towards the brown door to the left of the fireplace.

'Goodnight, and thank you both. It was a great evening,' I said, as I pointed my candle into the darkness at the other end of the kitchen.

I pressed the latch of the bedroom door, pushed it open, and reached automatically for the light switch. Of course, there wasn't one. My fingers met a small, cold object which fell off the wall with a scraping noise. As I brought my candle round the door, I saw another china Virgin. This one was smaller than the one in the kitchen and from her gathered skirts she was spilling Holy Water on my bed.

Thank goodness, no harm done. I put her back on the nail and swished the large drops of water away from the fat, pink eiderdown before they had time to sink in. The room was cold and the wind howling round the gable made it seem colder still. I undressed quickly, the linoleum icy beneath my

31

feet when I stepped off the rag rug to blow out the candle on the washstand. The pillowcase smelt of mothballs and crackled with starch under my cheek as I curled up, arms across my chest, hugging my warmth to me.

'And don't say the bit about getting my death of cold sleeping in a damp bed. It isn't damp. Just cold. And it will soon warm up.'

I laughed at myself for addressing my mother before she could get in first. She had beaten me to it last night in Limerick. Oh, the predictability of it. Like those association tests my friend Adrienne Henderson did in psychology. She said a word and you had to respond without thinking. My parents were good at that. I knew the key words. Or more accurately, I spent my life avoiding them. If I accidentally tripped over one, I could be sure I would get a response as predictable and consistent as a tape-recording.

The smell of the snuffed candle floated across to me. I was back in the small upstairs room of Uncle Albert's cottage. The candle wax made splashes on the mahogany furniture and I picked them off with my fingernails, moulded them and made water-lilies to float on the rainwater barrel at the corner of the house. Suddenly, I was there again, a ten-year-old, sent to 'the country' for the holidays.

Being ten years old didn't seem at all strange. I lay in the darkness, wondering if I would always be able to remember what it was like to be ten. Would I be able to do it when I was thirty, or forty, or fifty? Or would some point come in my life where I would begin to see things differently? For as long as I could remember, my parents, my relatives and those neighbours who were 'our side' had all assured me that when I was 'grown up', or 'a little older', or 'had a family of my own', I would come to see the world as they did. The thought appalled me.

Was it really possible that I could end up locked into the kind of certainty that permeated all their thinking? They always knew. They were sure. Indeed they were so sure, I regularly panicked that I would come to think as they did. What if there was nothing to be done to stop the process? What would I do if I found that thinking as they did was like going grey, or needing spectacles, or qualifying for a pension, one of those things that was as inevitable as the sun rising tomorrow.

As I began to feel warm I uncurled and lay on my back. Moonlight was flickering from behind dark massed clouds and gradually my eyes got used to the luminous glow reflected from the pink-washed walls. I distinguished the solid shape of the wardrobe at the foot of my bed and the glint of the china jug on the washstand. Then, quite suddenly, for a few moments only, the room was full of light. In the brightness, I saw a large, grey crucifix on the distempered wall above me. Crucifixes and Holy Water. Even more to be feared than a damp bed.

The room settled back to darkness once more and I closed my eyes. The door latch rattled and stopped. Then rattled again. Perhaps I wouldn't have to change after all. Perhaps I could just go on being me at twenty-one, or thirty-one, or any age, till I was so old there would be no one left older than me, to tell me what I ought to think. There was a scurry of feet in the roof. The wind whined round the gable and the door latch rattled again. The scurrying increased. Mice, of course.

And pisherogues. I had not the slightest idea what a pisherogue was. But whatever it turned out to be, it would not harm me. Indeed, in this unknown place at the edge of the world, I felt as if nothing could harm me. Tomorrow, I would ask Paddy what a pisherogue was and make a note about it. I was going to make lots and lots of notes. In the blue exercise books I had brought with me. Tomorrow.

Chapter 3

After three days tramping the lanes and fields of Lisara I was looking forward to my walk into Lisdoonvarna on Thursday afternoon. Paddy was sure I'd get a lift, but as I strode along, turning over in my mind all I'd learnt since my arrival, the only vehicles that overtook me were full of children and luggage. I was very glad when they waved and left me to the quiet of the sultry afternoon.

As I reached the outskirts of the town and turned up the hill by the spa wells, I was surprised to find there were people everywhere. Preoccupied and distracted, they wandered over the road, walked up and down to the well buildings and streamed back and forth to the Square. After the emptiness of the countryside and the company of my own thoughts, the sudden noise and bustle hit me like a blow. I wove my way awkwardly between family parties, strolling priests, and bronzed visitors, only to find that the Square too was completely transformed.

The empty summer seats were now packed with brightly coloured figures. Close by, a luxury coach unloaded a further consignment. Clutching handbags and carrier bags, beach bags and overnight bags, they queued erratically beside a small mountain of luggage and reclaimed matching suitcases from a uniformed courier.

I'd been planning to sit down for a bit but now even the stone wall of the war memorial was fringed by families eating ice-creams. Nothing for it but the first grassy bank on the way home.

The queue for the post office greeted me on the broken pavement outside. It moved slowly forward. When I finally got inside the door the smell of damp and dry rot caught at my nostrils. The place hadn't seen a paintbrush for years, the walls were yellowed with age and seamed with cracks. Behind a formidable metal grille, an elderly lady with iron-grey hair and spectacles despatched stamps and thumped pension books with dogged determination, apparently unconcerned by the queue of restless women with coppery tans, white trousers and suntops in violent shades of lime-green and pink.

I shuffled forward on the bare wooden floor. In front of me, an old lady cast disapproving glances at two women writing postcards on the tiny ledge provided. She glared at their bare shoulders and arms and the skimpy tops that revealed their small, flat breasts. Despite the heavy warmth of the afternoon, she was wearing a black wool coat and a felt hat firmly skewered to her head with large, amber hatpins.

The woman behind me fidgeted impatiently and shuffled her postcards as if she were about to deal a hand of whist.

'Gee, you Irish girls sure do have lovely complexions. How come you manage it?'

Her voice so startled me, I must have jumped a couple of inches but I went on watching the postmistress counting out money for the old lady, a pound note and some silver coins. Could her pension possibly be so small?

I felt a tap on my shoulder. When I turned round she was looking down at me. Waiting. Pinned to her suntop was a button which said: 'I'm Adele from New York City . . . Hi.'

'I think it's probably the climate,' I said, awkwardly.

The moment I spoke I knew it was 'my school teacher voice'. George often says I must never become a teacher. Women who do always lose their femininity and he couldn't bear that. He loves me just as I am so I mustn't ever change.

'D'you mean all that there rain we had in Killarney lass' week?'

She looked baffled, but something in her manner suggested she would not give up easily. People were turning to look at us and I felt my 'Irish' complexion grow a few shades more rosy.

'I think it's the dampness of the air here.'

I tried to sound suitably casual, but I just sounded lame. What else could I say? I could hardly explain the adaption of skin colour and texture to environmental features, could I? What on earth would George say if I did that?

'Gee, you Irish girls do talk cute.'

She beamed indulgently and gazed around at the women writing postcards, delighted to have got one of the natives to perform.

I was saved from further questions by the little lady in black who pushed past me, handbag firmly clutched in both hands, leaving me to face the postmistress who stared at me fiercely as I handed over my letters.

'You'd be a friend of Mrs O'Dara, then?'

I nodded awkwardly. Of course Mary and I were friends, but I knew that wasn't what she meant.

'I'm staying with Mr and Mrs O'Dara for a few weeks,' I said quickly. 'I'm a student.'

'We don't get many students here,' she said suspiciously. 'Is it the Irish yer learnin'?'

'Only the odd wee bit from Mr O'Dara. I'm really studying farming.'

That sounded a bit schoolmistressy too. Behind me, the queue was building up again and Adele from New York City was breathing down my neck.

'And that's nice fer ye too,' she said decisively, as she studied the envelope addressed to Mr and Mrs William Stewart.

'You'd be wanting to let yer paren's know ye was safely landed, indeed,' she said severely, as she turned her attention to my letters to George and Ben, and my thank you to the Hendersons.

'Oh, I did write letters on Monday, but Paddy the Postman took them for me.'

'Indeed, shure he wou'd take them for you, and why wou'dn't he?'

Her face crinkled into a grimace that looked like a friendly gesture, though I could hardly call it a smile.

'I'll be seein' ye again, Miss Stewart, won't I?'

'Oh yes, you will indeed. I'll be doing the shopping while I'm here.'

I was so glad to escape the smell of Adele's Ambre Solaire that I set off back to the Square at a brisk trot. But I had to slow down. Apart from the ache in my legs, the afternoon was getting hotter by the minute. Huge clouds were building up in threatening grey masses and it felt warm, sticky and airless.

The windows of the hotel with the summer seats had been thrown wide but there wasn't the slightest trace of a breeze. The net curtains hung motionless and I could see into the dining room where small black figures moved to and fro. Like the pale, dark-eyed girls I'd seen at the Mount, these girls were equally young, straight from school at fourteen.

I thought about them as I waited in the queue at the butcher's, drawing circles in the sawdust with my toe. I too

might have left school at fourteen if I hadn't passed the
Eleven Plus. Even then, I still might have had to leave if it
hadn't been for the Gardiners.

'Did ye hear that Mrs Gardiner today, bumming again?'

I was back in my bedroom in Belfast on a summer evening
towards dusk, reading in the last of the light. My parents had
come out into the yard behind the shop. There was a rattle as
my father filled his old metal can so he could water the
geraniums and the orange lilies which he grew in empty fuel
oil cans he'd brought home from Uncle Joe's farm. It was the
beginning of July, for the lilies were in flower but hadn't yet
been taken to the Lodge to decorate the big drums for the
Twelfth.

'Oh yes, she was in great form, and the whole shop full.
Did ye not hear? Ah don't know how ye cou'da missed her.'

The reply was indistinct. My father always speaks quietly.
Often, he just nods or grunts.

'There'll be no standin' that wuman, if that wee girl of hers
goes to Victoria an' our Elizibith doesn't.'

Eavesdroppers hear no good of themselves, I thought to
myself. But there wasn't much I could do about it. The
window was wide open and they were right underneath.

'Well, if Bill Gardiner is going to send that wee scrap of a
girl, why shouldn't we send our Elizibith,' my mother went
on. 'None of the Gardiners have any brains worth talkin'
about an' that shop of theirs is only a huckster of a place, not
even on the main road. It won't look well at all, Willy, if we
don't send her. People'll think our shop's not doin' well. I
think we should just send her. We're every bit as good as the
Gardiners. We'd have done it for wee Billy for sure.'

I stuck my fingers in my ears, for I hated them talking
about wee Billy and I knew that was wicked. You shouldn't
hate your brother, especially if he was dead. The trouble was

it didn't feel as if he was dead. They were always talking about him, what he liked and disliked, what he used to say, what age he would be his next birthday if he'd lived, where he would be going to school, or even what flowers they would take when they next visited the cemetery where he was buried. My Aunt Maisie once said to me that it was a pity I hadn't been a boy, for Florrie would never get over wee Billy now and her too old to have another.

I lifted Mary's shopping bag onto the counter and let the red-faced man put the brown-paper parcel inside. The butcher's counter was marble and the one in the shop was wood. I imagined myself standing behind it in a pink, drip-dry, nylon shop coat like my mother's, handing out papers and cigarettes and penny lollipops, ringing up items on the till, running up the rickety stairs to the stockroom for a new box of Polo mints, or a fresh carton of Players.

He counted out my change slowly, made a mistake and corrected himself. His fingers were smeared with blood. My father's fingers were yellowed with nicotine, the nails cut short to keep them clean. I could see him as he spread the day's takings on the table each evening. Piles of silver, mounds of copper, creased pound notes, and the occasional papery fiver which he held up to the light to make sure it was all right. Business was good, he would admit as he counted. Never better, my mother would agree. Everyone has money these days, she would continue, especially the Other Side.

It was the Other Side's money that let me stay at school to take A-levels. Then my scholarship had taken me to Queen's. After seven years passing the back of the students' union every day on my way to school, I got off the bus one stop earlier and stepped into a different world. It was luck. Pure luck. I had my books and my hopes for the future, these girls had their skimpy black skirts and their long hours of hard, poorly paid work.

'Well then, how do you fancy a career in catering?' Ben and I were sitting in our usual seats at the top of the double decker, our first week's pay envelopes torn open on our knees.

'Not a lot,' I replied. 'If this was all you had to live on you wouldn't have much of a life, would you?'

'No, not even if there were two of you and there was equal pay.'

I laughed wryly and counted the crumpled notes in my hand. We had worked so hard, sharing the same dreary jobs, working the same long hours. Ben had ten pounds, I had only seven.

'It's one thing if you're earning book money,' he went on, stuffing the notes into his pocket, 'it's another if it's all you've got. Are you going to have enough for going to Clare, Lizzie?'

I'd reassured him that I'd be fine for I knew he'd offer to help me. I couldn't let him do that for I knew what he was planning to buy. The newly published book he hoped might help him to make sense of his mother's condition would cost several weeks' work.

'It's exploitation, Ben, isn't it? But what can one do? What can anyone do?'

'Political action, Lizzie. Probably the only way. But that's not my way. It needs a particular sort of mind and I know I haven't got it. I'll have my work cut out to make a decent doctor. What about you?'

I told him I didn't really know about me.

The first thing I noticed as I opened the door of Delargy's shop was the smell. This time, unlike the post office, it brought the happiest of memories: small shops in Ulster, in villages where I had done messages for various aunts, places where you could buy everything from brandy balls and humbugs to groceries and grass seed, packets of Aspros and pints of Guinness. There had been many such places in my childhood and I had loved them all.

Surprisingly, the shop was empty but for a single customer, the little lady in the black coat whose hatpins I'd studied closely in the post office queue. A pleasant-faced girl in a blue overall had come from behind the counter to pack her shopping bag. As she fitted in the packets of tea and sugar, she listened sympathetically to what the old lady was saying.

'And they want to put me out and knock the whole row down.'

'But Mrs McGuire dear, they'll have to give you a new house, or one of the bungalows. Wouldn't that be nice for you now, and no stairs to climb?'

The girl glanced at me and made a slight move as if to come and serve me but I shook my head. 'I'm not in a hurry. Do you mind if I have a look round?'

'Do, miss, do. I'll be with you shortly.'

We exchanged glances over the head of Mrs McGuire, who was completely absorbed in her problem. Indeed, they were very nice, she agreed. And a nice price too. Where would she get seventeen shillings rent out of her pension?

I moved away in case my presence would disturb them and began to examine the contents of the long, low-ceilinged room. A solid wooden counter ran the whole length of one side. Behind it, shelves filled with packets and boxes rose to the ceiling, except at a central point where a large clock with dangling weights ticked out the separate minutes of the day. Against the counter leaned bags of dried goods, barley and rice, lentils and oatmeal, each with its polished metal scoop thrust into the mouth of the sack ready to measure into the pan of the shiny brass scales on the counter. Beyond the end of the counter, a low-arched doorway led into a passage which gave access to the stable yard outside.

On the opposite wall was the bar. Empty now. But the fluorescent light was on. It reflected in the rows of bottles and glinted off the well-polished seats of the high stools. At the furthest end of the bar, a new Italian coffee machine had just been installed. It sat, still partly draped in its polythene wraps, looking across the worn floorboards to a stand of wellington boots and a rack of Pyrex ware.

I wandered around slowly. Who would buy the bottles of DeWitts Liver Pills, the mousetraps with the long-life guarantee, the shamrock-covered egg-timers, the hard yellow bars of Sunlight soap? And what would the same people make of the contents of the freezer, tucked between a pile of yard-brushes and a display unit of the blue and white striped delft I'd met at the cottage. Prawn curry. Chicken dinner for two. French beans and frozen strawberries. Unlikely substitutes for the bacon and cabbage, the champ, or the stew Mary had cooked for our supper on these last evenings.

Below a small counter laid out with newspapers and magazines, I found some exercise books. The notebooks I'd brought with me were filling up rapidly and these had the wide-spaced lines I liked. As I turned one over to look for the price, I heard voices in the passage leading to the stable yard.

'Now don't worry, Moyra. You concentrate on Charles and I'll see to the stock. Paddy knows what's needed here and Mrs Grogan won't let you down in the hotel.'

There was a woman's voice too, light and pleasant but further away.

'I'll come in this evening to make sure all is well, but I won't come up to you. You look tired yourself.'

The voice intrigued me. It had something of the intonation of the voices I'd been hearing all around me since I arrived, but it was more formal. With her sharp ear for social distinctions, my mother would pronounce the owner either 'educated' or 'good class', depending on the mood she was in.

'Are you all alone, Kathleen?'

I glimpsed the figure who strode across the empty shop to where Kathleen had just closed the door behind Mrs McGuire. I busied myself with the stand of postcards as he followed her glance.

'It went quiet a wee while ago, so I let May and Bridget go for their tea,' she explained. 'They hardly got their lunch atall we were so busy. It's teatime in the hotels, that's why it's gone quiet.'

He nodded as he listened to her. I had the strange feeling he was watching me out of the corner of his eye. A rather striking man. What some people might call handsome. A strongly shaped face, rather tanned, dark, straightish hair. He seemed to tower over Kathleen who was about my own height.

'I've been talking to Mrs Donnelly and I've told her I'll take care of the stock till Mr Donnelly is better. Would you let me have a note of anything you can think of. It's so long since I've done the ordering I shall probably be no good at all.'

Kathleen laughed easily at the idea and said she'd start a list right away. He moved towards the door leading out into the Square and then, as if he had forgotten something, he turned and walked back towards me.

'I'm afraid the selection isn't very good,' he said, as I looked up from the postcards. 'We've some new colour ones on order from John Hinde, but there seems to be some delay.'

His eyes were a very dark brown and he was looking at me carefully, as if he was possessed by the same curiosity I had come to expect, but was too well-mannered to let it show.

'I don't honestly think they do justice to the place,' I replied, nodding at the inexpensive sepia cards on the stand. 'I'm glad you're getting the John Hinde, he's done some very good ones of Donegal.'

'But you don't come from Donegal, do you?' he replied promptly. 'I'd have thought it was more likely to be Armagh or Down myself.'

I had to laugh. Partly because it's a game I play myself, placing people by their accent, and partly because he was so accurate. Even after growing up in Belfast, my accent hadn't lost the markings of my earliest years when we lived with my grandparents down near the Armagh-Monaghan border.

'You're not far wrong,' I admitted, smiling at him. 'Very near in fact, but I live in Belfast now.'

'Yes,' he agreed, 'and you're staying with Paddy and Mary O'Dara at Lisara.' He held out his hand and made me a small bow. 'Miss Elizabeth Stewart, I presume. Patrick Delargy at your mercy.'

'How on earth did you know that?'

His hand was warm and firm and he was smiling broadly.

'Kathleen, come over here a moment. Come and meet the lady herself. Does she answer the description we had of her?'

Kathleen hurried over.

'Oh, miss, you made us all laugh, you did indeed. Didn't you put the fear of God into Michael Feely on Sunday. I hear he's not the better of it yet.'

Patrick Delargy leaned himself comfortably against the side of the freezer. 'I missed all the fun,' he said sadly. 'Kathleen had better tell you the whole story.'

'Ah miss, poor Feely came in here on Sunday evening and

we thought he had seen a ghost,' she began, her face horror-stricken.

I was so worried by the look on her face and the thought that I'd upset Michael Feely that I turned to Patrick Delargy to see how he was reacting. He appeared to be enjoying himself thoroughly.

'He came in here,' she repeated, 'and the bar full and he swore he had met a witch.'

Her tragic expression crumpled and she giggled. Patrick Delargy shook his head. 'Now, come on, Kathleen, this won't do. Tell Miss Stewart the story the way you told me.'

With an effort, Kathleen gathered herself.

'Yes, indeed. A witch. That's what he had met. And it took two large whiskeys before he could go on.'

I opened my mouth to protest, but Patrick Delargy held up a warning finger. Kathleen was not to be interrupted.

'He said that he had taken a student out to Lisara, a nice enough young lady and very well-spoken. And he says that she told him she had never been in the place before and didn't know anybody and didn't even know if the place was still there. And he said he believed her, for she was a very nice young lady and good-looking forby.'

She nodded towards me as much as to say, 'Now there's a compliment for you.'

'And then he says, he takes her out to look for this place she's never been to and the next thing is that she starts to tell him where every house and tree is and where he can park his taxi. And she knows every stone and bush of the place as if she'd been born and reared there.'

'But I'd only been reading the map . . .'

'Ach, sure, what would Michael Feely know about maps, miss? The man has no wit.'

Patrick Delargy was watching us both, a broad grin on his

face. 'What about bewitching Paddy O'Dara?'

'I was coming to that, Mr Delargy, I hadn't forgotten atall,' she reprimanded him.

'Apparently, miss, you went into O'Dara's cottage with Paddy, and you'd never set eyes on the man before. No relative, not even a far-out friend, and the next thing, back you come with Paddy as meek as a lamb to carry your case and you to stay for three weeks.'

Kathleen could certainly get value out of a story. When she imitated the look on Feely's face, I had to laugh myself.

'I do hope I didn't really upset him. I did try to explain. But he does jump to confusions, doesn't he?'

'He does that, miss. Whatever way you would put it plain, he always gets the wrong way of things.'

'But it was a serious case,' added Patrick Delargy, the light in his eye at odds with the soberness of his expression. 'I'm not sure how many whiskeys he was bought to help him over the shock and to elicit the full extent of his distress.'

'I think at one stage he thought I was going to write a book about his hotel,' I offered.

'Oh, he did, he did indeed,' Kathleen nodded vigorously, as the shop door opened and two girls in blue overalls appeared, followed by a group of visitors and a cluster of children. She left us to go back behind the counter. Patrick Delargy looked at me quizzically.

'And how are you proposing to get back to Lisara, Elizabeth? By broomstick?'

There were grey hairs on his temples and above his ears. His tie was one of those tweedy, handwoven ones with little irregular blobs of colour where the thread is thick. Like the one I'd nearly bought George for his birthday. Lucky I hadn't. When I showed him one in a shop window, a lovely yellowy mix, he said it looked just like scrambled egg.

'No, actually,' I replied, glancing at my watch, 'I must get a move on. The meat for supper's here in my bag, and I still have bacon to get from Kathleen.'

'Right. You get the bacon and I'll bring the car round. It's going to rain long before you get to Lisara. You do know about witches and water, don't you?'

Without another word, he disappeared down the passage and into the stable yard.

The car was the largest I had ever seen. It was American and very new. The front seat was long and squashy and the shelf above the dashboard wide enough to lay out a whole picnic. When Patrick Delargy settled himself behind the wheel, his solid frame seemed somehow smaller and a remarkably long way away. He drove slowly out of the Square, manoeuvred round a pony and trap abandoned in the middle of the road, paused for a group of visitors who appeared quite unaware they were strolling on a main road and stopped twice for pedestrians who simply crossed the road without looking.

I remembered an article I'd once read in a women's magazine about assessing a man's character by the way he drove. Patrick Delargy certainly scored well on patience. I saw him relax as he turned right at the crossroads beyond the wells.

'This is not exactly the best car for driving through Lisdoonvarna in September, I fear,' he said with a slight, apologetic smile.

I was puzzled by the car. The best word to describe it was opulent. And that was right out of key with its owner who was in no way opulent, either in dress or in manner.

'Well, it is rather large,' I agreed cautiously.

'Large, oversprung, difficult to handle and expensive to run. It was also a gift. What would you do?'

'I see the problem,' I began sympathetically. 'I used to have an aunt who gave me the most ghastly blouses for Christmas. I always had to wear them when she came to visit so as not to hurt her feelings. I do wish people would just sometimes ask what you really want and not just assume they know.'

He looked at me briefly but very directly, something he had done several times already. I was beginning to find it most disconcerting. Until I came to Lisara, I had found few people ever bothered to look at me and even fewer who paid the slightest attention to my reactions. As I met his gaze I knew I'd spoken far more sharply than I intended.

'Don't people ask you what you want either, Elizabeth?'

'No, not usually. My family all seem to know exactly what I want without any help from me. They then get upset if I point out that it's not what I want at all.'

'And what happens then?'

'Oh, a row of some sort.'

I couldn't for the life of me see how we'd managed to get ourselves into a conversation about my family. I was anxious to change the subject.

'Was it your family's idea that you came to Lisara?'

'You must be joking.'

'Well, I did rather wonder. Most of the Ulstermen I know think the west is a wild, barbarous place.'

'Do you know many Ulstermen then?' I asked, my curiosity getting the better of me.

'Not so many now. Years ago, I had cousins at Trinity when I was at U.C.D. I used to visit the north in the long vacations. My mother had relatives in Fermanagh.'

'What did you read?'

'English literature. Only for two years though. I had to give it up.'

His eyes were on the road ahead, but the soft tone in his voice and the set of his face spoke with more feeling than the words themselves. I wanted to ask why but something held me back. After all, I hardly knew him. I nodded and said nothing.

'My father died and then my brother was killed. Someone had to take over at home. So I packed up my books and became the squire.' He turned towards me, touched his forelock and mumbled, 'Yes, sur, no, sur.' He sounded just like an ancient retainer in a sentimental, Irish comedy.

I laughed aloud, delighted by the accent and gestures which were so exactly right.

'And what about the books?'

He had made me laugh, but beyond his mimicry I felt the shadow of painful memories.

'I still read. Oh, not as much as I'd like. But some. Have you read Tolstoy, Elizabeth?'

'Oh yes, but only *Anna Karenina* so far. I thought that was splendid, though I didn't like Vronsky and I just couldn't understand Anna. Kitty and Levin were much more interesting. I really felt for Levin.'

'So you like Tolstoy?'

'Yes, I suppose I do, but I shouldn't really say that.'

'Whyever not?'

'My English teacher used to say you couldn't possibly "like" a writer on the evidence of one book. You had to study the range of his work. But I liked Tolstoy from chapter one. I'm afraid it's a weakness of mine, I make up my mind far too quickly. That's what happened with the islands.' I waved my hand towards the familiar shapes which lay darkly below the massed thunderclouds. 'The minute I saw the islands, I knew I would be happy here.'

He pulled across the road at a point where it widened and

had a broad grass verge. He angled the car so that we were looking out straight across the turbulent white-capped water.

'Funny you should say that,' he replied. 'I always stop here on my way to Limerick and have a think. Perhaps the distance lends a certain perspective.'

His eyes were fixed on the far horizon where silvery rays pierced the dark storm clouds. A gust of wind spilled round the car, buffeting it as a curtain of rain descended, pattering on the roof. In a few moments, the islands had disappeared and we heard the first rumbles of thunder. I wondered what he meant about distance lending a certain perspective.

He turned abruptly and smiled at me.

'I must take you home, Elizabeth, or the locals will have us married off by tomorrow. I expect you've worked out what small communities are like by now.'

I nodded vigorously and told him about a man on a turf cart passing the cottage, who greeted me by name, and the way the postmistress had checked me out.

'I used to spend a lot of time in the country before I went to Queen's, but I've not been there very much these last few years. I've forgotten things I used to know. I haven't got my lines right yet. But I keep remembering things all the time.'

'I take it the work is going well.'

'Far better than I expected. My tutor really did lay it on about me being a woman and a Protestant in a male-dominated, Catholic community. He advised me not to come.'

'But you came anyway?'

'I was lucky. My tutor changed. The new one is an anthropologist and she's just come back from fieldwork with the Masai. She didn't see any problem.'

'Have you managed to get any figures for acreages and landholdings?'

'Oh yes. But I did explain I wasn't from the income tax or the Land Commission, that I just needed them for my examinations. They were very good about it.'

He shook his head ruefully. 'I think perhaps Michael Feely was right. You're the first person I've ever heard of who's got any real information out of them. I've known these people all my life and all I get is a version of the truth.'

'Yes, but you are the squire.' I touched my forelock and said 'Yes, sur, no, sur,' just as he had done, but I couldn't get the accent quite right. 'And I'm only a student who'll pass the time of day for a week or two and then disappear for ever. They can afford to be generous. I don't threaten them, because I'm only a stranger in the place.'

'You don't have the feel of a stranger,' he said promptly. 'You have the feel of someone very much at home here.'

He stopped outside the cottage and looked across at me.

'Yes, I am. I'm far more at home here than I ever am in Belfast. I'm trying to work out why. It's far harder than the land-use bit.'

'Will you apologise to Mary and Paddy for me? I must get back. Will you be in on Saturday?'

'Yes, I expect so. It's easier for Mary, if I do the shopping.'

'Come and see me when you've finished,' he said, as he came round and opened the door for me. 'I'll be shut up with the stock books, Kathleen will show you where. I'll be needing a spell or two by then.'

'Thank you for bringing me home. If I come on Saturday, I shall pester you with questions,' I warned him, as he walked back round to the driver's side.

'I shall look forward to that.'

He raised a hand and was gone.

Mary was standing in the middle of the kitchen with the empty kettle in one hand and the tin mug she used for filling it in the other. 'Boys, Elizabeth, was that Patrick Delargy's car I saw outside? That hyderange has grown so high I can't see a thing these days.'

'It was indeed, Mary. He gave me a lift back, for he said it would rain. Wasn't it nice of him?'

'It was, it was that, but shure he's a very nice man altogether.'

She stood peering out of the door. 'He's a great one for books, like yourself,' she said, as if the thought had floated in with the exhaust fumes of his departure.

'We were talking about books. He said he'd been to college, but had to leave.'

'Aye, he did, poor soul. Shure, it was a tragedy. First his father died, and then Walter was killed and their poor mother an invalid. They say she died of a broken heart. Poor lady, she was kindness itself.'

As I started unpacking the shopping on the table, she went to the bucket of spring water and filled the kettle.

'What happened to Walter?'

'Ah, it was a fall. He was a great man for the hunting. The whole family were great for horses, but Walter was mad about them. Well, it was the Boxing Day meet and he had this new horse. They say Patrick advised him not to ride it with the ground so hard. Oh, that was a bad year, Elizabeth. I found a wee bird in the haggard frozen with cold and I put it in a box near the stove, but it died, poor thing.'

She pulled back the rings of the stove and poked up the fire before she went on. 'But Walter would ride the new horse and it threw him on the road, just below the house. They say he never moved, his neck was broken.'

'But why did Patrick have to leave college?' I asked after a few moments. 'Was it because of his mother?'

''Twas partly that,' Mary answered sadly. 'Yes, 'twas

partly that, but indeed she didn't live long after Walter died. I suppose Patrick came home because there was no money for the girls. Patrick's father was a lovely man, but he was no use with the land, or the shop, or the hotel. He'd inherited them, but he had no interest in business. He left that to Walter. He was a doctor, you see, and the kind of a man that wouldn't send a bill to poor people that he knew couldn't pay. Oh, they might send him a dozen eggs or a fowl, if they could spare it, but that's not much good with two girls away at school in England.'

'So Patrick took over from Walter?'

'He did, and a great job he's made of it, so I hear tell. Anyways, his sisters finished their schooling in Dublin and went for a year in Switzerland forby, and one of them's married in England to some big man in the government there. In the Parliament, I think, but I don't know the right way of it. He's very high up, for shure. And the other sister married a man who trained horses. They run the hotel and shop and have horses as well. They're back and forth to Dublin and you'd see them in the papers regular with winners. It must be in the whole family.'

She poured two cups of tea and handed me one.

'Where's Paddy, Mary? If he's up on the far field he'll be soaked by now.'

'Ah, never fear. He's gone to Doolin for the pension and I'm thinking he's met somebody in Considine's.'

I hoped that Mary would go on talking, but she seemed lost in her own thoughts as she sat looking into the fire. 'Patrick Delargy is a rich man now, Elizabeth,' she said with an air of finality and sadness. 'All he needs is a wife and shure who would he marry here and him an educated man?'

She certainly had a point. In his position, he couldn't just marry anyone, nor could there be many suitable single women of his age around. It must be very lonely to be so old and not have anyone to go home to. I remembered the way he had asked me about Tolstoy and I wondered who he could talk to about Tolstoy in Lisdoonvarna. Then it struck me that I had never talked to anyone about Tolstoy either. At home, no one ever reads anything but newspapers. George reads *The Economist* because that's his subject and Alistair Maclean for relaxation. Good escapism, he always says. And don't we all need some low literature to keep our minds off things.

'That tea was marvellous, Mary. Can I help myself to another cup? What about you? Are you ready yet?'

To my surprise and delight, Mary held out her cup and let me refill it. All week, she had been pouring my tea and serving Paddy and me at the table, while eating her own meal by the fire. She had waited on others all her life. Now, at last, she'd let me do something for her. It delighted me, for I knew such a gesture could have only one meaning. As far as Mary was concerned, I was no longer a stranger in the place.

We finished our tea in silence. My legs were beginning to throb gently after the long walk and the standing in the shops. Mary had been on her feet all day too, feeding hens and calves, baking bread, separating milk and making butter. We were both reluctant to move.

Finally, Mary got to her feet, her hand to her low back in a familiar gesture. 'Have you writing to do today, Elizabeth?'

'I have, Mary, but I'll wait till we light the lamp. I'll help you with the supper first.'

Outside the cottage a van stopped. Mary moved quickly to the middle of the floor. 'I wonder who that is. Bad luck to that hyderange, for I can't see a thing these days.'

The van started up again and continued on up the hill. The fumes drifted through the open door. They were followed by the scrape of boots on the flagstones. A moment later, Paddy appeared.

He had shaved off the stubble which had graced his chin at lunch and was wearing his best suit of brown corduroy with the pink and mauve tie that had so amazed me on my arrival. His face looked as if it had been polished, the cheeks fresh and pink, his eyes even brighter than usual. From the top of his cap, perched on his shiny forehead, to the toes of his well-polished boots, he looked trim, collected and totally in command of himself.

Such a small man, I thought, as he raised his hand in the doorway. Small and compact and full of a compelling sense of life that related not at all to the lines on his face, the remaining wisps of white hair, or the gnarled fingers, thickened with age. How can a man be old and yet so full of life? Paddy would never be old.

He hung his cap on the hook behind the door, grinned at us cheerfully and walked into the room with only the slightest trace of a sway. He smiled again, a sideways smile directed mostly at Mary. It was like the look on a child's face, when it knows it has been naughty, but expects to be let off with a caution.

Mary said nothing, but I could see she was amused. We waited.

'God bless all here,' he said heartily. 'I'm sorry, Mary, that I was unavoidably detained. I met some Yankees from Australia.'

Chapter 4

It isn't Paddy who has the hangover this morning, I thought to myself, as I sat munching wheaten bread at breakfast next day. He had been in such sparkling form the previous evening that we had sat by the fire till midnight. He'd told me stories from every part of his life, moving back and forth across the Atlantic and the decades of his seventy-odd years with equal ease and a fluency that had me spellbound.

He had such a gift with words. Everything he said was put in a simple, direct way but out of that simplicity he built something much more complex. The atmosphere he created was so very potent that as I listened to his stories, some happy, some sad, some cautionary, I felt sure I was experiencing something quite beyond the actual events he was recounting. It came to me that Paddy's stories were like parables for in them he had concentrated the wisdom of a long life lived with passion and humanity. I had gone to bed, my head full of Paddy's stories, and spent a dream-haunted night reliving stories of my own.

'God bless all here.'

The dark-caped figure of Paddy the Postman stood in the doorway, a hand half-raised in greeting. I'd been so far away that I had neither seen the bob of his cap above the hydrangea, nor heard the scrape of handlebars as he leaned his ancient, regulation bicycle against the wall of the dairy.

'God bless you, Paddy. Sit down and rest yourself, till I get you a drop of tea.'

He sat down, his cape dripping gently from a sudden shower. 'Ah, miss, I have a handful for you today,' he said. He counted out three letters for me.

'Well, what's news in the world today?'

Paddy O'Dara put down his blue enamel mug. He'd persevered with the delft cup and saucer for two days after my arrival until Mary had absentmindedly taken the mug from the dresser. He clutched it thankfully and the cup and saucer did not reappear.

'Good news. Mary-at-the-foot-of-the-hill has a wee boy and all well. Seven o'clock this morning.'

'Ah, thanks be to God,' said Mary, crossing herself. 'I'll go down and see the poor crater after a while.'

'There's Yankees arrived at John Carey Thatched House and his brother's over from Kilshanny. There'll be a big party tonight, I'm thinking. Flannigan's lorry was there delivering crates of porter.'

Paddy finished his tea at a gulp and stood up. 'God bless you, Mary, that was good, but I must be like the beggar man, drink and go, for I've a packet for Flaherty's beyond the Four Crosses.'

'Ah, 'tis a good way that, Paddy, and mostly uphill,' Mary nodded.

'And we're not getting any younger,' said Paddy ruefully, as he settled his mailbag on his shoulder and put his cap on.

'Good luck till ye.'

'Good luck.'

I began to stack the cups and plates at one end of the table, but Mary stopped me.

'Sure leave them, astore. Aren't you going over to Bally-vore. And I've not much to do today.'

It was highly unlikely that Mary had not much to do. I had seldom seen her finish her daily round before supper. But I sensed that often she was glad to be alone, with me out pacing the fields and Paddy working on the land or in the haggard.

'Will I need my wellingtons, do you think, Paddy?'

'Ah no, it won't be that wet. The path is rough, but it doesn't flood and the wind's been drying between the showers.'

I collected my plastic folder of field maps, put the letters in my pocket and zipped up my jacket. 'I'll be back by one, Mary, is that all right?'

'As right as rain, astore.'

'Mind yourself, Elizabeth,' Paddy warned severely, 'Bally-vore is full of old bachelors and wouldn't they just like me to make a match for them with a nice, slim, young girl like yourself.' He laughed as he stumped off to the garden to dig potatoes.

Slim. I smiled to myself as I set off up the road. No one had called me slim before. After my 'skinny' phase in early childhood, I had begun to put on weight when I was about eight years old. Despite the removal of all sweets, chocolate and cake from my life and my mother's continuous nagging not to eat this or that, or anything I put my hand out for, it was my late teens before I suddenly shed the flabby layers that had made my late childhood and teens so miserable. For years now, I had shut out the memory of those unhappy times. The teasing at primary school was bad enough, but what happened at grammar school was even worse. The games mistress made me run round and round the gym every morning before prayers. Remedials, she called it. My face would prickle with heat, I'd get a stitch in my side, and afterwards I couldn't find my place in my *Songs of Praise*, because my hands were shaking and sticky with perspiration. Those days were long gone. Thank Heaven.

But slim. I could hardly think of myself as slim. Certainly not compared with Adrienne. Perhaps Adrienne was a bit too slim. George said she had a marvellous figure but he preferred his women cuddly, like me. He said he was glad I wasn't sylphlike. Often, when we were lying together on the sofa in his mother's sitting room, or on a rug on some beach or hillside, he would put his head in my lap and say that I was built for comfort. But Paddy thought I was slim.

I turned to look back at Lisara and to study the new perspective from the high point I had reached on the long curving slope of the road. Funny how people see you differently. George. Paddy. My mother. Mary. It made me wonder how you could ever tell what the truth really was when people offered you so many different versions of yourself.

Just over a mile from the cottage I came to a weather-beaten signpost. It didn't say anything for the arms had long ago dropped off, but the track which led away to my left was clearly used. It was rough, but some of the bigger holes had been filled with stones. Apart from that, there wasn't much other sign of life about. No houses were visible either behind or before me. The hedge boundaries were overgrown and the fields were full of rushes. The trackway to my right that led down to the cliffs was identifiable only by the parallel stone walls. Its whole length was filled with the luxuriant growth of grass and bramble.

The bank below the signpost was smooth and mossy. I sat on my plastic-covered maps and took out my letters. I fingered the two from George in anticipation and laughed at myself as I put them to one side. I always save the nicest things till last. Adrienne always says you can tell a great deal about a personality from that simple observation, but whenever I ask her to explain exactly what you can tell, she never does.

My mother's letter was a single large sheet. It had been written hastily in blue biro on the strange-smelling, pink paper she had been using for years, a line that hadn't sold in the shop. 'Dear Elizabeth,' I read,

> Dad and I were glad to get your letter and hear that you had found somewhere to stay. It sounds reasonable considering but be careful of a damp bed. You can't be too careful in these places. Things are much as usual. We are very busy in the shop. It's amazing how trade keeps up especially cigarettes. Dad had to go to the Cash and Carry twice last week. Everyone has money these days especially (the Other Side). I don't know how they do it what with the big families and what they have to pay the church. Of course they have the big family allowances and the national assistance. The house at the end of St Judes the one with the orange lilies has been sold to one of them. One of our customers says the church puts up the money for them. They're getting in everywhere round here.

I paused. Even the irony of the Other Side having bought the house with the orange lilies failed to raise a smile. My mother puts on paper exactly what she thinks. Given how I feel about most of what she thinks, it was hardly surprising I'd find a letter upsetting. I just hadn't been prepared for it. Listening to what she said, evening after evening, I had learnt to filter out the things that upset me, but seeing them written down in tangible blue biro was another matter. I couldn't filter out the words and what they meant. She'd even written 'the Other Side' in brackets, like a stage direction, to remind me of the customary lowering of the voice.

Mary and Paddy were 'the Other Side'. So was Patrick Delargy, a man who had talked to me as a friend and driven me home to save me a walk and a wetting. Just by being here in Lisara, I was doing something neither of them could accept. There would be no talk of my visit when I went back, no interest in anything I'd done. My father would put the event out of mind, as he always did with anything uncomfortable. My mother would wear that tight, thin-lipped look of hers, if I were foolish enough to mention the visit myself.

Once, long ago, I had made the mistake of suggesting that some Catholics might be quite nice people. I have never forgotten the look she gave me.

'Don't ever let anyone hear you say a thing like that,' she warned me, two bright spots of colour flaming on her cheeks.

My father had actually lowered his newspaper, a rare thing for him to do. 'Indeed, Elizabeth,' he said, in a tone intended to sound both conciliatory and wise, 'that's all very well, but when all's said and done, you know, you can't trust one of them.'

I never raised the subject again, or expressed any further opinion, but I did wonder what strange power it was that produced such hatred and fear.

I shivered in the chill wind and turned back to the rest of the letter.

Clare Roberts that you were at school with has got engaged to Clive Robinson the shop. They are going to live in Helen's Bay. Clive has got a big job with the Co-op and they have bought a lovely bungalow with an L-shaped lounge. Her mother says it is the last word.

She is very pleased I was speaking to her on Monday.
She also told me Mary Dalzell as was had a lovely baby
boy born on her birthday. What a coincidence. They are
calling it William John after the grandfather.

That was the trouble with the shop. It meant my mother
heard all the news. All the girls I went to school with, married
and having babies, or leaving their babies with their mothers
to take 'wee, part-time jobs' so they could buy the velvet
curtains for the L-shaped lounges, or clothes for their Spanish package holidays. Perhaps it was my imagination, but I
sometimes thought the only time my mother ever looked at
me was when she talked about my contemporaries. It seemed
as if she were waiting for me to say something. But whatever
it might be, I'd never managed to say it. Her face went hard
and disapproving, no matter what comment I made.

A graduation photograph on the piano in the seldom-used
sitting room over the shop and a married daughter in a lovely
bungalow in Helen's Bay. Was that the future she wanted for
me?

The single page of the letter was flapping in the stiff
breeze and my fingers were numb with cold.

Dad has started to do up your room. He thought it was a
good chance. Uncle Jamsey got us the paper from his
work 30% off. It is a nice big green leaf with gold on
white. Dad says it will dirty awful easy but you only
have a year to do. He has only the woodwork left. You
said white but he thought it would look a bit bare so he
got a nice cheerful yellow at the cash and carry. I have
no news at all from the country so will close now. Mum.

I suddenly began to feel very depressed. At first I thought

it was the green and gold wallpaper, which sounded hideous. Then I wondered what they'd done with my precious maps and postcards that I'd been able to sellotape all over the walls, because the paper was brown with age and long overdue for stripping. My mother was quite capable of throwing the whole lot out.

No, it was something deeper than wallpaper and the lack of respect for my possessions. It was L-shaped lounges and babies called after their grandfathers. That wasn't what I wanted. I didn't know what I did want but it certainly wasn't that. Just thinking about my mother's news of the girls I'd been at school with made me feel afraid. Perhaps such things could happen to me too. Just like one of those road accidents you couldn't possibly predict, where people get killed or injured, because they happened to be where they were at a particular moment.

I stuffed my mother's letter back in my pocket and started to open the first of George's. At that moment, the wind caught me. I looked up and saw the islands had already disappeared beneath the approaching squall. The grey, choppy sea had white caps and the first spots of rain fell chill on my cheeks. I put the letter away, stepped back onto the road, pulled up my hood and tied it awkwardly in place with my numb fingers.

A few minutes later, the squall hit me as I walked up the track to Ballyvore. Hail peppered my back and legs, bounced off the loose stones at my feet and drifted into the tangled grasses below the low stone walls. I bent my head forward and walked as fast as I could. I'd had a good look round and I knew there was no shelter anywhere. The only thing to do was keep going.

After the squally morning, the day improved steadily. By late afternoon the sky was a brilliant blue. Up on the floor of the quarry where I'd been collecting rock samples, I had to take off my jacket and then my sweater. When I opened the neck of my blouse and turned up my sleeves, I decided it was time to have a rest. I spread my jacket on one of the smooth surfaces at the foot of a layered rock face, stuck my rolled-up sweater behind my shoulders and leaned back in the blissful warmth. I thought about George.

In all the romantic novels, this would be the moment when he would come striding up the track. He would have come home unexpectedly, borrowed a car and driven down to find me. Now he would be in sight, looking everywhere, calling my name. But this wasn't a romantic novel. George and I hadn't seen each other since he'd gone off to England to his vacation job in the middle of June. I had wanted to go with him but the factory he'd found had no accommodation for women. That's why I'd ended up at the Rosetta.

Earlier in the summer I'd thought a lot about our reunion. Whenever things got bad at home or when I felt especially lonely, before I started my job, I'd let myself daydream. Particularly, I thought of his arms around me. Not of kissing him or of our limited lovemaking, but simply of being held, of being safe in his arms, of feeling warm and secure.

I stirred myself, for my sheltered corner was so comfortable I was in danger of dozing off. I took out the letters I had been carrying with me since the morning, saving them for just such a quiet moment. I opened them quickly.

They were both rather short. The first had been written from the vegetable factory in Spalding. It said how much George missed me, how he longed to put his arms around me and how awful the campbeds were. Their Nissen hut had no hot water and the bog across the yard had been bunged up for days. He said the crack was good and his crowd had taken over a pub which sold Guinness and that the fish and chips were the best he'd ever had. He said I wasn't to worry about him. He could cope with these things. The rest of the letter was an account of the practical jokes they had played on the supervisor to break the monotony of tending the pea belt, or watching the labelling machine.

The second letter was shorter still. The vegetables had come to a sudden end with a change in the weather, so he had packed up and caught the first boat home. He missed me terribly. None of our friends were around in Belfast, the students' union was still closed, and he couldn't have his mother's car. She needed it for work since they'd stopped the estate bus. How wonderful it would have been if he could just have driven down and whisked me away from all those strange people and found us a nice place where we could be alone together, just the two of us, a long way away from Belfast. He hoped the work was going well and that I'd be back *very soon*. I was to let him know by return when he could meet me at the Great Northern.

I reread both letters several times to see if there was anything I had missed. But there wasn't. Letters were such a poor substitute for being together, I reminded myself. And, of course, George didn't like writing letters in the first place. He always said that scientists have difficulty with literary modes. Geography wasn't really a scientific subject, he said, and anyway I'd always been good at English which was his worst subject.

Beside me a clump of tall, pink wildflowers began to sway in the light breeze. From their lower stems hundreds of tiny balls, like thistledown, drifted in front of me. They spun slowly in the sunlight, a hint of iridescence on their white fronds, some borne upwards by the warm air, some colliding, some few moving towards me, touching my warm skin,

catching in my hair. I looked down the empty track and tried
to re-enter my daydream. But I had the greatest difficulty
remembering what George looked like.

I thought back to our first meeting. It was in my second
year, a lovely, lively spring day just before the beginning of
term. I came out of the front gate of Queen's on my way up
to the Ulster Museum and saw Ben sitting on the wall
opposite the bus stop with a tall boy I didn't know. Ben had
hailed me, introduced George, asked if I had time for a
coffee. We'd gone to the espresso bar across the road, talked
for an hour or more and then gone for a walk in the Botanic
Gardens. A few days later George found me in the library and
asked me out.

It had been easy to get to know him. Although he lived on
a new estate near Lisburn with his widowed mother, he'd
gone to the same city-centre grammar school as Ben, so we
knew many of the same people either from schooldays or
from our first year at Queen's. We began going to the weekly
hops and to the film club. George worked hard and sometimes we would meet in the library and go to the union
together for coffee. I was grateful for his company, glad to
have someone to talk to when things got on top of me, when
I felt suffocated by the flat over the shop and my mother's
complaints, or when my tutor was being awkward, pressing
me for work I could only do if I had enough time to think it
through.

George was easy-going. Nothing seemed to upset him. I
had once thought I was easy-going, but I'd come to accept
that I wasn't. I was always getting upset over things and
having to be comforted. And George was very good at that.
What was the point in getting upset about things if you
couldn't alter them, he always said. It seemed he had a point.

I sat watching the swirling down and wondered about the

name of the tall plant that had shed its seedheads with such enormous generosity. I picked some silky fronds from my black trousers and waved away a floating fragment that tickled my nose. As I moved my hand, the sunlight gleamed on George's signet ring, the one he had asked me to wear before he went off to Spalding. I wore it on my right hand, but I knew very well that he hoped to replace it with an engagement ring as soon as we graduated. He'd never asked me to marry him, it just somehow seemed obvious that was what would happen. I hadn't really thought about it till now.

Everyone assumed that because George and I had been going out together for more than two years we would marry. My parents certainly assumed that my bedroom wouldn't be needed when I finished my degree and Adrienne Henderson was always asking where we would live and whether George would teach or try to get into industry, whether we'd stay in Belfast, or be prepared to move away for a time till George got established.

I took his letters out of my jacket pocket and looked at them again, the envelopes I had ripped open so hastily and my name written in biro on them. Miss Elizabeth Stewart. Perhaps it was being so far away that made my life in Belfast suddenly seem so very remote. What was it Patrick Delargy had said when he'd stopped to look at the islands? Something about distance lending perspective.

Perhaps, being so much older, he felt he had a lot to reflect upon. So much had happened to him. He had lost people he loved, given up a future he'd chosen to take up something he certainly hadn't chosen. But nothing very much had ever happened to me. I'd lost my Uncle Albert the year I got my scholarship, but he was in his eighties so I could hardly complain about that. I hadn't had to give up what I wanted to do and go and do something else.

'Not yet, you haven't.'

I heard Ben's voice as clearly as if he were sitting beside me. One of his favourite phrases. If ever I told Ben I couldn't do something, or I'd never been able to manage such and such a thing, he would always come back at me. Not nastily, but always firmly. You shouldn't make closed statements about yourself, he said, because people and circumstances change all the time. Surely there were things I thought now that I never used to think, things I did now that I couldn't do before.

I hadn't noticed before how different Ben's way of thinking about life was from George's. I wondered if I would have noticed the difference had I not been sitting in the sun, in an abandoned quarry, over two hundred miles away from the low, red brick wall where I'd bumped into the two of them on a bright, spring morning that now seemed a very long time ago.

Chapter 5

'Hallo, Elizabeth, I heerd you was here. Will ye come with me to the dense tonight? Me cousin Brendan has the van from his work an' he says there's room for wan more.'

As I stepped through the door of the cottage, a red-haired girl of about my own age hailed me cheerfully.

'Ah, shure do, Elizabeth, do,' urged Mary. 'Go to the dense with Bridget. 'Twill be company for her and it'll do you good. Ye can't be working all the time. There'll be a great crowd.'

'The dense is great gas, Elizabeth,' Bridget went on, tossing her short, coppery curls. 'Isn't the band down all the way from Belfast itself. They must have knowed you were here!'

It was a long time since I'd been to a dance without George, I was tired and I couldn't think what I'd wear, but because I liked her immediately, I let Bridget persuade me. There weren't many people I knew who'd walk two miles to offer a complete stranger a lift to a dance.

When Brendan's van started bumping its way round a huge, crowded car park full of buses and minibuses, cars and taxis, vans, tractors, motorcycles and bicycles, I could hardly believe that the long, low building ahead of us was a ballroom. With its rusting corrugated roof and boarded up windows it looked more like a warehouse or a battery chicken unit. Its breeze-block walls were plastered with the tattered remains of posters and flourishing nettles sprang from its concrete base but as I peered out into the darkness I saw a long line of people queueing up at its entrance and a tail-back of vehicles spilling out into the road behind us.

It was some time before we got inside. Only one half of the building's double doors was open and once over the threshold the four large men who were supervising the payment of seven and sixpences created a further bottleneck. Beyond them a wide, empty corridor led to the darkened ballroom itself. We were greeted by a solid line of backs.

''Tis the season,' Bridget explained, as we struggled through the press of bodies towards the dance floor. 'They come from all over in the season. And there's visitors forby.'

I felt a touch on my shoulder. Bridget winked at me and as I turned round, a young man asked me to dance. He put his arm firmly round me and energetically shouldered our way to the dance floor.

Despite the noise of the band and the speed of the quickstep, he asked me where I came from, what I was doing here, and whether I liked farming. Then, I danced with a farmer from near Ennis. He too asked me where I came from, what I was doing here, and whether I liked farming.

A few more partners and I was able to predict the questions. What was more I heard the odd snatch of other conversations. The same thing was going on all around me.

About eleven o'clock, I looked around for Bridget and couldn't see her anywhere. Probably Danny had arrived and they were settled in the back of Brendan's van for a while. No matter. As long as they turned up to take me home, I could look after myself. I manoeuvred my way towards the back of the hall and plumped down gratefully on the narrow bench next to an emergency exit, firmly locked and barred against gatecrashers. I wiggled my aching feet inside my high-heeled sandals and looked about me.

The dancers divided into two camps, women on one side, men on the other. Up by the stage, their ranks were six or seven deep. Down here, beyond the range of the beacon that bathed the dancers with alternate garish hues, they thinned out into a single line. On the men's side there was an intense scrutiny of the opposite camp. The women's scrutiny was just as intense, but they covered it by talking to each other and feigned indifference. Their eyes moved around just as much.

As the band started up again the dark wall of suits crumbled at its edge. The women held their ground as if nothing were happening and looked surprised or even bored as they were led onto the floor.

From time to time, a couple detached themselves from the moving mass of dancers and came and stood only a little way from where I sat. Not romantic encounters these. No affectionate gestures, not even the touch of hands. The faces were far too intent for it to be any kind of chatting up that was going on. I watched cautiously and saw that as each dance ended, the couples who'd been engaged face to face would either return to the dance floor together, or turn their backs on each other and rejoin their respective camps.

'Ah, sure many's the bottle of whiskey I've had, Elizabeth, for the making of a match. But sure, nowadays, the young people see to it themselves and save the expense of a matchmaker, more's the pity.'

Paddy had talked at length about the custom of matchmaking. I'd listened to every word, intrigued and fascinated by what he'd said. What I hadn't expected was to see it actually going on around me.

'I think the hardest match atall is when the family has no

money and the daughter is ill-favoured forby. There's a lot of work and if no good comes of it the matchmaker gets the blame from both sides,' he'd said ruefully. 'Another hard one is when there's a love match. The boy and girl have their minds set on each other but maybe one of the families is hoping to gain by the match and they think they're losing a great opportunity.'

What was clear to me from all Paddy had said was how good he was at the job and how much he enjoyed it.

'Ah well,' he reminded me, his eyes twinkling. 'There's a lot of grand eating and drinking at the expense of both sides while the negotiations are going on. An' many's the bottle of whiskey I've had if it came out right.'

Some of the women I could see were as young as fifteen or sixteen, others were years older than I was and some few were in their thirties. Small and fragile, large and matronly, warm and homely, large-boned and gingery, they were dressed in a variety of ways, everything from the latest fashion in bridesmaid's dresses to T-shirts and jeans.

I wriggled uncomfortably on the hard bench. It was one thing reading up the marriage customs of the Nootka or the Inuit and quite another to observe the customs in action. It didn't look to me as if 'love and marriage went together like a horse and carriage' as the song would have it.

Whatever I might like to think about how people behaved in 1960, the evidence was that out on that crowded floor young men were looking for a woman who would cook and clean for them, help with the farmwork and bear sons to carry on the work on the land as they themselves grew older.

'And the women? What about the women?' I said quietly to myself.

It looked as if they were just as hard-headed as the men. They had to be. What they wanted was a man to give them a place of their own, children and their status as a married woman. Until they acquired that status, be they fifteen or fifty, they would still be a 'girl'. And a 'girl' had no rights. She was someone who stayed at home, had no life of her own, did always what others told her to do, someone who could end up spending her whole life looking after aged parents or unmarried brothers.

Suddenly, I thought of my own Aunt Minnie, my mother's youngest sister, a tiny wisp of a woman married to a large, loud-mouthed man I'd never managed to like. Uncle Charlie was a greaser in the ropeworks, his hobbies were drinking, betting on greyhounds and sitting in front of the television in his vest. He and Minnie didn't get on. Often, they didn't speak to each other for days and when they did, it was only to complain.

'Yer Uncle Charlie's a dead loss,' she would say to me, shaking her head, when I went over to visit her in Short Strand. 'Yer grandfether warned me. "Minnie," he sez, "if ye marry thon pahel of a man ye'll have neither in ye nor on ye." An' he wos right.'

Standing over the chipped and stained jaw box in her shabby kitchen as she emptied the tea leaves into a cracked plastic drainer, she nodded at me and went on.

'All verry well, Elizabeth, but how wos I te get outa that aul hole at the back end o' Dromara? Yer mather upped and went as soon as she cou'd. I might 'ave been there till this day if I hadn't struck up wi' Charlie, bad an' all as 'e is.'

So it wasn't just here on the far western seaboard, 'the back of beyond', as my parents would call it, that women still married to escape an even more unwelcome future.

I shivered at the thought of it and decided it was time I looked for Bridget again. I stepped back into the glare of the rotating spot as the singer grasped the microphone and launched into 'April Love'. 'Our song,' George always called it, since that first date in April 1958 when he said he'd fallen for me.

'There ye are, Elizabeth,' said Bridget. 'We was lookin' for you all over. This is Danny.'

Danny beamed down at me, a gangly youth with a sharp nose and a good-natured manner.

'Pleased to meet you,' he said, pumping my arm. 'Are ye enjoyin' yerself?'

I was about to assure him that I was when a hand grasped my elbow. Bridget's eyes moved heavenward. I turned and recognised the only one of my former partners I'd actively disliked. He was small, about my own height, and fat. When we danced, he'd held me so close I was impaled on the buckle of his large leather belt. He'd breathed beer and super strong mints in my face and I'd got a crick in my neck trying to lean away from him. Now he was smiling and holding out his arms. There was nothing for it, I'd have to dance with him again.

'Ah, Elizabeth, shure I've been searching for you these last two dances. That's a lovely name, indeed it is.'

He smiled at me and held me at arm's length to observe my reactions. I couldn't remember him having smiled at me when we last danced. But then, I'd looked at him as little as possible. He really was quite repulsive. The kind of man who looks as if he's sweating even when he isn't. And at this moment, he was. Rivulets of sweat poured down from the bald dome of his head through the thinning black hair below.

'You were telling me,' he went on, 'that you were interested in farming. Now, isn't that a coincidence and I interested too? Were you brought up on a farm then?'

'Yes, but I live in Belfast now,' I said shortly, hoping to

discourage him. But he only nodded as if my answer was entirely satisfactory. I could almost see the wheels going round as he set about preparing the next question.

'And now, ladies and gentlemen,' boomed the Master of Ceremonies, who had become louder and louder as the evening wore on, 'for Maureen and Sean who have just announced their engagement, "True Love". Congratulations Maureen and Sean, and love from everyone at Ballymore Creamery.'

'Tell me now, Elizabeth, how many cattle could you keep on forty acres?'

He turned his head to one side playfully, this being a little joke between those of us who were interested in farming. He might be oblivious to the band, but I wasn't and trying to raise my voice over the well-amplified strains of 'True Love' was positively painful.

'That depends, doesn't it?'

'Oh, it does. It does indeed.'

He laughed merrily as if I'd said something amusing. But the gaiety was forced and beneath the smile there was an unpleasantly determined look about his face.

'Ah, now, Elizabeth, shure it's a lovely name, Elizabeth, tell me now what it depends on.'

'Well,' I said firmly, convinced now that he was trying to trip me up, 'if it's the dry land round Ballyvaughan you might keep ten, but if it's the wet land towards Liscannor, you'd do well to have four.'

'Ah, shure great, aren't you the clever girl I'm thinkin'. And haven't I got a nice farm of land, and a house, and a shop, forby. I suppose all I need now is a wife to keep me company?'

The question came out in the form of another joke. He wore a self-satisfied smirk that infuriated me. What was I supposed to say? That no girl could resist what he had to offer? He was making an enormous effort to be pleasant, 'fishing for compliments', as my mother would put it. Well, he wasn't going to get any compliments from me. That was for sure.

'You'll be wanting a good dowry with a nice place like that,' I said sarcastically.

The moment I spoke, I knew I shouldn't have tried to be sarcastic over the noise of the band, but even so warned, his response took me completely by surprise.

'Oh, never mind the dowry, Elizabeth,' he said, pressing his hot, damp cheek against mine and shouting in my ear. 'Never mind that a bit. If I could get a girl I liked I'd never mind the dowry. Didn't I work three years in a car battery factory in Dagenham to buy the place. And hasn't the house got running water and both my parents dead.'

'I'm sorry about your parents,' I said weakly.

A look of impatience glanced across his face and was then replaced by an indulgent grin.

'Shure you'd have no one to look after. There'd be just the two of us and the wee ones,' he said, squeezing me affectionately.

What wee ones? I began to panic. Somewhere in the conversation he thought he'd made me an offer. That was bad enough. But now he actually thought I was interested.

'Thank you,' I said hastily, as the music stopped at the end of the dance.

I disentangled myself and looked around anxiously for Bridget and Danny. No sign of them. In desperation I dived towards the line of women, but he was too quick for me. He slid an arm round my waist and held on tight.

'I'm shure you'd like a glass of mineral water. 'Tis very hot in the hall,' he said. 'Or perhaps you'd like a breath of fresh air. We could sit in my car or go up and look at the Spectacle Bridge.'

The mineral water was the lesser of the two evils, so we sat in the gloomy space where I had previously watched other couples. I tried to think of a way out of the situation, but short of making a terrible fuss, I couldn't see one. I blamed myself for what had happened. I should never have answered his questions in the first place. Pride, Elizabeth, pride, I said to myself. A good observer should remain detached.

He still had an arm round my waist but he was fully occupied with pouring the contents of a bottle of fizzy lemonade down his throat. I looked at my watch. Half past midnight. An hour and a half to go.

The next dance was a quickstep. The minute we were back on the floor his determined look returned.

'You'll come down tomorrow and see round the place, Elizabeth. I'll send a taxi for you. What time would suit you?'

'I can't do that,' I said, shaking my head hard. 'My boyfriend wouldn't like it.'

'And where's your boyfriend tonight?'

'In Belfast.'

'He's not much use to you there, is he?' he replied, turning on the indulgent smile he used whenever I said anything he considered irrelevant. 'Now what time will you come?'

I shook my head vigorously. 'I can't come. I have work to do and then I'm going back to the university.'

'What?'

It wasn't surprising he didn't hear me. The band were now playing 'She'll be coming round the mountain', and the dancers were joining in on 'when she comes'. I waited.

'Back to the university,' I shouted, before the downbeat.

'Sure, I'd pay for you to finish your education. Isn't that reasonable?'

I didn't know whether to laugh or cry. He thought my resistance was just a matter for negotiation. If I was selling myself, he probably thought I was entitled to try for the best price I could get. That nothing in the whole world would induce me to marry him hadn't entered his consciousness.

'Isn't that a fair offer?' he repeated, a touch of self-righteousness penetrating his smile. 'Ah, Elizabeth, wouldn't I give you anything you wanted, my darlin', if you'll just say the word,' he began, pressing his sweaty cheek against mine. 'You can have anythin' you want. I'd not expect you to work in the shop, or on the farm. You'd be a lady, Elizabeth, that's what you'd be. Mrs Michael Brady would be a lady.'

He released me again to observe the effect of this thought that had just struck him. Then he tried to kiss me. The music stopped and I took my chance.

'Mr Brady,' I said sharply, 'there seems to be some misunderstanding. It's time I was going home. Goodnight.'

I tried to free myself, but his hands locked tight on my wrists. Several couples nearby were looking at us. We were right down the far end of the hall, the worst possible position for my making an exit.

'Ah, now, Elizabeth, don't go. Don't go. Sure we'll leave the house for the moment.' He was wreathed in smiles again despite my look of fury.

'Blue moon, I saw you standing alone,' crooned the singer.

That's all I need, I thought bitterly. A slow waltz. A plan was shaping in my mind, but I had to be level with the exit close to where the four large gentlemen were standing guard. At this pace, it would take for ever. Around us, couples began to entwine, making small pretence of dancing.

'Elizabeth, I love you.'

He clutched me to him and breathed hotly in my ear. I ignored him.

'Elizabeth, I love you.'

This time the statement had an element of interrogation about it. Something was expected of me. For one wild moment, I wondered if the mutual consumption of fizzy lemonade had the same significance in this community as the drinking of chocolate among certain South American tribes.

'Elizabeth, I love you,' he repeated, loudly.

The rotating spot which had been giving trouble all evening rattled and stuck. His face turned green.

'Excuse me,' I said urgently. 'I must go to the ladies.'

I sped across the floor, dodged between the couples and then the line of unpartnered girls. I felt an enormous sense of relief as I shot out into the entrance corridor and turned towards the cloakroom. I reached for my ticket. Oh, no. Not only had I forgotten there was no pocket in my skirt, but in the fraction of a moment I had paused, a hand gripped my shoulder.

'Shure, I'll wait for you outside, darlin'.'

Panting for all he was worth, he escorted me proprietorially to the ladies' cloakroom. He squeezed me affectionately and settled himself to wait beside the cylinder of Calor gas the cloakroom lady had used to prop open the door so she could watch the comings and goings.

Tears of rage sprang to my eyes. The four large men had disappeared, Bridget had the ticket for my jacket, and there was no way of getting out of the cloakroom except past Brady and the Calor gas. I went into the lavatory furthest away from the entrance and shut the door behind me.

The lavatory was smelly and nasty from excessive use. I tried to open the window, but the catch was rusted through. It came off in my hand. I pushed the glass near the edge of the frame. To my surprise, it opened. Cold night air streamed in onto my face and arms. Funny there's no netting, I thought.

All the other windows I had seen were boarded up or netted over. I closed the lavatory seat, climbed up and looked out.

The explanation was simple. The ballroom appeared to have been built on a rubbish dump. The window looked down on a steep earth slope covered with nettles and strewn with beer cans and empty bottles. No one could get in this way. But could they get out? I thought of Brady waiting by the Calor gas, took off my sandals and dropped them gently out of the narrow window. I watched them roll down the slope into the nettles.

As I squeezed through after them, the moon came out from behind a cloud. The nettles sparkled after rain. Too late now. It was only a drop of about six feet, but I had to be careful. I could start an avalanche. I took a deep breath and clumped feet first into the soft earth.

I landed unevenly, my knees folded under me and I skidded downhill on my bottom. Not far. But it was unnerving to feel myself sliding and not be able to do anything about it. I came to rest on the apex of a pyramid of beer bottles, dislodging a few that clinked their way down the glassy scree, starting other smaller avalanches as they went.

I could feel the damp of the earth penetrating my skirt, but I was afraid to make any sudden movement. The music from the dance was so remote I had to make an effort to hear what they were playing. A deep silence swept in from the surrounding countryside. Against its calm density, the noise of the cascading bottles seemed outrageous.

One of my shoes lay nearby. I reached for it and slid a bit further. Slowly, I managed to get to my feet, find my other shoe and work my way across the slippery slope. It was such hard going I hardly noticed the chill night air. I stopped at the rough edge of the car park and put my sandals back on my muddy feet. To my delight, Brendan's van was only a short distance away.

I glanced through the windscreen cautiously. There was no one inside. I knew it wasn't locked. No point locking it, Brendan had joked, she wouldn't go for anyone but him. I climbed gratefully into the back seat, wrapped myself in a raincoat someone had left behind and huddled up in the corner from which I could see the moon riding high in a clear sky. The raincoat smelt of straw and tractor oil and reminded me of a time, a very long time ago now, when I had lived in the countryside myself.

I thought of Michael Brady with his self-satisfied grin parked against the wall by the Calor gas cylinder. Waiting for me. I shuddered and drew the raincoat round me more tightly. There are nasty people wherever you go, town or country. But so far, I had been lucky. So many of the people I had met in my early childhood and in my many visits to Uncle Albert had been good people. Kind-hearted, straightforward folk who would make you welcome, as I had been made welcome in Lisara.

I closed my eyes and let myself remember the country people I had known and the places where I had once been so happy.

Chapter 6

Shortly after my unscheduled exit from the Kincora Ball-room, thick cloud swept in from the sea. By two o'clock, when the departing dancers launched themselves towards their parked vehicles, rain was sheeting down. It poured across the unmade car park from the downpipes at each corner of the building, bounced from the roofs of the vehicles themselves and created lakes in every depression of its irregular surface. There were shouts and screams as women in high heels splashed between the expanding waterways and waited for drivers to fumble with keys in the drenching rain.

Of all this I remained blissfully unaware, asleep in the back of Brendan's van, till Bridget, her coppery curls drip-ping, Danny's jacket pulled round her shoulders, stuck her head round the door and woke me up. Despite the fact that I was the only warm and dry member of the party, Bridget was convinced I'd catch my death of cold. She begged me to call over and see her next morning to reassure her that I was all right.

The rain cleared in the night but as I turned out of the cottage and crossed the road, brown water gurgled and splashed in the ditches, tumbling its way downhill to join the stream in the valley below. The sky was a clear, cloud-scribbled blue and the road itself already dry in the breeze.

The air had that special, fresh feel of early autumn which made me think of frost and red berries and whirling leaves. As I clumped along in my green wellingtons, I felt how marvellous it was to be alive.

I was so sorry when it was time to leave the road and make for Bridget's house, a two-storey building of grey stone, roofed with slate, at the end of a long lane. If I hadn't known that she had three brothers, I could have worked it out from the neat and prosperous look about the whole place. The haggard was full of great stacks of hay, thatched with corn straw and firmly tied down against the winter storms. The pasture that stretched up the mountainside was smooth and green, no sign at all of the dark, spiky rushes which had begun to invade Paddy's land as soon as his last son left home.

About a hundred yards from the house their lane was flooded right across, just as Paddy had warned me. It was deep too. Even in the middle, where the centre ridge stood well above the cart-ruts on either side, there were six or seven inches of brown water. I waded gently through, so it wouldn't slosh over the tops of my boots and soak my socks. Ahead of me, by the gable, a wooden gate opened onto a flagged path which ran across the front of the house. There were some flowers under the windows, marigolds and nasturtiums, neatly barricaded in by a row of whitewashed boulders.

As I drew nearer, a dog appeared, barking fiercely. He sounded as if he were about to eat me. I smiled to myself as I approached him. At the beginning of the week, I might have been afraid of him, but since then I had learnt two things about the dogs of Lisara: they all looked as if they were offspring of Paddy's dog, Prince, and like Prince, they were all confidence tricksters.

'Hallo, boy,' I greeted him.

He stopped barking, growled menacingly, but waved his tail at the same time. He sniffed my outstretched hand, then my trousers. Satisfied, he began jumping up and down, trying to lick my face.

'Down now. Good dog, down,' I said, as I balanced myself on the doormat and began taking off my wellingtons.

'Ah shure, don't bother, Elizabeth. Get down, Barney. Away wi' ye. He'd destroy your clothes, Elizabeth, he's the divil for jumping up. He's young yet. Come on in.'

Bridget was wearing a short-sleeved green sweater and some tartan trousers. They suited her a lot better than the pink and gold brocade dress she had worn the evening before, but her bare arms were purple with cold and her hands were red and chapped. Even though I still had on my red jacket with its warm synthetic-fur lining, I felt shivery just looking at her.

'Sit down by the fire, till I get you some slippers. Shure you needn't have bothered.'

She disappeared and left me sitting in one of the easy chairs by the side of the stove. Opposite me, an old woman sat staring at me. Dressed entirely in black and terribly thin, her yellowed skin was stretched tight over her bones. Where her cheeks should have been, there were two matching depressions, as if someone had poked their fingers into freshly made dough. Her mouth had sunk to a thin line.

'Here, put your feet in these.'

Bridget held out a pair of high-heeled slippers with a deep pink, hairy decoration on the toes. Luminous, silky fronds waved like the tentacles of a sea anemone around a rhinestone clip.

'Me sister in Boston sent them. Aren't they great?'

She laughed as I held out my feet for inspection. The slippers were at least two sizes too small and looked quite ridiculous over a pair of my father's old winter socks. But it was a kind thought, for the stone floor had just been washed and was still wet.

The old woman continued to stare at me. I smiled, but there was no response.

'She's nearly blind now and very deaf got, she doesn't see you at all,' said Bridget quietly. ''Tis my friend Elizabeth, come to see me, Granny. She's staying at Mary's. Mary-at-the-top-of-the-hill.'

Granny stirred slightly and made a sound. Her eyes moved upwards to where Bridget shouted in her ear. The pupils were tiny and the large, protruding areas of white were bloodshot.

'Yes, Mary. You know Mary?' Bridget went on, her voice echoing off the stone flags.

The face crinkled slightly. She nodded sharply as if angry at the idea that she might not know Mary. She fumbled in the folds of the black blanket which enveloped her and slowly extended a tiny arm. It was so thin, I could have encircled it with one finger.

'She thinks yer Mary.'

I took the outstretched hand. It was cold and lifeless and so fragile I was almost afraid to move it. Her eyes flickered towards me.

'How are you today, Mrs Doherty?' I shouted in turn, hoping I had said what Mary would have said.

She smiled and said something. I knew she smiled because her eyes changed their vacant look. But there was no movement in her face. And I knew she said something, because I heard sounds. But there was no movement of her lips. The hand fell back on the blanket as if it didn't belong to her any more.

'She says she's grand, she's pleased to see you.'

Bridget put the old woman's arm back inside the enveloping black folds and lifted her chair nearer to the stove.

'Ye'll have a wee sleep now, Granny, won't you?'

Granny was already asleep, her head dropped forward on her chest, her mouth open. Her thin, white hair curled in wisps over the pink of her scalp. Like a baby's.

''Tis a pity of her, isn't it?' said Bridget.

I nodded silently, afraid that if I spoke I might cry. There was something so devastating about that fragile hand in mine and the flicker of memory from a time when she and Mary had been women in their prime.

'Ye'll drink coffee, Elizabeth, won't you? I've no cake atall to offer ye. Would you eat a biscuit?' Bridget asked anxiously.

'I'd love coffee, Bridget, but I shouldn't eat biscuits. I'm sure these trousers are tighter than when I came with all Mary's good cooking.'

I wiped my eyes surreptitiously as she pulled out a stool and reached into the top of a cupboard for a box of biscuits. I was grateful when her blurred tartan bottom regained its sharpness.

'Can I give you a hand with the coffee?'

'Not at all. Sit yer ground. I'll not be a minute. Draw up to the fire and warm yourself. I'm just going to the pump.'

She parked the box of biscuits on the table and lifted out two enamel buckets from underneath its well-scrubbed surface. Through the small, back window, I watched her hurry down the yard, dodging a line of washing which billowed in the wind. Sheets, towels, shirts and overalls, reached out to envelop her. She seemed not to notice either their dampness or the chill of the morning breeze which had followed the night's rain.

The sight of her bare arms made me shiver again. I spread

my hands to the newly made-up fire in the massive black stove. It was another Modern Mistress, the same as Mary's and Uncle Albert's, except that it was the larger size, with two ovens instead of one, and a large tank at one side which heated water.

The stove was beautifully polished. I sat looking at my own reflection in the silvered edges and recalled the ritual of cleaning it with black lead and polishing it with old newspapers, which were then burnt. The silvery bits round the edges were rubbed with emery paper, as was the fender below. Hard work, and hard on the hands. I could still remember trying to scrub the black lead off with a nail brush after my early attempts to help Uncle Albert, the year Aunt Nellie died.

Granny slept. She was so still I could not be quite sure she was breathing. I looked at her closely, deliberately, knowing I had to get used to her presence before Bridget came back. She was not the first old lady I had seen, fragile and failing, in chair, or settle bed, but there was something about her situation which I found almost unbearable. Here she sat, sleeping out the last weeks of her life, by the fire she once tended, on the hearth she once swept, in the house where she had been mistress. I wondered how many hard years she had laboured in this house to keep it clean and swept, with food for the table and fire on the hearth.

The latch on the back door clicked as Bridget came in and put the buckets down under the table. She came over to the fire, shivering.

'It would skin you out there,' she said, giving me her hands to feel.

'Here, let me rub them. You're frozen. I don't know how you do it.'

'Shure, I'm used to it,' she said, tossing her head. 'I'm in and out all day. I'd niver get me work done, if I was to stop and put on a jacket.'

She pulled her hands away from me impatiently. Most of her fingers were still white.

'Wait'll I put the water on. The coffee will warm me up,' she said quickly.

'Let me help.'

I jumped up, unable to sit still any longer, and promptly fell over.

'Are ye all right?' she asked, torn between concern and laughter.

I rubbed my ankle ruefully. I had forgotten my exotic footwear.

'Sit there and act the lady,' she added as she put the kettle on the stove.

'Doubt if I'd be much good at that, Bridget. Shall I say "frightfully nice" when you give me my coffee?'

I watched her move back and forth across the kitchen, fetching cream from the dairy, cups from the parlour, a lace cloth from a drawer in the dresser. She moved quickly, talking to me over her shoulder, asking questions as they occurred to her. I was fascinated by her deft movements. She lifted a wire cooler with freshly made cakes of bread one-handed from the table and spread the cloth with the other before replacing it.

If I tried that, I'd drop the lot, I thought to myself. But then, as she'd said about the cold, she was used to it. She probably baked bread every day. And cleaned the stove, and pumped water, and carried baskets of turf, and washed floors, and cooked food.

'Come on, Elizabeth, sit over now, do. D'ye take sugar?'

'Coffee smells marvellous, Bridget. What is it?'

'American. D'ye like it? My sister left it behind when she was here in June. She won't drink tea at all now. All coffee.

She brought six packs for three weeks, but there was some left. The boys won't have it, so I have it meself when I get them all out. Go on, have a biscuit,' she added, winking, as she pushed the plate closer.

She leaned back in her chair and snapped a chocolate biscuit with her teeth. She had nice even teeth and they showed when she laughed. Sitting there, full of gaiety and excitement, Bridget looked more like someone downing gin at an illicit party than a girl having coffee with a friend on a chilly, September morning.

Her laughter was infectious. Whatever sad thoughts I'd had when I saw Granny and remembered Uncle Albert, they disappeared with the first cup of coffee.

'Isn't it great, Elizabeth, I have no dinner to make the day. Paddy and Own are away with Da to the fair in Ennistymon. It's not often I get a day off.'

'You've three brothers, haven't you?'

'Yes. An' all with big feet.'

She laughed again. I couldn't see quite why it was so funny, but there was something irresistible about Bridget's good humour, so I laughed anyway.

'And two sisters?'

'Both in Boston.'

She pushed the plate of biscuits over again, leaned her elbows on the table and started to tell me about their lives, their houses and patios, barbecues and holiday cottages, their clothes, their children, the jobs they had, the presents they sent, and the places they visited when they didn't come to Ireland. It was all very fascinating and a long way from buckets of water from the pump and a line of washing the whole length of the yard.

'Would you like to go to America?' I asked, when she paused for breath.

'Ach, I don't know. 'Twou'd be awful strange. I might be homesick.'

She had been so enthusiastic in her talk, I could hardly believe the change that had come over her. She tossed her head and changed the subject.

'You'd like to travel, Elizabeth, wouldn't you? Have you been to America?'

'No, I haven't, I've been the other direction, across Europe and into Norway and Sweden. I won a scholarship with an essay about travelling.'

'Europe? Were you not afraid, going away over there. What was it like?'

I thought of the way Mary spoke of her daughters in Boston as if they were just round the corner and then lamented that her sons were 'away over in England'. Mary's map of the world was quite different to any I might find in an atlas. What Bridget's map looked like, I couldn't guess, but I did my best to pick out the bits of my adventures that might make her laugh.

Bridget was full of questions. She assumed I'd visited all the capital cities she could remember from schooldays. I had to confess that the only one I knew reasonably well was Paris.

'Did ye do the can-can when ye was there?' she asked promptly.

I laughed and remembered that by a strange coincidence the dance I'd learnt to do in Paris was 'The Waves of Tory'. I told her how we'd found a party of young Scots lads staying in the same place we were and how we'd celebrated Bastille Day, dancing in the streets with everyone else.

'D'ye mean the French people just get up and have a dance in the street?'

Her eyes were round with amazement as I told her how we'd danced with our Scots friends and then split up the couples and taken partners from the crowd who gathered to watch us.

'I had a little man with a black beret just like you see in pictures. He was a fantastic dancer, but I couldn't make out a word he was saying, never mind understand it.'

'Was he a better dancer than Michael Brady?'

After her worries about me last night and the soaking poor Danny got when he went back for my jacket, she was entitled to tease me.

'Oh, don't mention Michael Brady, I was a right idiot to get stuck with him.'

'I think he fancied you, Elizabeth,' she said, winking.

'Oh, he fancied me all right,' I agreed. 'He fancied someone to run his house, and keep his bed warm, and he wasn't too particular who it was.'

I hadn't meant to speak sharply, but the words came out with an edge I instantly regretted. Bridget tossed her head impatiently. Her habitual smile disappeared and without it, her face was square and plain and looked neither young nor old. Our laughter and gaiety vanished like snow off a ditch.

'Michael Brady's a right eejit,' she said, stirring her second cup of coffee vigorously. 'Everybody knows he's as mean as get out, but to hear him talk you'd think he was great. Did he tell you about his house?' she asked crossly.

'With the running water?'

She glanced out of the window and scowled. 'There's a tap in the yard, and they say it doesn't work. And hasn't he his oul' granny there. They say she smokes a pipe. Yer well out of it, Elizabeth.'

I couldn't think what to say. Bridget was treating the matter as if I were seriously considering the man, when I'd long ago seen the funny side and was quite ready to make a joke at my own expense.

'I must say I'd rather have your Danny than Michael Brady,' I began, hoping to revive her good spirits. 'He's awfully nice, Bridget.'

She blushed and fiddled with her spoon. 'That's just a bit of a cod.'

Again, I couldn't think what to say. I'd seen her bright, excited look when she spoke about him on the way to the dance. I'd seen them together later in the evening, arms entwined, quite unaware of anyone else. If Bridget had been pretending more interest than she felt, she had certainly fooled me.

'He's all right for a bit of carry on, but shure there's no future in it.' She glanced at me briefly, then looked away. 'His da's only forty, and he's got three sisters as ugly as sin.'

I didn't have to puzzle over that one. It might be years before Danny inherited the farm. And there mightn't be much of it left, if three ill-favoured girls were ever to make a match.

'There's a drop more coffee, Elizabeth. Have it, do,' she urged, collecting herself.

'No, we'll share it,' I replied, putting my fingers over the cup till she had taken some herself.

As she poured mine, I saw that all her nails were broken, and the skin of her fingers was so hard it was ingrained with fine brown lines, as if her hands were dirty. I thought of that ridiculous jingle on television. 'Now hands that do dishes can be soft as your face.'

I could see the inane smile of the model as she lathered her immaculately manicured hands with the latest washing-up liquid. Yes. And what about hands that scour milk churns and wash stone floors and rub black lead on the stove and scrub manure stains out of blue dungarees? And do that day after day, week after week, month after month, without any hope of things ever being any different.

'Would you and Danny think of going to England maybe?'

'Shure how would I leave Granny, and the boys, and Da? There'd be no one to look after them. And Danny knows nothing but farm labouring and odd jobs,' she said wearily, as if she had already decided it was hopeless.

'You'll not always have Granny,' I said, as gently as I could.

'I know. Elizabeth, I know. I see her failed over the summer itself. But there's still Da and the boys. There's not one of them could make you a cup of tea.'

She said it without the slightest hint of criticism. It was simply a fact. Like the fact that Danny had no future unless he got the farm. Like the fact that my father couldn't make you a cup of tea, either.

Oh yes, literally, he could. He was always brewing up in the storeroom behind the shop. But once out of the shop, he felt entitled to put his feet up, mentally and physically. The running of the flat was no concern of his. How often had I heard him ask where his clean shirt was, or when his meal would be ready, or what was he to tell the milkman, or where the money was for the insurance man, or how he was to clean the car without a rag. My father was no more capable of performing the simplest household task than Da, or the boys. He took it for granted, just as they did, that it was a woman's job to ensure a man's comfort and convenience. Neither he nor they had ever questioned it, nor had I seen it for myself until this minute.

'But Bridget, if you hadn't been here, they'd have had to manage somehow,' I protested.

I was incensed by the idea of her spending her life slaving away for four men and looking after an old woman. Surely no one could expect that of her. But I knew perfectly well that many would expect just that. The business at the Kincora

Ballroom last night had made that absolutely clear.

'Ach I suppose they might find someone,' she admitted reluctantly. 'But ye know, Elizabeth, things are so dear these days. How would I rear a family on what Danny could earn?'

She looked at me as if she thought I might have an answer. But the only answer I had, I could not give. Bridget was a Catholic and a country girl. For her, marriage meant babies. Perhaps one a year, like Mary-at-the-foot-of-the-hill. For me, babies need not be inevitable. Once again, I was lucky. I had options that Bridget didn't have.

Suddenly, I thought of Gloria Ramsang, my Indian friend. She would be married by now. We had parted in June, after our General Degree exams. She was returning to Madras, where she would meet her husband-to-be in the week before her marriage. She had been happy, totally happy. Her parents had chosen a suitable young man, she was quite sure they would come to love each other and create a loving family.

I sat digging a hole in the sugar. What could I say? Part of me wanted to cry out, 'Oh, Bridget, run away. Go to England. Or America. Get a job. Don't have children, till Danny gets some training for something.' But how could I? Was it so surprising that Bridget took marriage and a family to rear for granted in the same way that Gloria Ramsang accepted her arranged marriage?

With a sickening thud, the penny dropped. And what are you taking for granted, Elizabeth Stewart? What's lined up for you that you haven't even thought about?

'It's great to be brainy like you, Elizabeth. Shure you can go where you like and marry who you like and laugh at oul' eejits like Michael Brady. When are ye going to get married? Can I come to yer wedding?'

She laughed and immediately became her former pretty and good-humoured self; it was I who felt a sudden stab of anxiety. Was marriage just as much my fate as it was Gloria's or Bridget's?

'Of course you can come.'

I tried so hard to sound enthusiastic that the words came out sounding bright and insincere.

Bridget simply assumed I would marry George because I'd told her he'd been my boyfriend for two years. She'd also assumed that I'd always been free to do what I liked. But she was wrong there. I knew how hard I'd had to struggle to read the books I wanted to read, to wear trousers instead of skirts, to study on Sundays instead of visiting relatives I had no wish to see. And as for coming to Lisara! Without the excuse of my thesis, it could never have happened, any more than my European trip without the scholarship.

'Will ye live in Belfast, Elizabeth, to be near yer parents?'

Her question pulled me up short. 'I don't really know,' I replied truthfully.

I hadn't thought about it. But I could see immediately there was bound to be a struggle over that. Whatever George and I might want to do, we could be sure that his mother, or my parents, would expect something different.

'Will ye have a house, or a bungalow?' Bridget continued. 'Theresa has a bungalow. It's all open plan. She says it's great for the wee'ans with no stairs to fall down. Would ye like that?'

I went on excavating the hole in the sugar. Bridget saw my future so clearly. I'd get married, have children and a house or a bungalow to put them in. It was all so obvious to her. Just as it was obvious to my parents that women did housework and men didn't; that men marched on the Twelfth, while the women watched from windows, and cooked late dinners at the Orange Hall for when they got back from the demonstration.

'We'll have to see how things go, Bridget. The big thing is to pass my exams first and get a job.'

'Will ye take a job?' she asked, surprised.

'Oh yes,' I said, briskly. 'I don't know what yet.'

'Ye'll be a teacher, Elizabeth.'

She sat up straight, made her face look prim and severe and then laughed.

'I don't know. Everyone's always said I'd be a teacher, but I'm not sure at all. Perhaps I just want to be different for badness.'

Deliberately, I filled up the hole I'd made in the sugar bowl. 'George hates me fiddling with sugar bowls,' I said, apologetically. 'I'm sure it's bad manners.'

'Divil the bit of bad manners,' she retorted strongly, as if she were saying I had a right to do whatever I chose, because she liked me. Because we had become friends.

'I'm awkward, Bridget,' I said with a sigh. 'I always want something different from everybody else. That's what my mother says. She thinks it's daft for a girl to go to university and then just get married. Yet that's really what she wants me to do. And that's not what I want. At least, I don't think it is.'

'Maybe you're a Career Woman, Elizabeth.'

She said it slowly, with the kind of unease you notice when people use a foreign word and are not quite sure how to pronounce it. Said as Bridget said it, Career Woman sounded like the name of a rare species, one you might have read about, but which you never expected to meet face to face.

'I wish I knew,' I said slowly. 'It would save me a lot of bother working it all out for myself. Sometimes I think I'd just like to travel around, finding out things all the time. I'd hate to be stuck at home all by myself, away from everything.'

'But sure you'd have the children for company and a

lovely house. George'll have a big job after all his exams, won't he? Shure it'll be great. I'll come and visit you.'

She said it briskly with that dismissive tone I was beginning to recognise. The subject of Michael Brady had been too close for comfort for Bridget, and now the vision of a house or a bungalow with fitted carpets, children about the place, and Sunday tea with salad and in-laws was having just the same effect on me.

It had looked so different, her life and mine. I had seen hers as so limited, bounded by the demands of others and the heavy, physical work. Now, I wasn't sure how different it really was. If Bridget wanted to talk about houses and gardens to push away the reality of her life, then perhaps I had better play my part and push away the reality of my own.

'All right,' I said. 'You come and visit me and I'll make chocolate haystacks. They're the only thing I like making, because you have to bash the cornflakes in a paper bag with a rolling pin before you start. And we'll eat the lot and get fat.'

Barney barked a staccato protest and I heard the squeak of a wheel axle. Bridget jumped to her feet so quickly she nearly knocked her chair over. She blushed.

'That'll be Sean, back from the bog. He was carting turf.'

She glanced at the clock. 'He's early, but he'll want a bite to eat.'

Before I had time to stand up myself, she had whisked away the cups and the plate of biscuits and disappeared the lace cloth into the drawer of the table.

'I must go, Bridget. I hope I haven't kept you back.'

'No, no, not a bit. It was great crack.'

Already preoccupied with her own concerns, she handed me my jacket. A tall figure appeared in the doorway and walked across to stand in front of the stove. Bridget's brother was sixteen or seventeen, very like her in looks, except that he had bad acne. Patches of black beard which he had not been able to shave showed around the angry spots. He was painfully shy, his eyes firmly fixed upon the floor as if he were terrified of meeting my glance.

'Sean, this is my friend Elizabeth.'

Bridget may have been flustered by Sean's unexpected appearance, but she managed nevertheless to make her statement sound like a command. He extended his hand like an obedient child without lifting his eyes one degree from the floor.

'Pleased to meet you, Sean,' I said quickly, as I stepped out of my exotic footwear. 'I hope we'll meet again, but I must go now. Mary'll be expecting me.'

He made a sound, but it was no word I could distinguish. He was standing so close to the stove that the fire was drawing clouds of steam from his damp clothes. It swirled round Granny like a fog, as she slumbered on, oblivious to his presence.

'Come up and see us soon, Bridget,' I said over my shoulder as I pulled on my boots on the doorstep. 'And thank you for the coffee, it was lovely.'

'It was great gas. I'll be up soon. Mind yerself how you go,' she called from the door, as I tramped down the path.

Before I had opened the little wooden gate, she had disappeared to see to Sean's 'bite to eat'. I picked my way between the puddles until I came to the pool where the spring had flooded. The level had dropped a little, but I still needed to wade carefully. I watched the ripples from my progress break up the reflection of the sky above me and looked down at the wet mark on my boots to see if I could measure how much the water level had fallen.

It was then I saw the joke about the three brothers 'all with big feet'. Bridget had laughed and I had joined in without really seeing what was so funny. Now I saw why she'd laughed, but it wasn't funny at all. Sean had been wearing a large pair of rubber boots, tall ones, right up to his thighs with thick, ribbed soles. I knew they had thick, ribbed soles, because I had stepped over their prints as I left the house. Sean had walked straight in and tramped dark mud from the bog all over Bridget's clean floor.

Chapter 7

When I arrived back from my morning with Bridget, Paddy helped me fill in my sketch of the Doherty farm and told me about the family and their history. I must have eaten my lunch in a dream, for when I tried to make some notes afterwards I couldn't remember half of what Paddy had told me. This will not do, Elizabeth. I stared crossly at the blank page of the blue exercise book. You must keep your mind on the job. Just think what important information you may have missed.

'Oh, the Lord save us!'

I started up in alarm to find Mary staring at the ancient green enamel clock that stood in the middle of the mantelpiece below the framed portrait of John F. Kennedy.

'Ah shure it's old age, astore,' she declared, turning to look at me, her face crumpled with anxiety. 'Didn't Paddy the Post come after ye were gone to Bridget.'

She reached behind the clock and handed me a white envelope, so thick it had needed more than the standard postage. The handwriting looked very familiar, but for the life of me I couldn't think who it might be.

'Shure I put it where I'd remember,' she went on, shaking her head sadly. 'An' I forgot all about it till this minit.'

'Never worry, Mary,' I said soothingly, 'I've just forgotten what you said you wanted in town. It's not old age at all. D'you think it's infectious?'

She laughed her quiet, inward laugh that lit up her gentle face, erasing the lines of anxiety which always saddened me so when they appeared.

'Ah shure maybe yer right,' she replied wryly. 'Didn't Paddy go up the garden this mornin' with the spade to dig potatoes and divil a sack to put them in?'

I tore a piece from the back page of my exercise book and made out her list, pushed the letter into my jacket pocket, ran a comb through my hair and set off down the empty road, consumed with curiosity and quite determined not to open the white envelope till I'd worked out who it was from.

'You idiot,' I burst out, as I began the long haul up the far side of the valley. Who else could it be? Apart from my mother and father, only three people had my address and Adrienne Henderson wasn't likely to bother writing to me.

I felt strangely agitated. Unless it was enclosing a brochure or some newspaper cuttings, Ben's letter was at least four times the length of George's. I started looking out for a mossy bank or a stretch of stone wall with a flat top. I was going round and round inside my head as I always do when I'm worried about something. But what could be worrying about a letter from Ben? Besides, I'd solve my puzzles if only I'd sit down and read what he'd written.

I laughed at myself and chose a comfortable piece of sun-warmed wall, opened the envelope carefully, peered at the neatly folded sheets covered with well-formed script and saw that a further carefully folded piece of paper had been placed in the middle of them. To my amazement, it was a five pound note, one of the old, papery kind with a silver strip down one side. There was only the slightest breeze, but even so, I didn't dare glance at the letter until I'd pushed the large note safely into the back compartment of Mary's well-worn purse.

I read furiously for a few minutes and then began to relax. Ben has always been good at telling stories, but apart from the Rosetta Primary School Newsletter, I had never seen him on paper before. I sat back and laughed in pure delight as the story unfolded.

Dear Lizzie,

Before you start worrying about the enclosed £5 I can assure you that it is not a first attempt at printing my own, which would certainly solve some problems but possibly cause others. 'There's a story to that there fiver,' as my grandfather would say.

It was Monday lunchtime in the Rosetta, he continued. He was taking orders and serving up what Keith had already pushed through the hatch for him. Busy for a Monday with lots of regulars, including the elderly English gentleman with the military air we had nicknamed the Brigadier.

'Ham sandwich, sir? What can I get you to drink?'

'Bush, please, a double. Where's the young woman today?'

'Elizabeth?'

'Yes, that's her name, isn't it? Dark-haired girl, nice smile, very efficient. Got the day off?'

Ben had explained exactly where I was and then ticketed the order for the sandwiches. We'd often wondered why the Brigadier always had ham. The Rosetta is good on cold meat, the beef especially, something I'd mentioned to him once or twice. But he'd just smiled slightly and stuck to ham.

'Is she your girlfriend then, young man?' he asked, as Ben put the sandwiches and the whiskey down in front of him.

'We're old friends, sir. Went to school together.'

'Long way to go on her own. Are you in touch?'

'Shall be, sir, as soon as I hear from her.'

'Mmm.'

The Brigadier was still sitting over his coffee in the almost empty lounge when Ben finished loading the dishwashers and came back to collect abandoned glasses for the hand-wash.

'Young man, what's your name?' he barked.

'Ben, sir.'

'Student? Both of you students then?' he went on more graciously.

'Yes, sir.'

'I'd like you to do something for me, Ben, if you'd be so kind,' he said decisively, as he took out his wallet. 'I don't approve of tipping. It's demeaning. Damned condescending when chaps are just doing their job. You and that Elizabeth girl have worked jolly hard all these weeks and I daresay you don't get paid very well. Here, put that in your pocket and share it with her. Maybe have a night out when she gets back. Seems to me you get on pretty well together. See what she'd like. Let me know when you hear from her.'

So you see, Lizzie, you have another admirer, as well as me, that is. I'd love us to have a posh night out but this fiver might come in handy on your travels. If you need it, we could still have egg and chips at Smokeys and honour the one and nines when you come back! We owe the Brigadier a night out. At least that's my excuse and I'm sticking to it!

A sudden creaking noise, accompanied by snorts and snuffles, broke my concentration. I looked up to see a turf cart stopping on the road beside me.

'Can I give ye a lift, Miss Stewart?'

A tall man in a sailor's cap and a Fair Isle sweater hailed me cheerfully, as if I were half a mile away.

'I'm going as far as Nagle's bog.'

There was nothing for it. I said thank you, pushed Ben's letter back into my pocket, handed up Mary's shopping bag and climbed the spokes of the wheel into the rickety cart. The miles that followed left me no opportunity to reflect on what Ben had said and done, or how he'd seized the opportunity of the Brigadier's fiver to invite me out for the first time.

'Hallo, miss, how are ye? Shure I thought you weren't coming. Mr Delargy has been in twice to see if there was any sign of you.'

Kathleen came from behind the counter before I was properly through the door and stood waiting impatiently as I searched my pockets for Mary's shopping list. The moment I produced it, she whisked it out of my hand and marched me to the archway at the back of the shop.

'Down there, that door at the end.'

I had been looking forward to meeting Patrick Delargy again, but I'd not expected him to be waiting for me. And I certainly hadn't expected to be launched into his presence without even doing the shopping. I walked slowly down the corridor and found myself standing awkwardly outside the appointed door.

'Shure he'll not take a bite out of you.'

It was my mother's voice. The comment was her habitual way of offering encouragement when I was uneasy. For once, it made me laugh. I knocked on the door and opened it gently. Patrick Delargy was halfway across the room to meet me before it closed behind me.

'Elizabeth, come in if you can. I'm sorry about all this.'

The room was very large and almost as full of assorted objects as the shop. But unlike the shop, it was completely unordered. Crates and boxes were piled up all over the place. A stack of pink lampshades wobbled precariously as I stepped past the two filing cabinets where they'd been parked. But the room was bright. One whole wall was pierced by tall windows that looked out onto the stable yard and let the dappled sunshine beam across the room to a long wall, where equally tall bookcases held leather-bound ledgers and bundles of yellowing papers tied with string.

I manoeuvred round a stack of boxes of whiskey and saw the only sign of order in the whole place, a huge mahogany desk where Patrick Delargy had been sitting. On its well-worn surface sat piles of neatly sorted papers, all anchored under makeshift paperweights, a brass inkpot, a round stone, an old pincushion, a mug covered with shamrocks and a bunch of keys.

Nearby, a space had been cleared by the fireplace where a small turf fire glowed orange and blue. A carved wooden stool bearing a book, an empty glass and a plate with a few crumbs on it stood beside a battered leather armchair. He waved me into it and smiled.

'Not exactly the most efficient administrative system, I fear. I don't know how Charles ever finds anything. I shall be glad to get back to my study.'

I sat down and looked around as he brought the swivel chair he'd been sitting on over to the fire, a difficult operation, for a rolled up carpet lay between the desk and the fireplace. He swung the chair over and I had to rescue the empty plate and glass before he could knock them flying with its heavy base. He put it down and turned to see me still holding them.

'Oh, well then, let's put them up here.' He placed the glass carefully on the very narrow mantelpiece, looked quizzically at the plate and balanced it on its edge beside the glass.

Despite the general chaos of the room, there was something about it I liked. The ceiling was high and still had its moulded decoration of entwined flowers, the bookcases and desk were of polished wood, mellowed with age to a chestnut colour, a colour which blended so well with the warm golden tones of the faded ledgers lining the walls.

'It's certainly got character,' I said, stroking the worn leather of my chair and looking round. 'I rather like it.'

'That's what Charles says,' he laughed ruefully. 'I'd rather it had a filing system that worked and a bit less character. We really need a part-time typist and filing clerk, but where would we put one?'

'I suppose if you found someone small enough you could put them up there.' I nodded to the only unoccupied space in the room, the top of a very high cupboard.

'That would have the added advantage of providing a look-out post. From up there one might be able to see where things were.'

He leaned forward and stirred the fire. It blazed up cheerfully. One or two sparks glowed at the back of the chimney.

'There's a stranger in your grate.'

'I should hope so too. I thought you weren't coming.'

'So did I for a couple of miles. Have you ever had a lift in a turf cart?'

'No, I can't say I have.'

'Avoid it if you can. It was slower than walking, and it made me seasick. Thank goodness he wasn't going far. When he turned off into the bog, I had to sit down for ten minutes. My legs were so shaky I'd forgotten all the questions I'd saved up to ask you.'

'Are you feeling better now?'

'Oh yes, once I was back on terra firma I was fine. The questions have all come back too.'

He laughed and leaned back in his chair.

'Yes, I remember you threatened me with questions. I've been wondering if I can answer them. What do you want to know? Agriculture? Tourist industry? Government policy? Local flora? Now I might know something about that,' he added thoughtfully.

He stretched his legs out and sat looking at me. It struck me then that he was rather nice-looking. His face was tanned with wind and sun, his eyes, a deep, dark brown, were both steady in their gaze and yet lively. They moved rapidly whenever they watched or considered or assessed. Whatever his mood, not much would pass unobserved in the environment of Patrick Delargy.

Sometimes his eyes sparkled with humour and the whole face seemed lighter and younger. But what age was he? In his thirties certainly, perhaps as much as forty even. He didn't seem old compared with other people I knew who were up to twice my age, but there were grey streaks in his dark hair. But more puzzling than his age was the feeling of isolation that seemed to surround him like a cloud. It looked as if he didn't often have anyone to talk to and just now was rather enjoying himself.

There was a knock at the door. He jumped to his feet and navigated the obstacles with considerable skill. The smell of freshly baked scones was quite overwhelming as he returned with a loaded tea tray. For a moment, we were quite defeated as to where to put it. Then I removed his book from the stool and set it between us. As he balanced the tray carefully on it I parked the book beside the plate on the mantelpiece. It was a battered copy of *Anna Karenina*.

'Do you have milk, Elizabeth?'

'Yes, please. Rather a lot.'

He began to pour tea into my cup, but had to put the teapot down abruptly.

'I keep asking them to get some china pots,' he said as he rubbed his hand on his knee.

'Hold on a minute,' I said, wrapping my hanky round the handle and holding it lightly. 'What you need is a kettle holder. My mother must have dozens stored away somewhere. We used to make them at primary school in handwork. I'll send you a free sample.'

He blew on his hand and looked solemn.

'Ah yes, but can you maintain production? One has to be very careful with craft goods from small enterprises these days.'

'I'll bear that in mind if I have to go into production,' I laughed, as we rearranged the tray so that it wouldn't overbalance every time we lifted the teapot or the milk jug.

I sat eating my scone and listened as he answered my questions about the growth of Lisdoonvarna. It felt as if we had been having tea together for years. It was a strange feeling, very warm and reassuring, but puzzling and disturbing too. How could I be so easy with this man whom I hardly knew, a man from a different country, a different culture, and a different social group, when I felt just the opposite with my own family and even some of my friends?

'Yes, that's very helpful,' I nodded, as I spooned home-made jam onto my second scone. 'It pulls together what I've managed so far, but . . .'

'But,' he prompted.

I hadn't the remotest idea what I was going to say, but it seemed quite wrong not to try to explain what I was thinking.

'Well, it's all very well doing what I've been doing.

Acreages and crop rotation and average output and growth of
a local market centre, but what does it really tell you? I mean,
take two farmers with the same kind of land and the same
acreages. One has forty cattle and the other has five. That's
what I'd like to explain. It seems to me the economic is
related to the social, and the social to the emotional.'

I stopped, confused. 'Perhaps I don't mean emotional. But
it's something abstract, like a perspective on the world.
Religion would be part of it. What people believe affects how
they farm. At least I think it does. But it's not something you
can measure, and if you can't measure it, how can you say
anything about it? Or if you did, who would listen?'

I finished my tea, which was nearly cold.

'I think there would be some who would listen. But you
are right, most people prefer the measurable. And the university world doesn't seem much better than the business world
on that score. Or what I know of it, at any rate. Here, let me
give you another cup.

'What exactly do you want to do?' he asked quietly as he
handed it back to me.

I began to explain. At first I felt very awkward and was
sure I was talking nonsense, but whenever I paused, or
couldn't go on, he would ask a question, or sometimes a
whole series of questions, and that got me going again. It was
then I realised I had answers to some of the questions, but
until he asked me I simply didn't know that I had.

'What really intrigues me is how customs and practices
developed generations ago survive and go on being handed
down, even in the face of all the evidence that they don't
work or aren't true.'

He turned his head slightly and paused, his teacup in
mid-air, a look of concentration on his face. 'How do you
mean?'

'Well, I've noticed that what people say suggests they believe things that aren't true. But if you question them carefully, it comes out that they don't actually believe them, they just behave as if they did believe them, because everybody else does. But it means that things can't change when perhaps they should.'

'You mean a private disbelief is combined with a public declaration of faith?'

He raised an eyebrow and smiled. I wondered exactly what he was referring to. 'Declaration of faith' had reminded me Patrick was a Catholic and the very thought set going some old association: watch what you say, they're very easy huffed. You just have to think twice and pass yourself. I recognised the script only too well, put it firmly out of mind and continued as I'd begun.

'Take an example. The other day, I was talking to a farmer whose son wanted him to extend his house like Mary and Paddy have done, to have a room for visitors from America. The farmer told his son it couldn't be done. The only place you could add on was beyond the existing bedroom and that was where the stable was. The son then says, "But what about the other side, the kitchen side?" And the father replies, "But you can't do that, man. Shure isn't that the west side." '

From the way Patrick looked at me, I could see he knew just what I was talking about.

'So I come home to Paddy and say "Paddy, why can't you build on the west side of a house?" '

His face broke into a huge grin as he interrupted me, 'And Paddy says, "Shure Elizabeth dear, isn't there a fairy path runs down the west side of every house." '

I nodded vigorously. 'But then, I ask Paddy if Sean Own Mahoney believed in fairies, for that was who I'd had the story from, and Paddy said "No, not a bit of him. He'd be right angry if anybody thought that." Now what do you make of that?' I ended, as I swallowed the last of my scone.

He was still smiling, the kind of smile that said he'd been there too, had met just the same kind of contradictions and been defeated by them himself.

We were silent for a moment, looking into the fire. When he spoke his tone was light and easy.

'But surely, Elizabeth, you don't want these delightful people to lose their simplicity, their whimsical rural charm?'

'Whimsical, my foot,' I retorted sharply. 'Paddy and Mary are the kindest, most generous people I have ever met, but they're not typical. I'm not fool enough to think there are many like them. Most of the people I've talked to are so sure they know everything there is to know that they never question anything. Everything is fine so long as you agree with them, just like it is back home in Ulster, but try to say anything that doesn't and that's a different story. Even Paddy and Mary say things I just can't take, things that are just not true. I never know whether it's tact or lack of courage that makes me keep silent.'

I stopped abruptly. I was thinking of Mary, of her kind face and her responsiveness to anyone in need or distress. I felt overwhelmed by a sadness I could not understand. I put down my empty teacup and looked up to see Patrick Delargy's face looking shadowed and sombre.

'What would you say to a woman who has borne nine children in real poverty, who tells you that God never sent the mouth but He sent the bite to feed it, when you know that millions of children are starving, and not all of them in Asia, or Africa either?'

He nodded grimly and said nothing.

'It's simple all right, far too simple,' I added, as I thought of Michael Brady and his attempts to provide himself with goods and services and a further increase in his labour supply.

'Perhaps I thought you took the view of our friend Levin,' he offered, nodding towards the book on the mantelpiece. 'All virtue resides in the peasant.'

I shook my head firmly.

'No. I liked Levin, because he felt like a real person who worried about things and tried to think them out. I couldn't really decide when I read it whether I agreed with him or not. But now I disagree. Peasants can be cruel and pig-headed and take a pride in being so. That's the dark side. Oh yes, there's another side too and it appeals to me as much as anyone. But you've got to see both sides, haven't you?'

A look of deep sadness passed over his face.

'Perhaps I needed to be reminded, Elizabeth,' he said with a sigh.

'Of the dark side?'

'No. Of the fact that I'm not the only one in the world that sees it. Sometimes I go for months without hearing a single reservation about the values of country people, the small farmers in particular. There's an idea about that they and they alone remain in touch with what people call real values. You begin to feel as if you're the only one out of step.'

I knew so well what he meant. I'd felt it myself so often. 'Sometimes I wish I could change how I see things and hear things and just join the club,' I agreed, wearily. 'It would be so restful not to be out of step all the time, wouldn't it?'

'It would indeed. Though, if I may say so, I hardly think you'd much care for a restful life.'

He said it so lightly it could be taken as no more than a pleasant compliment. But I felt it was much more than that. Without quite knowing how it had happened, we'd discovered what was really important to each of us. It put us together on the same side of an invisible line and made us friends.

'It's McClennan from Limerick, sur.'

Neither of us had heard the soft knock at the door, nor saw the young barman till he was halfway into the room.

'Good God, is that the time?'

I stood up and put my jacket on quickly, but Patrick was not to be hurried.

'Mickey, tell him I'll be with him shortly. Take him into the bar and cast your eye down the list yourself. See what you think we need. Let him make out the order with the numbers blank till we check what's in here. I won't be too long. Send round for sandwiches and coffee, but don't for any sakes let him start drinking free samples with you till he's had something to eat.'

The young man smiled shyly and retreated.

'I'm so sorry I've kept you late, the time just seemed to go,' I said apologetically.

'I'm not sorry at all, but I'd better take you home now, unless of course you could stay and have supper with me,' he added hopefully.

I realised how disappointed I was that our meeting had come to such a sudden end. I'd have loved to stay for supper. 'Mary will be expecting me. She might worry.'

'Of course she would. Did Kathleen take your bag?'

I had forgotten the bag completely. I turned to speak to him and promptly tripped on the rolled up carpet. He caught my shoulder and steadied me.

'All right?'

'Serves me right,' I laughed. 'I wasn't paying attention.'

We moved together towards the door, his hand still resting lightly on my shoulder. I felt sorry to leave the room. Our seats by the dying fire looked so inviting, cramped as they were into the small firelit space, the tea tray still perched on the stool, the mantelpiece decorated with a glass, a plate and a copy of *Anna Karenina*.

'Patrick, are those your car keys?'

'What did you say?'

The look on his face was so strange that for a split second I thought he was angry. I had spoken without thinking. I had called him by his Christian name. But I could hardly call him Mr Delargy, could I?

'I just asked if those were your car keys,' I said uneasily, nodding towards the desk. 'I noticed them as I looked back.'

'But before that,' he insisted. He looked me full in the face as if it were of the utmost importance.

'Just your name, just . . . Patrick.'

The strange look disappeared instantly and he grinned, tightened his grip on my shoulder momentarily and stepped back over the carpet to pick up the keys. He twirled them round his finger and returned to me, smiling.

'It's a long time since a woman called me Patrick . . . in that way . . . with that accent,' he confessed.

I looked at him, wondering if he would explain.

He laughed and put his hand back on my shoulder as he opened the door. 'Come along, young lady,' he said severely, as we went out into the corridor, 'before you find out any more of my secrets.'

Once out of town he accelerated. The broad brown and purple expanses of bog which had seemed interminable from the lurching turf cart flickered past like the brief locating shots of a documentary film. We'll be there in no time, I thought sadly.

I turned to look at the islands lying on the horizon, beyond the falling slopes of the fields to the west of the road. The car slowed. This was the point where we had stopped two days earlier when Patrick had driven me back to Lisara after our first meeting. Surely he wouldn't stop today when he was already late for an appointment. For a moment, he didn't notice my puzzled look as he concentrated on drawing the car off the road.

As he put the handbrake on, I realised why he had stopped. The road was narrow at this point. About half a mile away, a large, black taxi proceeded towards us in the middle of the strip of tarmacadam. Or rather, it was in the middle to begin with. As we watched, we saw it weave gently from side to side as if the driver were just a little drunk.

The driver was pointing out the islands to his passengers. It was Feely. Sometimes with one hand, and occasionally with two, he was directing their observations while the car oscillated its way up the hill towards us.

Patrick shook his head resignedly and finally pressed the horn. It was a funny little pip squeak of a thing, quite out of keeping with the size of the car, but the effect on Feely was remarkable. He gripped the steering wheel and looked towards us in amazement as if the last thing he expected on this road was to meet another car. His passengers glared. Drawing level with us, with only inches between the two vehicles, Feely recognised us. He straightened up like an infantry man coming to attention, raised his ancient green hat and bowed over the wheel. He was so close I could see the whites of his light blue eyes.

Patrick raised a hand in salute. I waved. As the taxi passed, its four occupants turned their heads to stare at us, like a section of the crowd at Wimbledon, perfectly synchronised. They were dressed identically in black and white, for they were all priests.

'What a man,' said Patrick, 'I wonder how he survives.'

'He'd never have spotted us if you hadn't tooted,' I said, laughing.

Patrick eased the car off the uneven verge and began to drive slowly towards Lisara. I wondered if he were expecting any more Feely-like drivers. But after a moment he spoke.

'I'm afraid that meeting may have been unfortunate, Elizabeth.'

'You mean the way Feely jumps to confusions?'

He smiled momentarily, but remained serious. His face looked almost grim. Surely he wasn't worried about gossip. Why, he himself had joked about the natives having us married off when he last drove me to Lisara. Besides, there could never be anything between us, he a Catholic, me a Protestant, and he was so much older. They were bound to see he would never think of such a thing.

But perhaps the problem was just being seen with a Protestant. I didn't have to be reminded how angry people got in my family when Catholics and Protestants were seen together. There was sure to be a furious outburst from my mother if ever she saw the girls from the grammar school talking to boys from the local Christian Brothers School at the bus stop.

'But, Mum, they were only talking.'

'Only talking, indeed. There's no knowing where talking will get you.'

She was as outraged by their 'only talking' as if she'd surprised the offending couple in the act of making love.

'You won't get excommunicated or anything will you?' I asked, trying to keep my voice light.

'No, I'm not worried about them,' he said firmly. 'The priesthood gave me up as a bad job a long time ago. No, I'm more concerned about you. I don't want you running into trouble with your work. One can't predict what kind of prejudice might be generated.'

He paused for a moment. 'I'm sorry. I don't really need to tell you that, do I? You know it very well yourself. But I am concerned. You could meet a totally irrational response. On the other hand, you might not. It is all quite unpredictable and there's not a lot either of us can do about it.'

It was then I remembered my former tutor's dire warnings about the reticence I might meet, because I was a Protestant and a Northerner. I hadn't thought about it since I arrived. Along with the many other unhappy aspects of my life in Belfast, I had put it out of mind. Now, here it was again come to spoil the unexpected pleasure of my meeting with Patrick.

'It's so ridiculous, isn't it?' I said, shaking my head. 'It would be funny, if it wasn't so awful.'

He nodded and turned towards me as we stopped outside the cottage.

'I'd be very sorry if you couldn't come to see me again, Elizabeth. But I'd quite understand.'

His face was grave, his eyes shadowed. The lonely look had returned, clear and unambiguous. I knew he meant exactly what he said. I also knew I would be more than sorry not to see him again.

'I'd like to come,' I said quietly. 'But you're the one that has to live here. "Strangers in closed communities are usually of low status and little significance," ' I quoted from one of my text books.

'Good,' he said, sounding pleased and relieved. 'When shall I see you then?'

'Tuesday?'

'Splendid. I have some books I think might help over the Land Commission and one or two other things.'

He opened the boot of the car and picked out Mary's shopping. 'Don't worry about me, Elizabeth,' he said quietly.

'I have had long experience with the natives.'

There was a firmness in his tone I had not heard before. I glanced up at him and realised he was angry, just as angry as I had been, time and time again when I was forced to listen to the prejudice and bigotry that surrounded me at home.

'You'll have to apologise for me,' he continued, smiling once more. 'Tell Paddy and Mary I'll come and see them on Tuesday, will you?'

'No,' I replied, taking the shopping bag he handed me. 'I'll tell them you asked after them both. Do you want poor Paddy to spend the weekend redecorating the house?'

He clicked his fingers and laughed, and the warmth of his smile blew away the last of the shadows that had hovered around us since the untimely meeting with Feely.

'Thank you for tea, and for bringing me home,' I said quickly. 'I hope your man's not tight by the time you get back.'

'Not the same one, he's had too much practice. It was a pleasure, a great pleasure. Take care, won't you. Till Tuesday.'

'Till Tuesday,' I repeated as he drove off.

I stood watching for the car to reappear on the far hillside, a shiny, metallic object catching the light as it moved against the backdrop of rock outcrops and smooth green fields. Separate, self-contained, independent, it moved at speed on its ribbon of road. I watched until it was out of sight.

Chapter 8

The wind caught me as I stopped for breath on the edge of
the ridge that rose steeply behind the cottages of Ballyvore.
My eyes were streaming and I had a drip at the end of my
nose. The map attached to my clipboard flapped noisily as I
dug in my pocket for my hanky. All I could see of Ballyvore
was one well-mended roof set a little higher than its neighbours. Beyond the rutted track I had walked half an hour ago,
a Dinky toy of a van spun merrily along the main road, a dark
shape against the dazzle of Liscannor Bay.

I moved the rubber bands on my board to stop the racket
my map was making and turned my back on the sea. Ahead
lay a broad expanse of upland bog and moorland rich with
long, seeding grasses and broken by peat hags topped with
purple heather. Here and there, the bleached skeleton of a
long-dead tree stood out like animal bones in the desert.

I set off along the path Paddy told me I would find at the
end of my scramble up the rough track behind the last house.
After only a minute's walk, the stiff breeze disappeared and I
felt the sudden warmth of the sun on my face. I was so
surprised, I walked back to the edge of the ridge to make sure
I hadn't been imagining things. The sea breeze caught me
once again and I was glad to hurry back the way I'd come.

The sun poured down from a large patch of blue sky and in

the quiet I could hear the urgent murmurings of bumble bees swinging in the heather. In this light, everything looked wonderful, even the tattered remnants of the bog cotton and the dying bracken. The grasses were lush, some still green, some bleached to shades of gold and beige. I had seldom been in a place that delighted me more. I looked around for any sign of human habitation, but there was none. But for Paddy's dog, Prince, I was quite alone in this empty, sun-drenched landscape.

'Prince, here boy, good dog,' I called, as he dashed off, pursuing some irresistible scent. He ignored me and bounced on as if he was swimming through the tall grasses, only the white tip of his tail waving like a giant bog cotton.

Just at that moment, a harsh screech shattered the silence. Startled, I looked up and saw two large birds wheeling in the sky. I gazed up at them as I walked slowly on, following their leisurely drifting movements, till I was sure they were riding a thermal, flying round and round each other for pure pleasure. Black. Not crows, and far bigger than jackdaws. The huge wing span made me wonder if there could still be eagles in Ireland.

Before I came to any conclusion, the ground gave way below my right foot. I threw out my arms, had a brief glimpse of something green slapping me in the face and felt water closing over my head. I clutched frantically at the air. My feet touched something solid and I found myself standing up to my shoulders in brown, muddy water.

My eyes were smarting and there was a roaring in my head. Prince was barking like a mad thing. I rubbed my eyes, pushed my wet hair back on my forehead and removed some water weed from the bridge of my nose. Prince leaned cautiously towards me and licked my face. Then he started barking again. I couldn't stand his bark at the best of times and right now he was only six inches away from me.

'Good boy, that's a good boy. Don't bark.'

My ears popped. It sounded just as if someone had turned the volume up. At the same time, I felt water penetrate my bra and creep up round my breasts with an unpleasant tickling sensation. I shuddered violently and my teeth started to chatter. Come on, Elizabeth, you've got to get out of this. Think, woman. Think.

The boghole was about twenty yards long, but only two yards wide. I'd fallen in right at one end, a few more feet and I'd have missed it completely. I grasped a clump of heather and pulled cautiously. It came away in my hand, leaving a small cross-section of moorland soil which at any other time I would have found quite fascinating. Right now, shallow-rooted plants were going to be no help at all. If I could get my shoulders out of the water, however, I might be able to pull myself back up onto the path.

Prince stopped barking and began to whine.

'Much use you are. Just sitting there.'

I tested the area around me with one foot. It was all deeper than where I stood. Without the rock or tree stump I was standing on I'd have had to swim for it. I shuddered again. The water was icy cold, I could feel the numbness in my feet and lower legs already. I wondered what the survival record was for total immersion in bogholes.

'Get moving, Elizabeth,' I said to myself. 'Just get moving.'

I struggled out of my zip-up jacket. It was red and new. If the brown bog water stained there'd be hell to pay. And Hell or Heaven if you don't get out of here quick, I reminded myself. I found my handkerchief, squeezed it out and decided to tie it to Prince's collar. The minute I reached for him, he backed away. Then I remembered Prince didn't wear a collar.

The likelihood of his going home if I told him to was pretty low anyway.

A waterboatman paddled past my chin and explored the edge of the unknown, red continent my jacket had suddenly created. I raised my arm out of the water and looked at my watch. I was amazed it hadn't stopped. The guarantee had said it was waterproof, but I'd never risked putting it to the test. It was almost ten-thirty. Paddy and Mary wouldn't miss me until after one o'clock and Sean O'Struithan, whose cottage was somewhere behind the barn that had just come into view, didn't know I was coming. No one else ever came up the mountain. There was nothing to come for. The turf had been worked out years ago, leaving the land too broken for sheep.

Prince pricked up his ears, stopped barking, and dived off with the enthusiasm usually reserved for rabbits. Having got my jacket off, I was about to try swimming down to the other end when I saw through the gap left by the heather plant, a small figure striding purposefully towards me, carrying a long plank under one arm. Prince greeted him noisily, then fell into step placidly at his heels without another sound. I watched them approach, so amazed by Prince's behaviour and so relieved help was at hand that I made no effort to silence the incredible noise my teeth were making. Within minutes, the man was standing over me.

'Miss Elizabeth Stewart, I presume,' he said, as he dropped on one knee and held out his hand. 'Sean O'Struithan, your humble servant.'

We shook hands. His was warm and dry and had a firm, friendly grip. Mine was wet and white with cold. I apologised for it being damp.

'Don't mention it atall,' he said, smiling at me, as if it were the most natural thing in the world to shake hands with a young woman standing up to her chin in a boghole.

'Perhaps, Elizabeth, if I may call you Elizabeth, we might remove ourselves to a more congenial environment. Indeed, a little hot refreshment might not seem inappropriate in the circumstances. Allow me.'

He placed the plank squarely across the boghole and showed me how to use it to swing myself out. A few seconds later I was standing on firm ground again.

'Good, good,' he said, surveying me briefly. 'Now if you'll forgive me, I'll lead the way.' So saying, he picked up my sodden clipboard in one hand and the plank in the other and set off at a cracking pace, Prince trotting at his heels.

My boots were full of water, my hands too numb to take them off and empty them and my saturated jacket weighed a ton. I slung it round me and squelched off after them as best I could, leaving a thin trail on the dry path like a car with a leaky radiator.

The path seemed to go on for ever. Try as I might, I could not keep up with Sean O'Struithan's pace. By the time I turned the corner of the high roofless barn and dripped breathless into his yard, he was nowhere to be seen. Exhausted as I was, however, the sight of his cottage really lifted my spirits.

Thatched, freshly whitewashed, and as trim as a new pin, it stood some thirty or forty yards back from the remaining walls of the old barn. The windows sparkled in the sunlight, their wooden frames painted a pleasant green to match the open door. But it was not so much the well-kept cottage that amazed and delighted me, as the courtyard created in the broad open space in front of it.

There were no fallen roof timbers in the shell of the old barn, nor any of the junk I was so familiar with from the farmyards of Lisara – abandoned machinery, old carts, sheets

of corrugated iron, outworn tractor tyres. It had been stripped
bare so that its stone floor was continuous with the flagged
courtyard. Between the flags grass grew, but it was short and
entirely free of weeds. Throughout the large space and on
both window ledges were tubs and troughs of flowers. In old
three-legged pots, wooden wheelbarrows, half-barrels and
hollowed logs, geraniums, lobelia, marigold and fuchsia had
been combined to provide matching and contrasting patches
of colour.

As I dripped my way to the door, my curiosity increased.
One thing was certain, Sean O'Struithan was neither a
farmer, nor a shepherd, for there was not a piece of farm
equipment or a trace of animal manure to be seen. Prince had
settled himself to guard the threshold and he whined as I
approached, but for once neither barked nor jumped up to
greet me. As I bent to take my boots off, he acknowledged
my presence merely by sweeping his tail back and forth
across the smooth stone doorstep.

'Come in, Elizabeth, you're welcome. Now if you'll forgive the inadequacies of a bachelor bedroom, you might care
to make yourself more comfortable.'

He handed me a bucket, two large warm towels and a
dressing gown.

'I'll take your jacket now and if you put your wet things in
there, we'll see to them in a few minutes' time.'

The bedroom was immaculate and I was horribly aware
that I was dripping all over a lovely woven rug. I stripped off
as quickly as I could, stuffed my things in the bucket and
wrapped myself in one of the towels. The woven quilts on the
two single beds had a geometric pattern and looked as if
they'd been straightened with a ruler and a spirit level.
Reluctantly, I sat on the edge of one of them and started to
dry my hair and feet. I caught sight of myself in the long

mirror of the wardrobe door. My face was as white as a sheet, my hair stuck to my head and cheeks, and my make-up had vanished, except for my mascara which had redeposited itself in dark circles below my eyes. I found my silly little handkerchief with the pansy in the corner and tried to get rid of them.

I found a fine deposit of silt between my breasts and a tidemark across my shoulders. As I pulled the towel too and fro on my back I caught sight of my naked body in the long mirror. No, I wasn't slim like Adrienne, but I did have quite a nice figure.

I had a sudden thought about how my mother would react if she could see me now, undressing in a man's bedroom and observing my shape in his mirror. I had such an urge to roar with laughter that I had to concentrate hard on something to stop myself.

The room offered me plenty of choice. It was just as intriguing as the courtyard outside. Spotlessly clean and beautifully cared for, every inch of wall space was covered with photographs, posters in English and Irish, facsimiles of documents and signed portraits of men in uniform. As I wrapped Sean's comfortable towelling gown around me and put my damp things into the bucket, I knew there was only one label in my mother's language to describe Sean. He was a man with a past, an 'Oul' Fenian'. I could see her face contort with loathing as she spoke the hated word.

I walked back into the kitchen with my bucket and stopped abruptly. Sean was making up the turf fire on the hearth. Outside the pages of a text book, I had never seen an original hearth with turves burning on the bare earth beyond the edge of the stone floor. Above them spread a canopy deep enough to sit beneath. Wooden armchairs were placed across the fire from each other. Sitting in them, you could look up the chimney and through the smoke hole to the blue of the sky above.

He had moved my chair close to the fire and left a pair of moccasin slippers beside it. I smiled at him, quite unable to think of any way of thanking him for being so kind to me. I curled my bare toes forward on the warm stone flags till they almost touched the white ash from the fire. Spreading out my hands to the blaze, I took a deep breath and drew in the warm, sharp smell of turf.

'It's such a lovely fire, Sean, I thought I'd never feel warm again.'

He looked down at me with a satisfied smile as if it were he himself who was revelling in the warmth.

'I think I can appreciate your feelings. I have on many occasions found it necessary to place myself in close proximity to the elements. Sometimes in the not entirely adequate shelter of a stone wall, it did not seem reasonable to let oneself imagine even the existence of such delights as a turf fire or a dry bed.' He nodded sympathetically as I shivered again at the mere thought of it.

'I hope, Elizabeth, you have no moral or religious objections to the medicinal use of alcohol,' he went on, as he opened a door in the bottom of the dresser. 'I think it might be wise to employ the prophylactic qualities of a little hot whiskey.'

'No, not at all, thank you.'

I had never heard the word prophylactic before and though I could guess what it meant, it made me wonder about his strange way of speaking. He sounded as if he were reading from a very pedantic script, yet there was nothing contrived about how he spoke. Perhaps the vein of irony which touched all he said had once been calculated, but was now simply part of him.

'Mmmm, I think I've had hot whiskey before. Yes. Isn't it funny how a smell brings back a memory?'

'A recollection of times past, perhaps?'

'It's come back to me now,' I began, sipping cautiously as the fumes caught at my throat. 'It was when Uncle Albert used to take me to see my grandmother. I'd ride on the bar of his bike but I used to get frozen with the wind. When we got back to the forge he'd wrap me in a blanket and give me punch. I can't have been more than four at the time.'

'That would have been up in Ulster, in the forties, I assume?'

I nodded and found myself telling him about the small farm near the border where I had spent the first five years of my life, and Uncle Albert's home on the outskirts of Keady where I had gone on visiting till he died in 1957. He listened hard and asked questions about my family, my work at the university, and my interest in Lisara.

It came to me that I was once again talking at length to a complete stranger, with the kind of ease I had never imagined. It was almost becoming a habit. So often back at home, I could think of nothing to say to the only questions people ever asked me. I oscillated between silence and nervous chatter. I'd just about decided that I wasn't much good with people at all.

'So the study of a community in Ireland seemed to you an appropriate complement to that of the Nootka and the Imbembe?'

'I wanted to see for myself. I hate being told what to think and I got so much of that at home and at school, I was afraid I'd succumb. Having to write a thesis was a marvellous excuse. In my home, there always has to be a reason that makes sense to them, but sometimes I have reasons I can't explain, not even to myself. Lisara was like that. After I'd read Arensberg's book I knew I had to come.'

Sean nodded and pursed his lips. 'I thought you must be an exceptional young woman, Elizabeth Stewart. When my old friend Paddy O'Dara says he's too busy to accept a lift to the pub on a Saturday night, then there is something, or someone, of exceptional interest involved,' he said lightly, as he reached out his hand for my empty mug.

'Tell me, Elizabeth, what time does Paddy feed the dog?'

'About noon. Before we have our own meal.'

'Then I think our canine friend may serve as our Mercury. You will stay and have a little lunch with me, will you not?'

'Sean, I've been such a nuisance already. I can't take up any more of your time,' I began apologetically.

'My time is my own and I would welcome your company,' he said, as he took a sheet of notepaper from the drawer in the kitchen table. 'As they say in these parts "God made time and he made plenty of it." Entirely untrue, of course, but a nice conceit. I will inform Mr O'Dara that I shall accompany you to his residence in due course and that he need have no concern for your well-being,' he added with a flourish of his pen.

He folded the note, called Prince in a low voice, and attached the note to his neck with string. Prince stood perfectly still, made no attempt to remove his temporary collar, and ran off when Sean told him to go home for dinner.

'I fail to see why Mr Patrick O'Dara should monopolise the pleasure of your company,' he said, as he watched Prince through the window. 'The oul' divil,' he added unexpectedly.

'Sean, how do you manage to get Prince to pay attention? One word from me and he does what he likes.'

Sean's eyes softened as he turned back from the window. His eyes were a very light blue, and there were masses of lines round them, like someone who had scanned far horizons for a long time. His face was tanned and he had white, even teeth. I wondered if they were false and whether he were as old as Paddy, who had long, yellowed stumps. He seemed younger. Everything he did was done lightly, deftly. He moved easily and his clothes were not those of an old man, a comfortable checked shirt, a tweed jacket, corduroy trousers and well-polished brown leather shoes. Only his flat cap bore any resemblance to Paddy's habitual way of dressing.

'I like dogs,' he said. 'I once worked with an animal trainer in Vienna. I would like a dog myself, but I'm away for many months of the year. A dog needs continuity. Perhaps when I have to desert my retreat I shall have one then. In another hundred years or so.'

'Surely more like two hundred,' I said lightly, as I saw the look of sadness flicker across his face.

He leaned across the hearth to unhook the boiling kettle. Then he sat down opposite me and began to talk in a quiet, reflective manner, rather different from the ironic style to which I had now grown accustomed.

'I'm five years older than this century, Elizabeth, and my good friend Paddy has five on me. We'll be dead and gone before Ireland heals her sorrows, for all we thought we had the answers forty years ago. Perhaps your generation will be wiser and not seek short answers to long questions.'

He looked into the fire and I thought of the posters, the documents and facsimiles, the portraits of men in uniform.

'I suppose Paddy told you I was an Old Republican?'

'No, he wouldn't tell me anything about you. He just teased me. He said I had mortally offended you by not coming to call. And that was his fault. When I saw no track on the map, I assumed the house was derelict and he didn't correct me.'

'Paddy has a fine sense of humour,' he replied, nodding at

me. 'During the Troubles it was to my advantage that Paddy and everyone else around should think the house was derelict. We did our best to create that impression. With some success, I may say. There were times when we did have to take to the bog or the mountain, but in general, we were better off than some.'

As he spoke, I regretted again how very ignorant I was of even the basic facts of Irish history. Beyond stories of a very doubtful nature entrenched in family memory, my knowledge was limited to the patriotic songs I'd learnt in youth hostels in Derry and Donegal.

'Sean, I'm so ignorant I'm ashamed. Apart from marching to Dublin "in the green, in the green, with bayonets glittering in the sun" and so on, I really don't know what happened in the Troubles. Could you manage a history lesson?'

'Well now, Elizabeth. I think meeting your requirements would be easy enough, but I feel I should warn you that it might involve a high degree of reminiscence,' he began. 'It is a dangerous thing to offer a receptive audience to a man who has reflected much on the events of his life.'

I settled myself more comfortably in my chair. I was prepared to listen to Sean for as long as he cared to talk.

It was well after one o'clock when Sean paused, stood up and began making preparations for lunch. I sat looking into the fire, so absorbed by what he had told me that I didn't even hear him the first time he asked me if I could eat *omelette aux fines herbes*. He had indeed marched to Dublin, just like the song I had heard. And he'd heard 'the rattle of a Thompson gun' and seen men die at his elbow. He'd nearly died himself. Below the flat cap, a white scar seamed the top of his balding head. His brother, Seamus, had managed to drag him unconscious and bleeding from the building they were holding just before it was taken by British soldiers. The defenders were rounded up and the ringleaders later shot.

I watched as he collected crockery from the dresser, lit a small spirit stove and melted a knob of butter in a flat, well-used pan. I suddenly thought of Bridget Doherty. 'Shure how would I leave the boys and Da, there's not one of them could make you a cup of tea.'

Sean poured the beaten egg into the pan and added snipped herb from a flourishing plant on his windowsill. He rocked the mixture gently to and fro. After a few moments, he slid the omelette deftly onto a warm plate, wiped the pan and repeated the operation. Sean would be about the same age as Bridget's father. But then he had never left Ireland. While Sean had travelled the length and breadth of Europe, earning a living any way he could, with pick and shovel or his father's trade of tailoring, later with his pen, his classmate Michael Doherty had stayed at home and gone no farther than the fair in Ennistymon.

We said little as we ate our omelettes with fresh wheaten bread. I was very hungry and the omelette was excellent. It was not till Sean made us coffee that I broke the easy silence that had come upon us.

'It's splendid coffee, Sean. Is it American?'

'It is. Seamus brings me a supply from Boston when he comes in the summer and then I collect some more when I'm over in the winter.'

'In Boston?'

I thought I had stopped being surprised at any detail of Sean's most unusual life, but I had not.

He laughed cheerfully.

'Indeed, my economic activities, whether with pen or needle, would hardly rise to such gallivantings, but Seamus is a very rich man. Bywater's is the largest tailoring business on the East coast. He has no great joy of it, however. When his wife died some years ago, he wanted to come back and settle here, but his daughters protested. So he compromises. It is, you might say, a symbiotic relationship. Without me, Seamus could not maintain his link with Ireland and this house, which is as dear to him as it is to me. Without him, I should have little leisure to pursue my scholarly pleasures. Our relationship was tested in very limiting circumstances and it has served us well. Together, we transformed our lives and our thinking most radically. That makes a very powerful bond.'

He lit a cigarette, flicked ash into the glowing fire and looked at me directly.

'Have you ever wondered, Elizabeth, what it is that makes people change the whole direction of their life?'

'Yes, I have. Often.'

He blew smoke up into the dark cavern of the canopy and looked towards the patch of blue sky visible beyond the swirling smoke.

'If anyone had told me at twenty that I would be leading the life I now lead, or think the thoughts I now think, I would have said it was pure fantasy. Yet, when I consider the matter closely, it is clear to me that the possibility was there. All that was required was the catalyst.'

He put down his coffee cup and leaned back in his chair.

'The Troubles, as I told you, were a very strange experience for Seamus and me,' he began. 'There's a book I'll lend you by a friend of mine, Mike O'Donovan. You would know him, I expect, as Frank O'Connor. Mike gets the feel of the very mixed quality it all had. Passion and dreams and real heroism mixed up with sheer romanticising and total incompetence. The Troubles gave people what they wanted. If you wanted illusion, it was there. If you wanted disillusion, you could have that too. It was a matter of personal taste. What it did for Seamus and me was take us away from Lisara. It created an opportunity to test the facts of our life. You might say, for the first time in our lives we were confronted with a reality we had to interpret for ourselves.'

I nodded vigorously. I wished I could write down exactly what he was saying and keep it handy. In one sentence, he had told me why I had to come to Lisara. For the first time in my life, I was able to have experiences of my own and have to decide for myself what they might mean. There was no official hand-out thrust at me, no party line I was expected to toe. I was truly free to make up my own mind without the customary struggle against those who knew the answers I ought to get before I'd even asked the questions.

He dropped his cigarette butt into the fire and watched it flame briefly among the turves. 'My own feeling, Elizabeth, is that the battles fought in the interior of one's own skull are of more importance ultimately than the kind beloved of our countrymen.'

'But what did happen after the Treaty, Sean? How did you and Seamus manage then? And who won that particular battle?'

'Interesting questions, Elizabeth. To all of which there are a variety of answers, but to do them justice I think we must reserve them for our next meeting.'

He stood up, crossed the room and picked out a well-thumbed volume from one of the two massive bookcases which stood on either side of the dresser. He leafed through a few pages. Finding what he wanted, he turned and read it to me.

'Apparently the only proof one had of being alive was one's readiness to die as soon as possible: dead was the great thing to be, and there was nothing to be said in favour of living except the innumerable possibilities it presented of dying in style.

'One part of your answer to what happened after the Treaty lies there. Too many people have been obsessed with the delight of dying for Ireland. The Troubles did lead a few to think again, Seamus and myself included. Since those days, there have been some ready to live for a possible future rather than die for a glorious past. But their influence was not felt for a long time and they are still a minority as far as I can see.'

The phrase 'glorious past' struck me immediately. I heard again the batter of the drums, the tramp of marching feet, the succession of perspiring figures. True, they carried no guns, wore no military uniform, but weren't the banners and the emblems just as potent? 'No Surrender' inscribed on fences and posts, and the gables of rows of terraced houses? Wasn't the Orangeman's determination to fight to the death rather than live to make a future, however difficult, just as potent and dangerous and misguided as the struggles of 'the Other Side' he so disparaged?

'I think living with the problems of the present must be much harder work than planning to die for what has been, intellectually that is,' I said sadly.

'It is, Elizabeth, it is. But considerably more rewarding, as you will most certainly discover.'

He collected up my warm clothes from the drying rack by the fire and handed them to me. With a twinkle in his eye and a tone full of his usual irony, he said: 'But "living" does have some great advantages, Elizabeth. It does put you in good company. Many of the martyrs I have known were very vulgar fellows, but the intellectuals are a much nicer type.'

My clothes were beautifully dry and smelt of turf smoke. I put them on quickly and spent a few moments more looking at the photographs on the walls of the bedroom. Next time I came I would ask Sean to tell me about each one of them. I felt sure that if I did I would do much more than improve my knowledge of Irish history.

Chapter 9

When I arrived in Patrick's stockroom on Tuesday afternoon, a second armchair and a low table had appeared in the small space by the fire. It meant that sitting down was even more difficult than before but, once we'd managed to fit ourselves in, having tea itself was a good deal less hazardous.

Patrick wanted to know how the work was going so I promptly launched into an account of my adventure in the boghole. His face was quite horror-stricken when I began, but as it became obvious I was none the worse he began to relax. By the time I'd unfolded the full drama of my futile attempts to escape, he was laughing heartily and shaking his head.

'I take it Prince won't be auditioning for Lassie?'

'No. Total disaster was Prince, except for the one thing.'

'What was that?'

'Barking. He nearly did for my eardrums while I was in the water and I kept trying to get him to stop, but that's what Sean heard. He hopped up to his lookout with binoculars and saw me. So Prince has to get the credit after all.'

'You know, Elizabeth, you do tell a good story. I don't know when I've laughed as much. Despite the fact it was *not funny*,' he added, severely.

We began to talk about all sorts of things, but all through tea his words echoed in my mind: 'You do tell a good story.'

It certainly wasn't what George would say. Nor Adrienne either. Whenever the three of us meet up, George always addresses himself to Adrienne and finds some excuse to tease me. It wouldn't be so bad if Adrienne and I were intimate friends, but we're not. I've known Adrienne a long time, but she's the sort of person who only uses me to fall back on when she's fallen out with everyone else, something she does regularly. George knows this perfectly well but he still treats her as if we were bosom friends.

One occasion at the end of my second year sprang back into my mind, so vivid I could see myself sitting with them and the whole thing happening all over again.

'And this smashing bit of stuff in a yashmak goes wiggling past these American soldiers,' he began.

Our table in the union was packed full but he stood up, waved his long arms and wiggled his body just the same.

'So, one of them follows her.'

He stuck out his chest, shaded the lower half of his face with his hand.

'He points to himself and says "Me Bob". And she turns round and says "Me thirty bob".'

'Oh George, you are naughty,' laughed Adrienne.

'Me thirty bob,' George repeated loudly. 'Get it, Elizabeth?'

'Oh, Elizabeth, you are the limit. Don't tell us you haven't caught on yet?' Adrienne screeched, before I'd even opened my mouth.

Then they talked about me as if I wasn't there. I had no sense of humour. I could never see a joke, and I certainly couldn't tell one. As they warmed to their task, a deep silence descended upon me. I grew more and more depressed. Was I really the kind of humourless person they were describing?

Patrick laughed again and I was suddenly aware of his

eyes, a rich, dark brown, bright and mobile. Their gaze only left my face to follow the movements and gestures of my hands. If I could make a man like Patrick laugh, could I be so lacking in a sense of humour after all?

The more I thought about it, the more I felt making Patrick laugh might be quite an achievement. Although this meeting was as happy and easy as the others we'd had, I'd seen a shadow pass across his face which made him look both old and grim. It was such a momentary thing, but when it flickered I felt sure some deep unhappiness had marked him.

'My goodness, it's six o'clock already,' I said as I caught sight of my watch.

He stood up immediately and manoeuvred towards his desk. I followed him cautiously and looked at the pile of books he had brought for me.

'What lovely illustrations.'

'They are good, aren't they? That one's very rare now,' he said, looking over my shoulder at a spotted orchid. 'But we still have some in the Burren. Thank God.'

'I shall have to read this,' I replied. 'I'm not very good on plants. Can I have the Charlesworth too? I did pack mine but then I couldn't lift my suitcase. I had to leave most of my books behind.'

'Of course, have anything you want.'

It was not until we were driving along the Lisara road in the bright sunshine that he spoke again.

'I'm afraid I have to go to Dublin for a few days, Elizabeth. I've been putting it off. But I shall have to go on Thursday.'

My heart sank and I could think of nothing to say. I told myself it was quite ridiculous to feel so disappointed. He'd been friendly and helpful and now he had to go. So why on earth should I be upset?

'When will you be back?' I asked as steadily as I could, afraid my voice might give me away.

'Tuesday or Wednesday of next week. As soon as I can get away. You won't be gone, will you?'

'I'm not sure, Patrick. Some friends may come down to collect me and I can't really refuse if they do. But I'd like to stay on till the end of next week. I had planned for three weeks if things went well.'

For a moment, he concentrated on the road, then he nodded and said, 'I have some calls to do tomorrow, mostly around Ballyvaughan. It's interesting country. I think you'd like it. Will you come and let me show you the Burren?'

Relief poured over me. And delight. I had to work hard not to let my feelings show too obviously. 'Yes. I'd love to come, if you're sure I won't be in the way.'

'Of course you won't. How could you be? I'll pick you up when I get my desk clear and Mrs Brannigan will pack some lunch for us. We may even get another day like today,' he added, as he drew up outside the cottage where Prince was sleeping in the sun.

'That would be lovely. Do you think you could also arrange for Mr Feely to be touring in the opposite direction?'

'I thought we might go in disguise.'

'I'd like to see this car disguised as a Mini,' I countered, as he handed me Mary's shopping and my carrier bag full of books.

'Aren't you the lucky one, Elizabeth? Shure I don't know when we had weather like it. The sun has hardly stopped shinin' since that mornin' you went to Ballyvore and got hailstoned.'

Paddy stood at the gate as I came out of the house, my arms bare, my feet clad in some summer sandals Mary's daughter had left behind. It was hot already. The islands were so clear against the perfect blue sky that we could see the white shapes of the houses on Inishmore and the dark shadows of the stone walls that surrounded the tiny fields.

We stood by the hydrangea and looked out over the familiar acres of Lisara, Paddy pointing out details with the stem of his pipe, until the sun glanced off a small, moving object on the far ridge.

'See ye enjoy yourself, Elizabeth. I must away and dig potatoes for Mary.'

I smiled to myself as I got into the car. I couldn't decide whether his rapid exit was a form of tact or merely due to the fact that his chin was bristling with the stubble accumulated since his last visit to Considine's.

'Don't you ever get thoroughly fed up driving through this place?' I asked sympathetically, as we wove our way through Lisdoonvarna.

'Ah, shure haven't I the patience of old age,' Patrick replied, his mimicry quite perfect.

'I hope you've got your wheelchair in the boot,' I retorted.

He grinned, but did not take his eyes off the road. Having pulled round a turf cart, we were now faced by three bullocks. Despite the efforts of a panting sheepdog and a man with a stick, they stared at us, paralysed. Patrick put on the handbrake and leaned against the steering wheel.

'Well then, what age do you think I am?' he said, his tone light but challenging nevertheless. 'Surely you have a page on me in that green file of yours.'

'No, I haven't,' I confessed. 'I only write down what I think I might forget.'

Without any warning, one of the animals lunged forward between my side of the car and a parked vehicle. Its horn caught the open window and its huge eyes rolled as it passed.

I moved away so fast I almost fell into Patrick's lap. He put an arm round my shoulders and steadied me as the other two creatures followed in a headlong dive.

'Nasty creatures, I don't like them either,' he said comfortingly. 'Perhaps it's their capacity for uncoordinated action.'

'Mmmm. Like some people,' I said as I straightened up. 'They can't help hurting you. It's not intention, it's just how they are.'

Patrick accelerated sharply and within moments we were clear of the town, bowling along an empty road between sunlit fields where the cattle stood in dappled shade and the hedgerows were bright with a second blossoming of wildflowers.

'You haven't answered my question.'

For a moment I hadn't the slightest idea what he was talking about. I was absorbed in the countryside, its rich greenness and the distant glimpses of the Hills of Burren.

'Er . . . let me see,' I began.

He stuck out his chin, pursed his lips and tapped the cheek nearest to me. 'That's my best side.'

The mood was light and easy and yet I sensed my reply was important. At home, everyone jokes about how touchy women are over their age, but I'd found the men of the family every bit as easy to upset.

'I should think a well-preserved fifty,' I said firmly.

'Wretch! I shall abandon you and make you walk home.'

We had been climbing steadily since we left town and had just breasted a very steep rise. At the highest point the verge widened to make a viewpoint. He pulled over and stopped.

'I'm thirty-five,' he said as we got out. 'Does that seem entirely ancient?'

'No, not entirely.'

I wasn't sure how to react. He was much older than any of

my friends and yet it seemed to make no difference to our friendship. At the same time, I was grateful he had not said forty. Forty would have been a shock, a blow. Thirty-five, I could manage. But what did I mean by that? Why should his age be of any significance to me?

The view spread out below us was quite magnificent. We leaned against the bonnet and gazed over the vast panorama.

'Age is a funny thing,' I said abruptly, when I realised how silent I had been. 'When I was ten I knew a girl who was fourteen and I just couldn't imagine what it would be like to be fourteen. But when I got to fourteen, I felt I was still me. I've never felt any different because I'm a year older. I did once expect to, but I still haven't. When I get to thirty-five, I'm sure I'll still feel I'm the same Elizabeth.'

He nodded and moved forward to the very edge of the lay-by, gave me his hand so I could climb up on the low stone wall.

'Corkscrew Hill. Now what does a human geographer make of that?'

Although the drop was only a few hundred feet, the road turned back on itself in a far more extraordinary manner than any of the famous Alpine passes I'd seen on film. No wonder busloads of tourists stopped just here to take their pictures. But it was not just the extraordinary contortions of the road that held me, it was the luxuriant landscape, every detail of hedge-row and stone wall, pasture and woodland, pin sharp, fresh and clear in the morning sun. Suddenly and quite unexpectedly, I felt as if I had always known and loved this place, as if I were merely returning to it after a long absence rather than coming to it for the first time. I felt a surge of joy rise up in me, bringing tears to my eyes, but I couldn't say why.

'I have the One Inch and the Geological in the car, if you'd like a look.'

His words made me aware I'd fallen silent yet again, so confused and puzzled was I by what was going on inside my head. I tried to say something about his calls and having delayed him, but he just shook his head: 'Don't worry. The first call is down there in the trees. John Carlyle, the blacksmith. I doubt if John even has a clock. If he does, he pays no attention to it whatever.'

We pored over the maps looking at the pattern of roads and settlements. It was the first time I had shared a map with anyone except another geographer. And George, of course. Maps were another thing George teased me about. He said he couldn't understand why a geographer who is supposed to know everything about maps can never tell you which way to go at a crossroads.

I'd had another letter from him at breakfast time. Only a single sheet by the feel of it and written in haste by the look of it. I was going to read it when I was getting ready to go out, but I'd sat talking to Mary and left myself short of time. Then I'd found I had no flat sandals to wear with my summer skirt and we'd had to search around to find the ones Mary thought Bridget had forgotten.

I felt a sudden stab of guilt that it was still unopened in my bag, but as Patrick traced the outline of the brilliant white hills which lay beyond us, I pushed it out of mind and gave all my attention to the scene before me.

'Paddy says the people on the limestone are different from the people on the shale, the "wetland" he calls it. What do you think?'

'Certainly people around here are better off than around Lisara. The grazing is very good. They do a nice line in young calves. And sheep, of course. Too wet in Lisara for sheep.'

'Do you think that sort of difference can affect personality? Paddy says the limestone people are "close".'

'I'll have to think about that one,' he replied as we folded up the maps.

Just then we caught sight of a small, black car as it began to weave its way up Corkscrew Hill. The noise of the engine reached us over the song of larks and the twitter of small birds in the hedgerows nearby. Patrick winced as the driver crashed his gears. We waited, not wishing to meet this particular vehicle on the steep descent.

'I'm not entirely sure that car's going to make it,' he said, as the sound effects became more dramatic.

'Patrick, you don't think . . .'

'Who else?'

'We could hop over the wall and hide.'

'And take the car with us?'

We got back into the car and sat waiting. It was indeed Feely. For a few seconds, as he came out of the last bend, his bonnet pointed straight at us. With a wrench at the wheel, he was past. He had no chance to recognise us, but his passengers certainly did.

'I think they were the same ones we met last Saturday.'

'Could well be. Priests usually stay a fortnight. Moyra's got a dozen or more at the hotel. Don't worry about them. As I said before, they gave me up as a bad job a long time ago.'

I said nothing, for the descent was difficult in such a large car and Patrick was driving slowly so I could enjoy the view. I glanced sideways at him and saw a person I barely recognised. The lines on his face were hard and deep-etched as he concentrated on the hairpins. This was a quite different person from the one who had shared the landscape with me only minutes ago. Uneasy and sad, I felt as if the brightness of the morning itself had been shadowed by threatening cloud.

We stopped in front of a rusty five-barred gate. At the end

of a lane shadowed by sycamores, I could see the shabby plaster of John Carlyle's house. As the engine died away and the buzz of insects and the sound of birds came back to us, the heavy air filled with the ring of hammer on anvil. My unease disappeared as suddenly as it had come and my spirits soared.

'Could I come with you or do you want me to stay here?' I asked, my words spilling out so quickly I nearly stuttered. 'I do speak fluent blacksmith,' I added, hopefully.

'Yes, of course you do. Do come if you want to but I'm not sure what you'll make of John. He looks like Abraham and he's not much of a ladies' man,' he warned.

Beyond the lane the cobbled yard was full of ploughs and harrows and bits of reaping machines. From a low, white-washed building with a black, felted roof, fresh smoke rose and hung almost motionless in the still air. As we approached, the hammering stopped and a tall figure bent under the low lintel, his eyes screwed up against the light.

He did look like Abraham. The flowing white beard and craggy face reminded me immediately of my *Child's Illustrated Bible*. He was at least six feet tall and his height was accentuated by high boots and the long, worn leather apron which covered his working clothes.

'Good day, John.'

'Good day, sur.'

'It's a good day for the work.'

'It is, it is . . .'

'This is Miss Stewart, John. Miss Stewart is a student, she has an interest in these parts.'

John Carlyle grunted and kept his eyes fixed on Patrick. He looked about as comfortable as if someone had brought him a wild animal on a piece of thin string.

'How is he then?' asked Patrick.

'Good. Ye'll see him improved. He's in the low field. 'Tis very rough.'

He marched off without a backward glance. Patrick paused, disconcerted.

'I'll wait here, Mr Delargy,' I said loudly, signalling to him to follow John Carlyle's disappearing figure. 'Mr Carlyle won't mind if I look at his forge, will he?' I raised my voice so the departing figure could object if he chose.

Patrick still looked anxious lest I were offended, so I grinned broadly and shooed him towards the low field. This time he caught on, his relief palpable as he hurried away.

I had met men like Carlyle before, but not for a long time. Shy, rather than unpleasant, they used to sit on the wooden bench in Uncle Albert's forge, or lean against the entrance to the shoeing shed. Given time, they would get used to you and offer the odd word. Many a one had ended up saving sweets for me. They would slip them to me when no one was looking, sticky and hard to unwrap from having been carried round in an inside pocket.

Still smiling to myself, I walked over to the door of the forge, looked into the darkness and breathed the old, familiar smell. A mixture of smells really. Smoke, certainly. A thick, creamy rope of it wound upwards from the damp slack on the fire. And dampness, too. Always in summer the stone walls of a forge transpire their stored up moisture, cooling the air inside. There was the acrid smell of metal. And axle oil. Burnt hoof from a recently shod animal. Blended together, the smell brought back to me what I now understood as the very best days of my childhood.

I could see Uncle Albert in his leather apron, the strings tied behind and then in front, a horse's hoof between his knees, pressing the hot iron shoe against the hoof so that it singed and smoked and left a mark that he could read. The shoe would go back into the fire, the bellows pumped till the metal glowed orange. The forge would fill with the ring of hammer on anvil.

'Mind yerselves, childer,' he would call out as the sparks flew, tracing bright arcs in the dimness. And the children would scatter, pushing and laughing, delighted to be frightened by the pursuing fragments. But I never ran away. My place was the corner by the bellows the sparks seldom reached. There, I would wait for my favourite moment, when the hammering stopped. A silence and then the water tank swallowed up the hot metal, seething and bubbling like a witch's caldron, a cloud of steam enveloping me.

I was never frightened in the forge as other children were. I knew when to move and when to keep still, when to ask questions and when to stay silent and watch, and how to drink scalding tea from an enamel mug with my hanky wrapped round the handle.

John Carlyle's forge was bigger than Uncle Albert's. It had three anvils, all mounted on tree stumps sunk into the earth. There were long work benches, too, covered with tools and a machine for drilling holes in metal. A newly drilled bar of iron leaned against the wall and bright silvery filings glinted on the patina of black coal dust that covered the floor.

I walked slowly across to the anvil and picked up the heavy hammer Carlyle had been using when we arrived. A ten pounder. A favourite one, for the wooden shaft was polished smooth with use. As I put it down the metal rang on the anvil and Uncle Albert's words came back to me: 'Each anvil has a different note. A smith can always pick out his own, even in a factory workshop with twenty going at once.'

I drew a small hammer from the rack and struck each anvil in turn. Yes, they were all different. But what made them different? Was it the size? I experimented further and found that the second anvil was the one most like Uncle Albert's. I tapped it thoughtfully, an old rhythm stirring on the edge of consciousness. Uncle Albert never just hit a piece of metal. He made the hammer dance, moving from metal to anvil and back again. There was a pattern in it like the stresses in poetry.

'Tum ta-ta tum tum. Tum ta-ta tum,' I sang to myself. I tapped out the tune with the light hammer, but it didn't sound right. Well, of course it wouldn't, would it?

'Silly girl,' I said aloud. 'You'd never use a hammer that weight on the anvil.'

I went back to the ten pounder and tried again. Yes. That's more like it. But the rhythm was too slow and the blows too tentative. I tried again. And again. Each time it got better, but although my arm began to ache with the effort, it still wasn't right. If I could get the pattern, I'd be back in the forge. I had not the slightest idea why I needed to get back to the forge, but with every attempt I grew yet more determined.

A shadow fell across the anvil as I raised my arm once more. John Carlyle was in the doorway, his face dark in shadow, his arm outstretched for his hammer. His large figure seemed menacing as he strode towards me. I held out his hammer and retreated before him. Immediately, the forge filled with sound which echoed and vibrated from the walls and roof.

'Try it again, miss. Ye were holdin' it too tight.'

He moved towards me, a patch of sunlight falling on his face. He was smiling broadly as I reached out and took the hammer from his hand.

Chapter 10

By the time we left John Carlyle's, it was nearly two o'clock, the car was like an oven and we were ravenous. Patrick drove a short way, stopped in the broad entrance to a cornfield and nodded across the sun-bleached stubble towards a line of trees, a narrow band of deep shadow round their feet.

'There's a stream over there if you don't mind the walk.'

'I'd walk a mile for a stream,' I answered truthfully.

'So would I, usually. But today I might expire.'

He handed me one of the picnic baskets, picked up a rug from the car and we set off. The stubble was very prickly and pieces of thistle poked through my sandals and stabbed my bare toes. The heat had built up since noon and it was further than it looked, but a few minutes later we were able to collapse on a mossy slope at the foot of a tall beech. We sat for a few moments just listening to the stream. There was very little water in the deep cutting it had made for itself, but what there was fell in a series of steps and filled the air with its splash and gurgle. Under the trees, the air was cool and full of the sound of birds.

'How many people did Mrs Brannigan expect for lunch?'

'What?'

He looked up from the bottle he had just unwrapped, a

preoccupied look on his face. He laughed when I repeated my question.

'Just two. But I think Mrs Brannigan has been talking to Mr Feely. She doesn't usually put in a bottle of my best sherry when I ask for a packed lunch.'

'Well, there's enough here to feed the five thousand,' I declared, as I unpacked the larger basket.

He handed me a glass.

'Sherry, madam?'

She certainly intended we shouldn't starve. There were sandwiches in greaseproof packets, both beef and ham, a box of biscuits and cheese, two pieces of apple tart and a bunch of grapes. Packed in the basket with the sherry was a thermos of iced water and another of coffee. We leaned against the smooth tree trunk in silence, watching the wagtails dart about amongst the stones. After a while, I took out two mugs and balanced them on a flat stone.

'Coffee?'

He had been thinking and I saw the familiar shadow on his face as I spoke. It vanished when he turned and saw me struggling with the cap on the bottle that held the milk.

'Can I help?'

I gripped tighter and tried again. It was an old half-bottle that had once held whiskey and its rough metal cap dug into my hand. I took out my hanky and wrapped it round the neck. This time it gave.

'Milk?'

He was laughing and I laughed myself when it struck me how persistent I'd been with the wretched cap.

'Elizabeth, you are a very determined young lady. Did you know that?'

'Very unfeminine, so I've been told.'

'Who told you that?'

It was George, of course. But somehow that was a name I had no wish to mention. I'd just been thinking what a fuss George made about unpacking a picnic basket whenever we went out together. Patrick had simply handed me one and tackled the other himself.

'Oh, my grandmother for one,' I began. 'She thinks a woman should only think what her husband thinks and pretend she can't do things so as to bolster his morale. She says men don't like women who know too much.'

'She has a point there, I suppose. Not every man would appreciate an incisive mind like yours. Some of them set greater store by the homely comforts ... "*kirche, küche, kinder*".'

'Church, kitchen and children,' I repeated tentatively, sure enough of the words, but not at all sure what the expression really meant.

'It's an old German expression for the lot that properly becomes a woman,' he explained. 'I believe it was a man who first said it.'

'Naturally,' I agreed, as I tucked the expression away for future use. It summed up very nicely something I had been trying to put my finger on. 'Grandma Stewart used to nag my mother about my going to university.'

'You mean she tried to stop you?'

I nodded, surprised at his sudden anger.

'And how did you manage it?'

'Luck mostly. I won a scholarship and the headmistress sent for my father. I don't know what she said to him, but I think he may have got a bit of a shock. Miss Mannering is rather elderly, a little person, rather bird-like. She used to wear lace blouses with cameo brooches or pearl chokers. I always liked her, but I think she really surprised Dad. After his interview, he wouldn't even go to Prize Day.'

'She sounds quite a woman.'

'Yes, she was. I think most people underestimated her, because of how she looked, but she always managed to get her own way once she worked out what she felt was the right thing to do.'

'She sounds rather like an attractive young woman of my acquaintance.'

I wondered who he meant and was about to ask but I saw he was smiling at me in a way even I couldn't miss. I had absolutely no idea what to say.

'Look,' he cried urgently, swinging round towards the river. 'Did you see him?'

'Only just. Was it a kingfisher?'

'It was indeed. I've seen him here before. I hoped he might honour us. Come over this side, he might come back.'

I moved over beside him and shared the one small space where we could both see the pool where the dappled shadows had glinted with blue. We sat very still, talking in whispers. But I couldn't concentrate on what he was saying about the habits of kingfishers. Inside my head, a dialogue was going on so fiercely that I wondered if it was the effect of the heat or the sherry, or both.

'Attractive young woman,' said one voice. 'Incisive mind,' said another. 'Nonsense,' came the reply. 'Always did have a good opinion of herself,' shouted the other. 'Too sure of herself by far. Mark my words, educate a woman and she loses leave of her senses.'

If I was losing leave of my senses, I'd like to know which ones. I'd seldom felt my senses sharper. I was fully aware of my delight in Patrick's company, the uneasy excitement of his physical closeness, the warmth of his body through the thin, creamy fabric of his shirt.

'There he goes.'

As we moved forward together intent on the blue-green flash our hands touched and clasped. Unaware of his breathless audience, the kingfisher flew up and down the stream for a full fifteen minutes after.

'I'll not ask you to come with me this time, Elizabeth,' began Patrick, when we drew up outside a handsome, two-storey house a few miles further north. 'John Joe is as deaf as a post and never stops talking. I'll be as quick as I can.'

I let my arm rest on the open window in the hope of cooling off. But it didn't help. I thought of my cologne stick, reached for my handbag and found George's letter. Before I paused to think, I had ripped it open.

My darling Elizabeth, I got your letter yesterday and was so disappointed that I'll have to wait a whole week till I hold you in my arms again.

When was yesterday? There was no date on his letter and the postmark was fuzzy.

Last night a crowd of us went to Bostock. It wasn't very good and I missed you terribly. I gave Adrienne a lift home and we agreed there was no one there worth dancing with. But I have good news. Mum says I can have the car on Saturday but I must have it back on Sunday night. I'm sure you can be ready on Saturday. That old man seems to have been a great help with getting your maps done and counting the houses. I rang your mother and she says it would be lovely if I could collect you, it seems such an out of the way place. I don't mind how far it is, darling. I just want you back home again. Write soon or phone Mum at the office to tell me you'll be ready, afternoon probably. Must dash for post. Passionately yours, George.

Panic overwhelmed me. It couldn't possibly be this Saturday, could it? Today was Wednesday. That would leave only two more days. I must have made a mistake, I told myself, as I went through the letter again. There was no mistake. He was planning to come in three days' time, before I'd even had a full two weeks.

My face felt hot and cross as I applied fresh lipstick. I examined it in the mirror of my compact and was so shocked by my expression I attempted a tender smile. But I wasn't in the mood for tender smiles. Yes, I probably had covered most of the material I needed, but that wasn't the point. This was the part of my work I did best and thought most important and George had reduced it to drawing maps and counting houses.

I remembered the carefully folded fiver that had arrived in Ben's letter in case I might need it and the questions he'd gone on to ask about topics I'd only mentioned briefly when we were at the Rosetta. 'Comparisons are odious,' my mother would say, but it was hard not to notice that after two years listening to me talk about my work, George hadn't registered as much as Ben had in just a few weeks.

I thrust George's letter into my handbag. Why on earth couldn't he have asked me when I'd be ready to come back? It was far too risky now to write and tell him not to come, I'd have to ring his mother. A five mile round trip tomorrow morning to the nearest phone, the bookies in Roadford, and an international call at peak rate to the busy income tax office where she worked. Goodness knows how long it would take to get through and how much it would cost when I did.

'Duty done. At your service, ma'am.'

Patrick was stripping off his jacket and dropping it with his briefcase on the back seat.

'Have you really finished?'

'Yes. But for one quick one over on the coast. I thought we could do it on the way home.'

He opened up the map, ran his finger along the road that cut straight through the hills to the sea, and waited.

'That would be marvellous.'

I was still feeling desperately agitated and anxious as we set off. The thought of being torn away from Lisara on Saturday was bad enough, but what troubled me even more was why I should still be so angry and upset when I had already made up my mind I wasn't going.

It was the Hills of Burren that finally calmed me down. Every geography student has seen slides and film of limestone pavement, Malham Tarn, if it's a British Isles course, Yugoslavia if it's Mediterranean Lands. I'd seen both, but nothing had prepared me for the sight of these white Hills of Burren, under a cloudless sky with the sea a sparkling blue backdrop.

Patrick was enjoying himself and his enthusiasm and delight were infectious. He drove slowly and stopped often, sometimes to let me look at the naked rock, fretted and fluted by wind and rain and seamed by great crevasses, sometimes to examine a spring, or a group of plants. At one point, we climbed up a few hundred feet above the road and sat looking back at the green country where we had spent the early part of the day.

'It's incredible,' I said. 'I'm beginning to wonder if I'm going to wake up and find myself in Belfast . . . in the rain.'

'You don't exactly seem to relish the prospect.'

He looked at me steadily and I noticed the fine lines around his eyes and mouth. He had a way of picking up things from what I said and offering them back to me.

'Don't I? It's the sun,' I said lightly. 'It's always made me want to go and do impossible things.'

'What sort of impossible things?'

His voice was gentle, casual almost, but he was watching me carefully.

'I don't really know. My mother says I never know what I want. I hate to admit it, but there's a sense in which she's right. All I seem to be really sure of is what I don't want.'

'But surely that's more than halfway there?'

'You know, I never thought of it that way.' I paused to let his words sink in. 'At least if I know what I don't want, I suppose I won't be trapped by it,' I continued slowly, 'even if I haven't found out what I do want.'

'Trapped?'

His voice was questioning but at the same time reassuring. I tried to work out what I did mean.

'Do you remember when you told me about your car being a gift? Not what you'd have chosen. Well, the more I look at it, the more I feel I'm surrounded by people who expect me to think what they think, do what they do, enjoy what they enjoy. Mostly, I don't. And sometimes I'm afraid I'll give in, because I'm tired of struggling and always being made to feel the odd one out. Does that make sense?'

'Perfect sense.'

He had been listening so intently, I was surprised when he said nothing more and just went on looking down into the shadows of a deep crevasse.

'Come over here, there's something I want to show you.'

His hand was firm around mine as we knelt on the smooth surface and peered down between the jagged edges of the deep fissure. Growing out of the tiniest scrap of soil imaginable on the rock several feet below us was a small plant with delicate, fernlike leaves.

'But it's lovely. How on earth does it manage it?'

'Yes, it is a lovely plant. But there's more to it than that. Down there, it's out of the wind. Cooler in summer, warmer in winter, and always moister than here on the surface. And that's only a beginning. That particular plant cannot tolerate lime. Yet here it is in the middle of a desert of limestone. It has picked its spot and it survives, though everything in the local environment round about says it can't.'

I nodded and smiled to myself. There was a lot more to his words than an interesting botanical description. He helped me to my feet and we stood side by side, held by the sheer immensity of the scene, two tiny figures in a vast empty space created out of rock and sea and sky. Irresistibly, the thought crept over me that were I with Patrick, wherever I was, I would never again feel the ache of loneliness.

'Just one more call,' he said, as we got back into the hot car. 'An old lady who lives down by the beach at Drennan. If we go back by the coast road, you can watch the sun go down on Galway Bay.'

We had reached the highest point of the extraordinary lunar landscape. Ahead of us, in a triangle bounded by the hills and the horizon, lay a vast expanse of sea still densely blue and shimmering under a sky just beginning to lose its colour. Away to our right curved a long line of beach. Beyond the splash of tiny waves, the wet sand gleamed in the yellowing light. Where the storm beach had been enmeshed in drifting sand, grasses waved in the gentle breeze, vivid shades of green and blue-grey set against the darkened fragments of shattered limestone.

'I'm an absolute idiot,' I exclaimed. 'I've been living on Galway Bay for ten days and the penny hasn't dropped till now.'

'Not surprising really,' he replied. 'You've been focused on Lisara. But I'm told some of the tourists really are daft.

Apparently they expect to see an arrow on the skyline with a notice saying "Next sunset: today 7.45 pm" like the one near Old Faithful in Yellowstone.'

I laughed and looked out to where the islands lay on the misty horizon. My mind went back to the first time I had laid eyes on them, the Sunday afternoon of my arrival. I'd become so used to seeing them from Lisara, they looked strangely distant from this different perspective.

'What did you mean when you said distance lends perspective?' I asked, turning towards him.

'Did I say that?'

'Yes, when you drove me back to Lisara, last Thursday. You stopped to look at the islands and said you often stopped there on the way to Limerick, because the distance lent perspective.'

'Remind me never to get drunk with you around. You've too good a memory. Was that only last Thursday?'

I nodded and waited as he turned right onto the coast road. It was after six o'clock and there was a scatter of traffic around, mostly family cars with beachballs in the back windows and folding prams strapped to their roofracks.

'I think I meant that events often seem different when you look back on them from wherever you are now . . . if you see what I mean.'

I laughed, for the final phrase was mine.

'Yes,' I agreed, 'it's a pity one couldn't speed up time now and again, so that you could see how something would appear when . . .'

I broke off, for the situation ahead looked most awkward. A line of cars were nosing their way out from the field above the beach. One car had stopped and the driver was having an argument with an old woman who was waving and gesticulating angrily. Behind them, other cars were tooting and revving their engines impatiently. To my surprise, I saw that we were signalling to turn left into the field on the deeply rutted sandy track where this angry scene was taking place.

Suddenly, the old woman spotted us. With a hasty gesture she dismissed the irate driver and waved the line of cars aside so that we could come in. It was a very awkward manoeuvre. Once free of the departing cars, Patrick headed for the sea. He stopped with the bonnet pointing at the horizon where a small fishing boat was perfectly reflected in the calm water. As the last cars disappeared behind us leaving the beach deserted, I saw the old woman come hurrying towards us. Patrick took an envelope from his briefcase and put it in his pocket as we got out together.

'Ah, Mr Patrick, sur, I thought it was you. Shure, you're welcome.'

She clutched his hand and looked up at him, her face burnt brown from the sun. She was dressed completely in black but for a faded green velour hat which she wore on the back of her head and a stripy apron with large patch pockets.

'And you're all well I'm sure, your father and mother and Walter and Moyra and Helen. I say a wee prayer for you every night and you all so good to an old lady.'

She didn't appear to have seen me and I wondered if I could slip away behind the car and leave them to their conversation. Patrick had given her the envelope and she was thanking him profusely, catching his arm and calling various blessings upon him.

'Tell your father, I never forget him, nor you neither . . .'

She broke off and turned to me as if she had just registered my presence.

'Ah miss, I didn't see you. Shure you're welcome too. I'm glad to see you back so soon. It will not be long now, miss, shure it won't and I wish you joy. It's to be October isn't it, and that not far away now.'

I agreed that indeed October was not far away, though what it was that was to be I had no idea. She pressed my hands and muttered to herself. I caught 'Mr Patrick' and 'joy', but she was talking to herself now in a high-pitched voice which sounded as if she were weeping. Patrick moved towards me and held out his hand.

'Ah shure, go on childer, away for your walk. Isn't everybody gone home except old Mary Coyle and she wishes you joy. Take your time. I'll leave the gate for you and lock it later.'

She stood waiting as we moved to the stile where a path led down to the beach. She waved as I got over and was still waving as we set off across the shingle beyond the grassy sward.

'Do you mind if we walk for a bit? She'll go away as soon as we're out of sight,' Patrick said, without looking at me.

His face looked old and tired as I glanced at him out of the corner of my eye. I wondered if it was the reference to Walter that had upset him. And yet, he had seemed easy enough with her. He'd done what I'd done myself many a time, when I'd nodded to old people who had forgotten the loss of those once known so well to them.

No, it wasn't when she spoke of his family that he'd stood rooted to the spot. It was when she had turned and spoken to me. 'It will not be long now and I wish you joy.' There was only one possible meaning for those words when spoken to a woman with a man at her side.

We walked in silence along the shore, moving automatically towards the firmer sand left by the receding tide. It was very quiet, only the slight swash from the long ripples on a calm sea and the occasional cry of a gull. I looked studiously out at the islands, wondering whether the stricken look had gone from his face.

At last, I had to turn to look at him. I found him watching me closely. I dropped my eyes to the wet sand at my feet, studied minutely the pattern of tiny shells left by the tide. They were pink and cream and white.

'I'm sorry. Was it long ago?'

He smiled his familiar smile and squeezed my hand.

'Six years ago . . . a long, long time ago . . . but it has taken till now to get the right perspective on it.'

Watching the sun dip lower in the sky, we walked on till we found a smooth-polished tree trunk cast up on a sandy bank. We sat and talked quietly, about the islands and the yellowing light and the way the ripples crossed and recrossed each other on the gently sloping beach. A slight breeze sprang up from the sea as it often does at the end of a hot afternoon. I shivered slightly.

'Are you cold?'

He put his arm around me and drew me closer so that I could feel the tweed of his jacket on my bare arm and the touch of his cheek on my forehead. We sat in silence, watching the seabirds wheel and dip. I knew what had changed in me: even when you have no idea where you are going, sometimes you have to go to find out.

I also knew that if I turned to Patrick, he would kiss me. All day, I had been evading the look in his eyes, a look of loneliness and longing. I could evade it once more. And perhaps I should. For there could be no knowing where his longing could lead us. All I had to do was stand up, or bend forward and pick up a shell, any trivial act to take me beyond the shelter of his arms.

But I did none of those things. I turned towards him, felt his arms close around me and was overwhelmed by a loneliness and a longing of my own.

Chapter 11

Tiny puffs of evening cloud were turning to blue and grey as we hurried back along the beach. They began to drift across the orange and gold radiance the westering sun had spread out across the whole width of the horizon. Sunset itself would be spectacular. But we couldn't stay to watch, nor share the soft hush of the early evening, for Patrick was already late. Back at the hotel, there was the spirit store to unlock, supplies to be checked out for bar and dining room, while in Lisara, Mary and Paddy would be waiting for me, supper ready and long since put in the oven to keep warm.

Returning by the direct route was so rapid, there was little time for talk.

'I'll come and find you as soon as I get back,' he promised, as he pulled in behind a red car drawn up on the verge beside the cottage wall.

I knew he wanted to take me in his arms again but we'd both seen Michael Flannigan strolling up the road. As he moved closer, his eyes firmly fixed upon us, his goat on its long tether stopped and nibbled in a leisurely way at the roadside grasses.

We exchanged a wry look, clasped hands below the level of the dashboard and got out together. Moments later Patrick was speeding back across the far ridge.

'Ah shure good, girl, there you are. We was just speaking of you. I said ye'd not be too long.'

Mary was smiling broadly as she drew me over to the fireside. An elderly man sat in her chair. In his ancient duffle coat and wellington boots, he looked like many a neighbouring farmer, though he could easily have been a passing tramp. Whoever he was, Mary's unexpected animation told me he was important to her.

'Isn't it great now that Professor McDonagh is here for a day or two, Elizabeth, and you so interested in the old stories,' she said enthusiastically as she introduced us.

The professor stood up, shook my hand and enquired politely after my own professor at Queen's whom he said he knew very well professionally but not personally. His eyes were a pale blue, his hair thinning and gingery, his face creased with age and worn by wind and sun. It was his voice I noticed particularly, soft but very pleasing, full of a gentle humour, a voice you could listen to for a long time without growing weary.

'Come on now, it's time we had our supper,' said Mary, with unaccustomed firmness. 'Elizabeth, astore, would you fetch me the cloth from the bottom of the cupboard?'

It was a memorable evening, Paddy in great spirits, Mary more talkative than I had ever known her. I was so heartened and encouraged by the happy atmosphere round the fire that I offered some fragments of stories I'd heard as a child. I was amazed at how much I was able to recall. Before he went back to his hotel, Professor McDonagh asked me if I'd like to join Paddy and himself on their visits to the local storytellers. When he said it would be a great help to have an informant from another part of Ireland I was so excited I could hardly believe my luck.

For the next two days I listened and scribbled as they

worked their way round the area, sometimes meeting the storytellers in their homes, sometimes taking them to the local pub. Mary had often sung the praises of the professor and now I could see why: he was a genuinely nice man, thoughtful and kind. He was also very good at making people feel comfortable and getting them to talk freely even with a tape recorder running.

By the time he left us on Friday night, I'd heard so much and seen so much I wanted to write for a month. But I hadn't got a month. After my call to George's mother I knew I had to make a decision about going back, so, when I sat down on Saturday morning to record as much as I could about my time with Professor McDonagh, I began by writing notes to my parents and George to let them know I'd be coming home the following Saturday, by train from Dublin.

All through that morning I wrote fast, keeping my mind firmly fixed on what I was doing. By lunch time, I felt I had something I could work with once I was back in Belfast. I let myself relax a little and immediately my mind filled with thoughts of Patrick. Since we'd parted so hurriedly outside the cottage, I'd had no time at all to explore what I felt about him. Each evening I would look forward to having that time before I went to sleep, but my eyes closed the moment I climbed into bed. As I put my notebooks away and laid the table for lunch, I longed for the empty countryside, the six-mile walk into town and my first piece of quiet since the soft stillness of the beach at Drennan.

I strode down the hill, looked up at the gathering rain clouds, and gave thanks. With rain threatening, there would be few passing cars to interrupt me and I was unlikely to get a lift. I scanned the horizon. Today the islands lay heavy on the grey water, muted shades of purple and grey, the white shapes of the cottages barely visible, the stone walls lost in the dimness. How different they had looked from the bare Hills of Burren, shimmering in the heat, the sea dazzling around them.

'Distance lends enchantment,' I murmured to myself, as the images of that day flooded back into my mind. It was a day I would never forget. I felt sure of that, but of little else. What was it that had made the day so memorable? That I'd been kissed by a man a good deal older than myself, a man from a different culture, a different background, a different social group? My parents would be horrified if they knew, George angry, Mary and Paddy delighted. Bridget Doherty would think my good fortune nothing less than a triumph.

It was all a matter of perspective. Each had their own way of looking at it. What really mattered was how I saw it. That was much more difficult. To be honest, I wasn't sure. Certainly, I had responded to Patrick's kisses, been delighted and warmed by his tenderness, but if I had expected to feel something more, something dramatic enough to do justice to the fact that this was a new and forbidden relationship, then I hadn't.

I laughed aloud, remembering all those love scenes I'd viewed over the years at the Curzon Cinema, when I'd been sent off every Saturday afternoon to get me out of the way. Down at Drennan, there hadn't been so much as a solitary violin hidden behind the marram grass, never mind the full orchestra lurking in the sand dunes just waiting for its cue.

No, I hadn't expected anything ridiculous like that. I'd made up my mind a long time ago that instant, overwhelming passion was only to be found in that same fantasy world where heroines crash through jungles pursued by natives, wild animals or King Kong himself, and emerge with spotlessly clean blouses and their mascara still on their eyelashes. But excitement, or elation, or even something that might grow to passion? Had I experienced anything like that?

I brushed the trailing grasses by the wayside and set the heavy seedheads bobbing. When Patrick kissed me, I had to confess, what I really felt was relief. A sudden wonderful sense of comfort, and ease, as if some great burden had just melted away, leaving me feeling calm and happy and ready to return his embrace.

Did that mean I loved him? Or was my response simply a new experience, something sure to happen once I moved out of my own familiar world, full of boys I had grown up with, whose sisters I'd met on the hockey field, or in the Schools Challenge Cup debates, or a university club or society.

Although in Patrick's arms I'd felt nothing I would recognise as passion, equally I knew I'd be happy to make love with him. And there was no disguising the fact that the thought shocked me. Not the actual thought of making love itself. No. The problem was that I'd always insisted I could only make love to someone I was absolutely sure I loved. But that thought hadn't touched me at all as we clung to each other.

If Adrienne Henderson had had any idea what was going through my mind at this moment, she'd laugh her head off. She's always saying how terribly old-fashioned I am, because I don't make love to George. And I've always argued back that it was only sensible to wait, because the risks were far too great. Besides, I couldn't bear the thought of making love in the back seats of cars and on other people's sofas, furtively and hastily, part of me listening for the sound of someone coming. It just didn't seem as if that could be the right way for something that was supposed to be so very important.

But she declared she'd make love to anyone she really fancied. It was entirely my upbringing which made me so inhibited. Then she'd hint that if I really did love George, I wouldn't be able to stop myself making love whenever we had the chance. That really began to worry me, not because I hadn't, but perhaps after all, I hadn't really wanted to.

Troubled and uneasy, I sat down on a low stone wall. The islands had disappeared. The curtain of rain which had enveloped them was clearly outlined as it swept south, drawing cold air across my perspiring face. I shivered and remembered the enclosing warmth of Patrick's arms around me, the sense of well-being they had brought, the comfort and security I felt as we sat together on the tree trunk, sea and sky open before us.

I tried to remember what we'd said to each other. I laughed again, as lines of torrid dialogue from the ninepenny novels circulated at school repeated themselves in my mind. How marvellous it would be if writers actually told the truth about passionate encounters; admitted that lovers got caught in each other's spectacles, got cramp at an absolutely critical moment, found ants in their knickers, or that a parting embrace had been written out of the script by Michael Flannigan and his goat.

We hadn't produced much in the way of torrid dialogue. In fact, after the first long kiss, we'd said very little to each other. When we were not kissing, we sat silently side by side, and I watched the second hand of his watch sweep away what little time we had, before we had to walk along the empty beach and drive back to Lisara.

'You know I'd cancel this trip if I could?'

'Yes, I know.'

'I'll try to be back by Tuesday. You'll still be here, won't you?'

'Yes. I'll be here.'

In the middle of the deserted beach, we had paused a moment, kissed again and then run hand in hand to the car, hoping that Mary Coyle would not be there to delay us. He had not said he loved me but I felt sure that he did. What I was quite sure of was that I was longing to see him again.

'Miss Stewart, can I give you a lift?'

For a moment I didn't recognise the young man who stopped his van and pushed open the passenger door for me. It was the barman from Delargy's. One look at his face told me he was as uncomfortable about giving me a lift as I was about having to accept one. But the rules were clear for both of us. He could not pass a known person on the road and I could not refuse a kind gesture.

'Thanks, Mickey. It's beginning to look very like rain.'

'Aye, it rained further back. It might rain here yet.'

Why was it so many young men were so desperately shy, I asked myself, as I set about finding some topic of conversation to help him through the next four miles.

He parked in the stable yard just outside the stockroom. As I got out and thanked him, I could just distinguish the outline of Patrick's desk among the cardboard boxes and the crates. There were no lights and no fire. Painfully aware of his absence, I walked round to the shop entrance and wished I didn't have to go in. But I had Mary's list.

Not all the visitors had gone home after all. The shop was full of them, buying cups of coffee or postcards, or just wandering aimlessly around. Kathleen was nowhere to be seen and by the time one of the younger girls was free to serve me, my back had begun to ache with a dull throb.

Full of irritation with the visitors who were also filling up the Square, I wove my way through them and up to the post office. The sky had turned grey and to the west the heavy cloud had a darker tone. A few spots of rain fell on the pavement and evaporated almost immediately in the warm breeze.

The queue at the post office did nothing to improve my temper. My head had begun to ache and when I discovered I'd put the shopping into Mary's bag on top of the letters for the post, I nearly burst into tears. I stood behind a crumpled green anorak and fished for them one-handed as we shuffled towards Miss Molloney's window.

Mary's two letters were under the tea and sugar, my thank you to Professor McDonagh emerged badly creased, but search as I might I couldn't find the two notes I'd written to George and my parents. Surely, I couldn't have forgotten to put them in. If I had, it would mean yet another expensive phonecall and an awkwardness I would much rather avoid. If I rang the shop my mother would complain about my extravagance, but if I rang George's mother instead, she'd complain about hearing at second hand.

I breathed a sigh of relief when I found them under the squashy brown-paper parcel of bacon. You really must get yourself better organised, I berated myself, as I caught up on the green anorak who had made several strides forward. The sight of the Belfast addresses reminded me that a week today I'd be on my way back. The thought depressed me utterly. But then, if I hadn't phoned George's mother, I'd be on my way back at this very moment. Better be thankful for small mercies. I still had a week, a precious week, and so much to do with the new ideas from my time with Professor McDonagh. And so much to resolve between Patrick and me.

I wiped my forehead. The post office was warm and steamy and I had thoroughly upset myself panicking over my letters. Come on, Elizabeth, calm down. Not long now. Out of town at speed and then a quiet walk home. Doesn't matter if you get soaked, you've plenty of dry things at the cottage.

'Four letters and three cards, please.'

I pricked up my ears. The voice was English, rather formal

and slightly hesitant, like the kind of public school boy George enjoyed imitating, the ones who are supposed to say things like 'Frightful bore' and 'What ho, Carruthers'.

There was a pause. It had taken me a little while to discover that as Miss Molloney pressed the stamps on the damp sponge pad, aligned them carefully and smoothed them thoroughly, she was busy reading the addresses. She had long ago identified my parents and George. The third time Ben's address appeared she'd enquired coyly if he was another boyfriend. When I explained that Ben was just very good at writing me letters, so obviously I wrote back, she'd made a funny noise like a hiccup.

I'd no idea how to interpret this sound, but I was planning to tell Ben about it tomorrow when I wrote again. I knew he'd enjoy being vetted by the local postmistress, because so far he'd enjoyed all my stories. After he'd had my first long letter thanking him for the Brigadier's fiver, he'd asked for more details about the people I'd mentioned and how various aspects of my work were going. In his most recent letter he said he thought I was doing so well I ought to take as much time as I could manage. He insisted I was to be sure and use the Brigadier's fiver if I was tight for money. How lovely of him to call it 'the Brigadier's fiver' when actually half of the money was his.

But that was just like Ben, looking for the best in any situation. Working at the Rosetta was far better than I expected, because Ben was there to point out what I was missing. He always saw the lighter side of things, made people laugh, and yet underneath the easy manner there was a thoughtfulness and a seriousness most people missed. When he came up against exploitation, or prejudice, or indifference, he'd get just as angry as I do. But whereas I always try to stop myself being angry, because it upsets me so badly, Ben believes anger is perfectly proper and can be very productive so long as you decide what you're going to do with it.

'All right, Lizzie, so the man next door practises the violin at midnight. Every night. And he's no Yehudi Menuhin. So you get angry. That's fine. You have a right to be angry. It's what you do after that really matters. Wiring up the seat of his loo to the ring circuit is not appropriate.'

I grinned broadly, then hastily straightened my face in case someone might think I'd gone mad. But I felt cheered. As I shuffled another few feet and felt the dull ache in my back again, I did a quick calculation. Too obvious for words. I'd brought one box of Tampax, of course, but as the minutes dragged by I began to worry what I'd do if I needed more and the medical hall didn't stock them.

'Could you possibly tell me how to get to this address?' green anorak enquired politely.

'Ye'd be a friend of Mr O'Dara's then?'

'No . . . er . . . I'm afraid I haven't met Mr O'Dara yet.'

'Ah, yer going to visit him, is it?'

Green anorak cleared his throat nervously. I was beginning to feel sorry for him. He wasn't going to get anywhere with Miss Molloney unless she got more information out of him than she herself was asked to supply. Being English and reticent, he would never think of saying more than was necessary.

'I have a letter of introduction to Mr O'Dara, but I've not been able to find Lisara on the map.'

That makes two of us. I peeped round the side of his jacket to see how Miss Molloney was reacting to a letter of introduction. She was frowning crossly at the piece of paper with the address written on it. The young man was tall and thin, with a pale, rather pointed face and very dark straight hair. A few strands of it kept falling down on his heavy-rimmed spectacles and he ran his fingers through it in a vain attempt to keep it back. He spoke with the kind of deliberation that suggested he might once have had a speech impediment.

'D'ye know the road to the Cliffs of Moher?'

'I'm ... er ... afraid ... I don't.'

'Well, if you go down to the Square you might find a Guard. He'll put you right.'

Miss Molloney dismissed him with a curt nod and as he thanked her and moved away, I saw how tired and anxious he looked. When I touched his arm and said I thought I could help, he blushed as if I'd just propositioned him.

'Is this a friend of yours, Miss Stewart?' broke in Miss Molloney.

'Any friend of Mr O'Dara is a friend of mine,' I said innocently, as I spread my letters out to be inspected.

To my amazement, she creased her face at me and peered sideways through her grille at the young man.

'He's too old for a student,' she muttered. 'And he's English.'

'Some English students are awfully old,' I assured her in a whisper.

'Ye'll be going home soon, I expect?' she said, reverting to her normal tone and giving me her full attention as she checked out my letters.

'Yes, indeed. Next Saturday. I'll be sorry to go.'

'Ye will, indeed. I'm sure ye've enjoyed yer stay.'

This was my cue for more information, but I ignored it politely and told her I would see her again before I left.

'I say ... it's frightfully ... good of you to ... er ... help me out like this. My name's ... Llwellyn-Jones, Geoffrey Llwellyn-Jones,' he said, thrusting his hand towards me when we got outside.

As I said my name, I wondered why I'd never learnt to think before I offered help. So much for my quiet walk back to Lisara.

'I have my car parked . . . down in the Square . . . unless Mr O'Dara lives nearby.'

As we wove our way back to the Square, I explained where Lisara was and that I was staying with Mary and Paddy.

'What a . . . tremendous piece of luck . . . meeting you. My directions weren't very clear. I should have been here two days ago, you see, to meet someone who would have helped me, but the car packed up . . . she does sometimes.'

We had come to a halt beside a battered Morris Minor. I wasn't surprised she'd packed up, I was only surprised she'd got going in the first place.

'I'm sorry . . . it's a bit of a mess,' he said, disappearing inside the car to unlock the passenger door.

To clear the front seat for me, he had to move a pile of books, a plastic raincoat and a tape recorder. These he tried to accommodate on the back seat with some rubber boots, a pile of maps, a Norwegian sweater, two thermos flasks and the remains of a packet of sandwiches. I settled in the passenger seat with Mary's shopping on my knees, but when he saw the large black bag he insisted on putting it in the back. I gazed through the grubby windscreen while he tugged and pulled until he managed to perch Mary's bag on top.

He looked quite exhausted as he got back in and turned on the ignition. The engine coughed, whirred, and died.

'She's sometimes a bit difficult to start.'

It had grown heavier through the afternoon and now the strip of sky above the roofs of the shops was the same dark colour as their slate. A sudden rattle of thunder was followed by rain that lashed on the windscreen so fiercely that the buildings ahead were completely blurred.

He tried again. To my absolute amazement, the car started perfectly. He pressed the accelerator, the engine noise increased encouragingly and we moved slowly across the now deserted Square. After a few yards, he stopped again and switched off.

'I'm frightfully sorry . . . do you mind if we wait . . . a minute or two . . . the windscreen wipers . . . haven't been too good.'

He looked distraught. For the first time that afternoon my sense of humour came back. I could just picture Mr Feely on one of his regular circuits of the Square seeing me in a car with Geoffrey and all his worldly goods. What else would he think but that we were eloping?

I couldn't exactly share the joke, but it made me feel better. I was about to make some encouraging remark when a thought struck me.

'Geoffrey, you aren't by any remote chance connected with Professor McDonagh?'

'Why, yes. I was to meet him here in the Square on Wednesday, so I could go with him to Mr O'Dara. However did you know?'

For all the slowness of the journey back to Lisara, the problem of conversation did not arise. Just as Mickey Coyle had sprung to life when I'd told him about my problem getting a good head on a pint of Guinness, so Geoffrey was transformed at the mention of Professor McDonagh.

Once he began to tell me about his research fellowship and his work on Celtic myth survivals in the oral tradition of western Britain, the change was nothing short of miraculous. His hands relaxed on the wheel, he stopped running them through his hair, and there was no trace whatever of the hesitancy in his speech. Once, he actually looked at me long enough for me to notice he had rather handsome, brown eyes with surprisingly long dark lashes.

There were several questions I wanted to ask him, but as he was still talking when we came up the hill, I had to use hand signals to indicate that we had arrived and to show him where to park. The moment he stopped talking, things took a turn for the worse. He stepped out of the car, caught his sleeve on the indicator lever and snapped it off. When he bent down to retrieve the broken piece from the floor, he bumped his head on the steering wheel. I wondered if I should fetch my shopping from the back seat myself, but that might upset him more, so I waited patiently and listened to the landslide he generated in the process of getting it out.

By the time we'd walked out of the yard and round to the front of the house, he was running his fingers through his hair at five-second intervals. Something would have to be done to help him. I parked the shopping on the garden wall and waved him over to the other side of the road.

'Look,' I said, pointing out to an expanse of sea south of the islands. 'That's where Kyle Stefeen lies lost below the waters with its houses locked and barred. And it's a girl with six fingers will find the key and she'll find it in the sands of Liscannor Bay,' I said quietly, mimicking the rhythm and intonation of the storytellers.

His face lit up. He beamed and said something about an Atlantis myth.

'You won't mind if I just call you Geoffrey, will you?' I asked, pausing before we went in. 'The O'Daras are very informal people. You'll like them.' I really couldn't imagine what Mary and Paddy were going to make of his decidedly upper class accent.

He nodded, but continued to look very nervous as we entered the kitchen where Mary and Paddy sat by the fire wearing the unmistakable signs of people trying to pretend they're not expecting a stranger to appear at any moment.

'Mary and Paddy, this is Geoffrey. He's a friend of Professor McDonagh. I heard him asking for you, Paddy, in the post office. Wasn't that lucky?'

'Yer welcome, Geoffrey, yer welcome,' said Paddy, rising to his feet and jutting out his hand.

'Professor McDonagh is it?' said Mary.

Geoffrey was about to reply, but Mary wasn't listening. From the ecstatic look on her face I knew exactly what was coming next, a Professor McDonagh story I'd heard at least three times.

'Ah shure he's a gentleman, Professor McDonagh. He's a lovely man. For all he's educated, you'd not feel one bit strange with him. He'd come in here and sit down in that chair like any one of the neighbours and talk away as if he were in his own house. Shure one time he came and didn't he take a packet out of his pocket and it a pound of steak. Ah, shure the butcher hadn't wrapped it half-right and the blood had come through on his pocket. But he never said a word. Just that he thought I mightn't have been in town and it might come in handy for the supper. Wasn't that nice now?'

Geoffrey agreed that it was, his face turned towards her bearing no trace at all of his former anxiety. Paddy took up the story. For another ten minutes, Geoffrey said so little his accent hardly noticed and by the time they got to asking him about his relationship with Professor McDonagh and the nature of his visit, the kettle was already down and the blue striped teacups waited on the table.

I smiled to myself as I watched Paddy curl his fingers round his blue enamel mug. Only two weeks since I had first sat drinking from the best flowered china cups, wondering how I would deal with the problem of money, the absence of a bathroom, and the hazard of my alien religion.

I looked at my blue striped teacup. Best china for female visitors, because women notice such things. Second best china or delft for male visitors, because men don't notice such things. Mugs or chainstore cups for children and tinkers, because what they might or might not notice doesn't matter anyway. The ritual hierarchy of teacups. I'd make a note on it and try the idea on Patrick.

Patrick. The name resonated in my mind and comforted my weariness. Outside, it was settling in for a wet evening, the wind gusting round the gables, spots of rain hissing down on the glowing fire. Geoffrey still wasn't saying very much, but he was proving himself a good listener. His questions were very simple, but just what was needed to carry on the easy flow of talk and reminiscence. Already, I could see the gleam in Paddy's eye. He was enjoying himself. Any minute now, he would start to tell one of his stories.

When he did, I could move into that strange world of fantasy I found so intriguing, or slip away unnoticed into my own thoughts, where Patrick was with me, watching me, talking to me, asking me questions. Happy as I was in the small gathering round the fire, there was one place I would rather be. And that was with Patrick.

Chapter 12

Whatever anxieties I might have had about Geoffrey Llwellyn-Jones when I brought him back to the cottage, they disappeared as the hours passed. Beneath the shyness and his quiet manner, I discovered a remarkable capacity for accepting people and situations without the slightest fuss. He didn't say a lot, but he listened closely to all Paddy and Mary said, a warmth in his dark eyes I had not expected to find in someone from such a very different background.·

When he arrived back the next morning with his tape recorder and a hand mike, Paddy settled down to tell stories as if this was as much a part of his life as digging potatoes. I sat in a corner by the stove, working on my own notes, while Mary crept round the kitchen trying to do her usual jobs without making any of the usual noises. I glanced at Geoffrey from time to time and saw he was perfectly at home, his only anxiety the oscillations of the green lines on his portable machine.

At the end of Sunday's efforts, I heard him persuading Mary to let him peel the potatoes for supper. I was amazed when he succeeded and even more amazed when I noticed how competent he was. I watched him across the table as I scraped the carrots and remembered the way George insisted he was no good at the job. Certainly the amount of potato he left on the skins made his point. Geoffrey was a different story. With his shirt sleeves rolled up and a cheerful grin on his face, he tweaked out the odd sprouting eye like a professional and left a mere handful of peelings at the end.

By the time I took Geoffrey to visit Sean O'Struithan on Monday afternoon, he'd made further progress with his shyness. On Saturday, even meeting my glance looked as if it might have dire consequences but today he could look at me as if I were a normal mortal rather than a close cousin of the Morrigan.

'You do seem to have made a lot of friends in a fortnight, Elizabeth,' he said, as we turned out of Sean's courtyard and took the short path that led to the steep back wall of the quarry.

'There are a lot of nice people around. It wasn't very difficult,' I said, over my shoulder, as we tramped in single file through the spiky heather.

'I say . . . Elizabeth . . . I . . . I've been wondering . . . well you're so good at these things . . . I wanted to . . . ask your advice.'

I turned to look at him, startled and dismayed to hear the old hesitancy return.

'Well, you always seem to come up with exactly the right thing to do or say . . . as if you knew every single custom or habit of this whole community . . . I've never met anyone half as good as you are at getting on with people in the field.'

I was completely floored. He'd paid me a very sincere compliment, but the way he put it I could hardly say thank you in the usual way. I muttered something feeble about always being glad to help in any way I could.

'It's Mary and Paddy actually,' he went on. 'They've been so kind to me, and so generous, giving me supper and putting up with all my questions. I'd like to express my appreciation, but I can't think how to do it. I can't do the flowers and chocolates thing. At least I can see that's not right. But I can't manage the pound of steak in my pocket one. I'm sure I'd just end up embarrassing them. What would you do?'

Now he'd got it out, he seemed easier. Certainly I felt easier because I knew I could solve the problem once I gave my mind to it.

We had emerged from the wide expanse of heather. The path now led across a broad stretch of short grass starred with tiny wildflowers. I studied them closely as we walked along side by side.

'Yes, mmm . . . money in any form is taboo . . . and what you do has to fit the relationship you've made. Can you drink Guinness, Geoffrey?'

'Oh yes, most certainly.'

'That means you could take Paddy to Considine's,' I said happily. 'But then I expect you want to include Mary too, don't you?'

He nodded emphatically, so I tried again.

'Something that makes life easier, or pleasanter, or a little more comfortable, but where money is not visibly involved.' I turned to him, beaming, as it suddenly came to me. 'The rates. That's it. The rates.'

He burst out laughing. 'I'll believe it, if you say so.'

When I explained, he looked relieved as well as delighted.

' . . . so you need to pretend you have to get a sight of Ennistymon for the benefit of your work,' I began. 'Then you can ask them if they would like to go along for the outing. When they say yes, which they will, because otherwise they'd have to hire a car, you could ask them if they would have lunch with you. The place the farmers go to does a very good meal for five shillings and they've been there before. How about that?'

'Splendid . . . absolutely splendid . . . but for one thing.'

'What's that?'

'I'd so like it if you could come, Elizabeth. If you could manage it, that is,' he said apologetically. 'I know you haven't got much time left, but I'm sure Mary would like that.'

I hesitated. Then I looked at him and weakened. He was a very kind person and Mary had become quite devoted to him, but I knew that although she listened to him with total attention, often she didn't understand what he said.

'Could we go early and be back for tea?'

'Yes, of course, whatever fits your programme.'

We stopped at the end of the path and gave our total attention to the shallow steps cut in the steep back wall of the quarry. Safely down we moved across its floor and then turned and looked back.

'He's absolutely right, isn't he?'

Geoffrey gazed up at the descent we had just made. Sean had said the steps were invisible and they were. Unless you'd been shown the markers and taken down yourself, the grey cliff which ran the whole length of the old workings appeared exactly as Sean wanted it to appear, a barrier to anyone trying to approach his mountain hideout.

A few minutes later, as we passed through the gate into the uppermost of Paddy's fields, we agreed that Wednesday would be the best day.

'Splendid,' he said again, as we moved into the next field. 'I knew you'd have the answer.'

When I opened my eyes on Tuesday morning the first thing I thought of was Patrick. I could hardly believe the six days since our parting had disappeared so quickly. But I was grateful they had, for I was sure I wouldn't be able to manage a day longer without seeing him. There was so much to tell him, so many new and interesting things to share with him. And I wanted to see what he thought about the ideas I'd been shaping for some real research of my own.

As I set off down the hill to visit the elderly lady who had taught in Lisara when it still had a school, even the mizzling rain did nothing to dampen my spirits. I waved to the laden carts as they passed on the way to the creamery. Last week, I had met and talked to all the farmers as they waited in the long queue to unload their heavy milk churns. I'd learnt a lot, added to the green file material for my thesis and notes towards this other project which hadn't any name yet.

In fact, the green file was now full. Not another sheet of punched paper could I coax between the bulging rings. Patrick would laugh when I told him, for he referred to the Green File as if it were some friendly creature following upon my heels, ever hopeful of being fed with one more delectable sheet covered with my observations.

I was some way beyond the creamery when I noticed a strange object on the now empty road. Black and shiny. With a high back. It looked like a giant beetle moving towards me. I tramped on steadily, the rain becoming heavier as I approached my turn down towards Ballahaleine. The strange object declared itself as I got closer and I laughed aloud. Head down over the handlebars, enveloped in his huge regulation cape, the wind inflating the dark, shiny material, Paddy the Postman was cycling towards me. I stopped by the turn and waited for him to reach me.

'I've two letters for ye, miss. Will I fetch them out?'

'Oh, Paddy, I don't want to trouble you in this rain.'

'Shure I wouldn't keep a lady from her love letters,' he said with a wink, as he took the envelopes out and put them into my hand.

'I'll let you know tomorrow if they're any good.'

The moment he'd gone, I ripped open the thick, white envelope with a Dublin postmark and an unfamiliar, spiky writing. I knew it was from Patrick and I was sure it had to be bad news. It was. His elderly uncle had died suddenly. He wouldn't be able to return before the funeral which was to be on Friday. He would come out to Lisara just as soon as he arrived back. He very much hoped I would still be there.

Tears sprang to my eyes. Friday. Three more whole days to wait. But before I'd even grasped that unhappy fact a worse one came to me. I was to leave Lisdoonvarna on the ten o'clock bus on the Saturday morning. That left only Friday evening, assuming Patrick would actually be back by then. A brief meeting at the cottage. Perhaps a drive to the cliffs. So little time to resolve what had been begun between us.

I blew my nose hard. Maybe it would have been better if we hadn't gone to the Burren together. Then all I'd have was a happy memory of someone I'd met and had tea with a couple of times. I pushed the damp envelope into my jacket pocket and stared at the other letter. It was from George, written in haste. He had left out 'Doolin', the postal district for Lisara, so although it had been posted on Saturday it had taken an extra day to get to me. I had to read it through twice before it finally sank in that George was planning to arrive tomorrow, Wednesday. He was coming with Dicky Sinclair in Dicky's new car, which he'd just had for his twenty-first. They hoped I'd be ready to leave on Wednesday, but in case the letter didn't reach me in time, Dicky had thoughtfully agreed to spend Wednesday night in Lisdoonvarna and set off for Wicklow on Thursday morning. Dicky had friends in Wicklow who had invited us all to a party and we could stay overnight with them. How wonderful to be together, just the two of us, at last.

'No. No. I can't,' I said aloud. I couldn't just go off like that. If I did I would miss Patrick completely. And what about Geoffrey's outing for Mary and Paddy? There wouldn't be time to say goodbye to anyone, neither Patrick, nor Sean, nor Bridget, nor Mary-at-the-foot-of-the-hill, nor any of the neighbours who had done so much to help me with my work.

I stuffed the letter into my other pocket and marched furiously down the road to Ballahaleine. However pleased I might be to see George, it upset everything for him just to appear like this. Our letters had crossed. Today, he would have mine telling him I was coming back on Saturday. But that wouldn't have much effect on him, if Dicky had already decided to go to Wicklow by way of Lisdoonvarna.

On top of all my distress at George just thinking I would drop everything and be delighted to drive off to a party in Wicklow with people I'd never laid eyes on, was the fact that he was coming with Dicky Sinclair. I could understand him wanting us to be together again, but to land me with the company of one of the few people at the university I really loathed and detested was a quite different matter. What on earth could he be thinking about?

The answer was simple: he wasn't thinking at all. If there was a prize for the person I would least like to inflict upon Mary and Paddy, Dicky must surely win it. Rich, spoilt and insincere, I'd disliked him from the moment I'd set eyes on him. Son and heir to Sinclair Textiles, good-looking, wealthy by any student standards, I'd always thought his main aim in life was to collect admirers by using his looks, his money, or both. Surely I'd said as much to George often enough for it to sink in. How often had I complained about Dicky's clever talk, his attempts to shock, his sudden synthetic enthusiasms and his affected, modish slang.

The awful thing was there was absolutely nothing I could do. George's mother was having a week off so I couldn't phone her office. A telegram would cost the earth. Besides, how could I say anything other than 'Don't come'? And how could I say that? I sniffed miserably and wiped my eyes again on my damp hanky. There was something so terribly wrong about having to go with plans broken off and promises unfulfilled.

By the time I had walked back to Lisara after my morning with Miss Crawford, I was feeling a bit steadier but I just didn't know how I would tell Mary and Paddy about going. I was sure Mary would be very upset.

'Hallo, Mary, where's Paddy?' I asked, as I stood on the doormat, taking off my boots.

'Ah shure good, there you are. I was just putting on a bit of griddle bread for us, astore. Paddy's away to Careys-the-low-road. He's helpin' Jamsey with the t'atch. He'll not be back till supper. Are ye hungry?'

'The smell of that would make anyone hungry,' I said truthfully, as she poured the bread mixture on the smoking griddle. I wasn't really hungry, which was most unusual, but I wasn't going to say so.

I hung up my jacket and put my notebook in the window recess where I kept most of my writing stuff. The little pile of books Patrick had lent me were there with the few I had brought with me. I would have to write Patrick a note. He would come to the cottage and Mary would explain that I'd had to go.

Mary's comfortable shape blurred as I watched her turn the bread. I went and fetched a clean hanky from my room and said how the wind had made my eyes water. Our last lunch together, I thought, as Mary cut the fresh bread into pieces and fried bacon for us in a small, battered pan. And tonight when we sit round the fire, it will be the last evening I'll listen to Paddy's stories.

I scolded myself thoroughly for letting myself think such negative thoughts, but I made up my mind at that moment I was not going till Thursday. Even though I'd had the letter in time to be ready tomorrow, I was not cancelling our visit to Ennistymon. You can't just plan to come back next year, expecting people who have worked so hard and endured such hardship, over so long a life, still to be there for you. Dicky might not like it, but George was bound to understand I couldn't just leave without even a day's warning.

'Is it anyways?' enquired Mary anxiously, as I slowly ate my hot, buttered bread.

'Mmm,' I replied, nodding with my mouth full. 'It's great, Mary, just great. I was thinking I must get the recipe before I go.'

I was going to tell her about the griddle Uncle Albert had given me once and how I was going to take it out and try some of the things she had cooked for us, but I could see she'd already guessed something was wrong.

'Mary, I had a letter from George this morning. He's going to come down for me tomorrow with one of his friends who has a car. I'll be going back on Thursday.'

'Ah, shure that's very soon.' Her face crumpled and she put her teacup down with a jerk. 'You'll hardly have time to say goodbye to your friends. We'll miss you for shure. And I'm thinking we'll not be the only ones.'

'It's quicker than I wish, Mary, but George wants to save me the journey home and he has no car of his own. I suppose beggars can't be choosers.'

'You'll be going into town today, I suppose?'

She was too shy to mention Patrick's name, but I knew what she meant.

'I will if you need anything, Mary, but I thought we could shop tomorrow in Ennistymon. I'm afraid I won't see Patrick today. I was expecting to, but his uncle has died in Dublin and he can't come back till after the funeral.'

'Ah, the poor man.'

I thought she meant Patrick's uncle, but her look made it clear it was Patrick himself she was concerned for.

''Twill be very hard on him to come back and you gone.'

I nodded, for I really couldn't trust myself to speak. Every time I thought of the note I would leave with his books, I felt tears in my eyes. Mary was looking as miserable as I was feeling.

'Ah, we'll not see Ennistymon tomorrow, astore,' she said sadly.

'Oh yes we will, Mary,' I said firmly. 'It's a brand new car, so they'll have to take it slowly. I can't see them getting here till suppertime. It's over two hundred miles and there are some really bad bits of road round the border. No, we must go tomorrow. We can't disappoint Geoffrey, can we?'

She smiled that soft, slow smile which always made her face look so lovely. Geoffrey treated her with a gentleness I found quite touching and Mary had responded with an affection rivalling even her feelings for Professor McDonagh.

I finished my tea and looked at the scatter of leaves in my cup. 'Come on, Mary,' I said encouragingly. 'Look into my future and tell me when I'm coming back. I am coming back, you know. I can tell you that for sure.'

She brightened visibly as she reached for my cup. The moment she picked it up her face changed and she issued her usual disclaimer. 'Ah, shure I'm no good at all at the cups.'

It was not true. Among the material in the green file was a note on the language of fortune-telling. It listed some of the formulas I had been intrigued by, the way the fortune teller never says 'next week' or 'next month', but uses expressions like 'within a three' or 'within a seven'. But beside my note on the actual use of language was a record of the predictions Mary had made for me since I'd arrived. Letters, unexpected meetings and surprises. Her predictions had been quite amazing. Try as I might to dismiss most of them as coincidence or luck, there was one I just couldn't argue away.

Two days before Patrick and I had gone to the Burren she had picked up my cup after lunch and said that 'she saw me kneeling down with a man who stood in the best of loving hearts to me and we were looking at something below the ground'. Patrick and I studying the habitat of a maidenhair fern and considering the possibilities for survival in a hostile world was hardly the sort of thing Mary could have guessed at.

I watched her as she fell silent turning the cup in her hands. Always when she read my cup she sat very still, absorbed, a frown on her forehead. It was not only the change in her language I'd noticed, her face too took on a quite different aspect. She sat now, intense, remote and silent.

'Ah astore,' she began at last. 'I see tears and a journey, and the tears are beside that journey. And there's a ring. The ring is beside a dark-haired man a journey away. There's another man here too, but smaller and fair. He's holding something up to his face. I don't know what it is atall. Like a piece of stick, but thin. But you'll have words over that fairish man for your back is turned against him. And I see a meeting with a man in dark clothes, in a bright place with birds flying. And that meeting is within a three. And I see papers, a whole case full of papers. And that case is blue. Aye, 'tis darkish at the top, but please God, lighter further down.'

She put the cup down and looked across at me as if she had

suddenly become aware I was there. The distant look had gone, her tone of voice had come back to normal.

''Twill all work out with the help o' God. Save us, what was that?'

There was only one thing could make the sudden noise which had startled Mary. I laughed as I stood up.

'It's all right, Mary. I think it's Geoffrey. Shall I fetch another cup?'

Chapter 13

On Wednesday morning the rain had cleared completely, the air was fresh and still, the islands so pin sharp they looked as if they'd been moved nearer in the night. By the time Geoffrey arrived the sky was a perfect blue and I'd had to change my trousers for a blouse and skirt.

Geoffrey had been hard at work. Not only had he cleaned the car itself, he had unloaded all his gear and swept out every scrap of sand, mud, gravel, turf dust and breadcrumb he had accumulated in his summer's travels. He had donned a jacket and flannels and looked relaxed and cheerful.

We set off in good spirits and the day unwound just as it had begun. The car behaved perfectly, the rates were paid, lunch was enjoyed, and afterwards, while Geoffrey and Paddy compared the quality of the Guinness in a sample of the many bars, Mary and I did the shopping and visited a tiny, overcrowded store where we chose a minute, embroidered dress for a newly arrived grandchild in Boston.

Back on the coast road and heading for home, we were all feeling pleased with ourselves. Geoffrey's shyness had disappeared so completely that he actually began to tease me. That made Mary laugh. Then he began to tell stories which made us all laugh and finally on the last stretch past the Cliffs of Moher he broke into song.

'Anyone would think we were drunk,' I said, laughing.

'Not at all,' broke in Paddy. 'Shure we only had the one to wash down our lunch. Isn't that right, Geoffrey?'

'Shure you never could count atall, old man,' added Mary good-naturedly.

'I can count well enough, so I can,' retorted Paddy, pretending to be huffed.

We laughed again, Geoffrey started another verse, Paddy and I joined in, but we didn't finish it. As we rounded the final corner into Lisara, we saw a shiny, red sports car parked below the hydrangea. Nearby, sitting on the wall, dangling their legs, sat George and Dicky Sinclair.

We drove past, turned off the road and stopped in front of the stable door. The one glance I had of the pair of them was not encouraging. As George looked up and smiled I saw he was unshaven. Dicky was staring out to sea, a glazed expression on his face, so absorbed he failed to notice our arrival altogether. He was dressed completely in black and it looked as if he too hadn't shaved for several days.

I helped Mary out of the back and wondered how long they had been waiting. 'Hallo, George, hallo Dicky,' I said brightly as they came round into the stable yard. 'Mary, this is George Johnston and Dicky Sinclair.'

Dicky clutched Mary's hand. 'I'm so pleased to meet you, this is an *enchanting* place, absolutely *enchanting*. I've just been sitting here absorbing the quiet and the beauty. Elizabeth *darling*, however did you find such a *paradise*?'

My heart sank. Before I left Belfast, Adrienne had said something about Dicky going through an aesthetic phase, but I hadn't paid much attention. Dicky was always going through something. But this was worse than anything I had imagined.

'Yer welcome, George. Yer welcome, Dicky,' said Paddy firmly as he and Geoffrey came round the car to shake hands.

I watched Dicky run a calculating eye up and down Geoffrey. That's routine with Dicky. If his victim is male he is costing the outfit, if female, judging how easy it would be to get her to remove it.

''Tis a lovely day,' offered Paddy. 'A good day for yer journey.'

George agreed that it was, and Dicky launched into another eulogy about the beauties of the Irish countryside. Mary was now looking anxious and uneasy. She whispered that she'd away in and get the tea ready, and scurried off, a worn, bent figure in her best black coat and hat, hardly recognisable as the woman who'd laughed so happily at Geoffrey's stories only half an hour ago.

'Have you been here long?'

'Oh ages, *darling*, simply ages.'

'About an hour,' added George, more reasonably. 'We left early this morning. About six.'

'Yes indeed. Quite the most *beautiful* time of the day, don't you think?'

Dicky was staring at Geoffrey as he spoke. When Geoffrey hesitated and muttered something unintelligible, he transferred his gaze to Paddy.

''Tis as good a time as any,' he replied, agreeably enough, but I saw his eyes narrow and his chin jut out a fraction more than usual.

I could see George was trying to signal to me, but I felt I daren't take my eyes off Dicky for as Paddy walked away, I'd seen his eyes narrow as he focused his attention on Geoffrey once more.

'And do you find the Morris a *pleasant* car to drive?'

'No . . . actually,' Geoffrey replied, with only a slight hesitation. 'She's rather uncomfortable . . . and . . . temperamental. But she suits my purposes.'

'Which are?'

Dicky cocked his head to one side as if to underline his intense interest in Geoffrey's activities.

'Geoffrey is doing post-graduate work.'

The minute I'd spoken I wished I hadn't, but all I could think of was the way his nasty little mind worked. I remembered the time he had been introduced to a girl I knew from school and he'd promptly asked her if she and her boyfriend were friends or if they just slept together.

'We had rather a job finding you,' said George easily.

Geoffrey took his chance, collected the rest of Mary's shopping from the boot and followed Paddy into the cottage.

'Oh my, *yes.*'

Dicky turned his gaze full upon me. '*Really*, Elizabeth *darling*, your directions were somewhat *vague*. The place you gave us was *miles* away.'

'What directions?'

'Dicky means the address you sent. Doolin is miles away, as he says.'

'Yes, *miles* and *miles*. We thought we'd never find you.'

I ignored Dicky, turned at last to look at George and was completely taken aback by what I saw. George is rather keen on clothes. He always wears socks to match his sweaters and often talks colour co-ordination and how badly some women manage it. His mother encourages him and is always buying him things in *his* colours. So why was he wearing an ancient black polo neck so worn there were grey pills round the neck and under the arms? Not only was it grubby but the jeans he had chosen to go with it had shrunk so much they revealed inches of white, hairy leg pushed into battered old sandals I'd never laid eyes on before.

'But I didn't give you any directions, George. I didn't know you were coming till yesterday, so how could I?'

I stared at him as if his answer to my question might explain why he looked such a mess.

'Oh, never mind. We're here now and that's all that matters,' he said soothingly. 'Presumably we can go off when we've had tea. Dicky knows a nice little place near Limerick we can spend the night.'

Just then, Mary appeared at the door and looked anxiously towards us.

'Just coming, Mary.'

I waved with a cheerfulness I certainly did not feel and led the way across the stable yard.

'George, I can't leave just like that. We can go for a walk after tea and I'll explain. I'll be ready first thing in the morning.'

He looked most put out, glanced at Dicky to see how he was reacting, and said nothing.

When I saw how Mary had laid the table, I knew just how uneasy she was about Dicky. Not only was there a starched linen cloth and cut-glass butter dishes, but there were only five places laid. Mary had not taken her meal by the fire since my first week at the cottage.

Dicky excelled himself over tea. 'But how unique,' he exclaimed, as he looked up at the darkened rafters under the thatch. 'How quaint,' as he took in the dresser with its well-worn plates and cups. 'What a marvellous *flavour*,' as he spread Mary's wheaten bread with a large quantity of the week's churning.

He waxed lyrical over the truly simple things of life like bread and butter, went on to speak of natural ingredients and the delights of homebaking, and made sure he acquired the largest piece of cake. Geoffrey's eyes caught mine and a ghost of a smile passed between us. We knew the cake came from the grocer's in Ennistymon.

George didn't say much during tea, but Geoffrey made an effort to include Mary and Paddy in the conversation whenever Dicky paused for breath. Like all bad dreams, it did finally come to an end. Dicky offered around his gold cigarette case, said 'You don't mind, do you?' and took a long, lacquered cigarette holder from his pocket. I had never known George smoke before, but he accepted a cigarette and lit up.

Geoffrey thanked Mary for his tea, said he must be getting back and that he'd call tomorrow on his way south. Only after he stepped outside did it strike me that I'd probably not see him again.

'Excuse me a moment.'

Geoffrey was already in the car as I ran past the window. I called to him but he couldn't hear me. I arrived in the stable yard breathless, as he started to manoeuvre.

'Elizabeth!'

He wound down the window, but did not stop the engine. I knew he daren't, for she might not start again.

'Geoffrey,' I panted, 'I may not see you in the morning if we leave early. What about your notes? Could I keep them for a little and send them to you? I wouldn't forget, you know.'

'Of course you wouldn't. I won't need them till I start to write things up. Can I give you my address in Oxford?'

'Thanks. I'll send you some of those photos I took today.'

He poked around in his wallet and produced a little sticky label with a printed address.

'I'd be awfully pleased to hear how your work goes, Elizabeth. We didn't get back to our conversation . . . perhaps . . . if you were sending the papers, you could . . . let me know,' he finished with a rush.

'Oh, yes. I'll write. I'm a compulsive letter writer, I warn you. But you must write back and tell me how you get on in Dingle and the Blue Stacks.'

'I will, I most certainly will.'

'And explain a bit more about structural linguistics?'

He laughed and I had to step back, for the fumes from the engine were so awful I was beginning to choke.

'Good luck, Geoffrey.'

'Bon voyage, Elizabeth.'

He drove off in a cloud of exhaust smoke. I stood watching him go with a most enormous sense of loss. I waved as he went down the hill and would have waited for him to reappear on the far ridge but I remembered Dicky and dashed back into the house.

He had fallen silent and sat looking uncomfortable as he blew smoke rings from his long holder. George had stubbed out his cigarette on his tea plate and was now stacking the best teacups in an attempt to be helpful. Mary was eyeing the pile with unease, but saying nothing.

'Well then, how about a walk?'

I was horrified at the sound of my own voice, Joyce Grenfell playing a games mistress in an Ealing comedy.

To my surprise, Dicky rose to his feet instantly. 'Marvellous, *darling*,' he said, making for the door.

I had not exactly planned to include him in my walk with George, but I couldn't exactly leave him with Mary and Paddy either. I didn't even offer to wash up, for one look at Mary's face told me she'd rather wash all the cups in Clare than have him for company.

'Won't be long, Mary,' I began, 'we'll just have a walk up to the quarry before George and Dicky go back into town.'

'My God, Elizabeth, I'm *bursting* for a pee,' wailed Dicky. 'Haven't your friends ever heard of lavatories?'

'That's it up there, or you can nip behind the stable wall.

Take your pick. The view's better up there.'

He disappeared at speed, closely followed by George. What in heaven's name did he expect? And why hadn't George warned him? I'd told him the story about 'going to see to the goose' in my very first letter.

'Hallo, darling.'

George's arms slid round my waist as I stood looking out at the islands. He so startled me I jerked away just as he bent his head to kiss me.

'Where's Dicky?'

'In the car,' he said absently, as he pulled me into his arms and kissed me, his lips hot and tasting of continental cigarettes.

'No, George. Please, not here,' I said, pulling away.

'Why not? What's wrong?'

'Someone will see us,' I said, striding off across the field.

'So what, you're leaving anyway. We can leave right now. Look, why don't we go now,' he urged as he caught up with me. 'No one knows us in Limerick, we'd have a room of our own. Come on, Elizabeth, you could be packed up in no time, you've only one suitcase.'

'George, I can't leave just like that. I've told you already. Mary and Paddy have been so good to me, they'll miss me when I go. It's been so sudden. The least I can do is spend an evening with them and not just dash off after we've had an outing together.'

'It's a bit hard on us to have to spend a night here so you can say a fond farewell. Dicky's been very good to come down with me.'

'No, it wasn't good of Dicky. He never does anything that isn't entirely for his own benefit. I don't know why he decided to come, but you can be sure of one thing, it wasn't for your benefit and it wasn't for mine.'

'I don't think that's fair at all. It was damned decent of him to help me out when you couldn't make it last weekend. I think you might be a bit more appreciative.'

George's face had turned slightly red and his Adam's apple, which is rather prominent, was going up and down more than usual.

'It's nothing to do with being appreciative. It's just that I can't drop everything to suit Dicky.'

'Never mind Dicky, what about me?'

We crossed the highest point of the upper field and dropped down towards the quarry floor, alone now, not a farm or cottage in sight. I headed for a flat bench of rock where we could sit and talk.

'Where are you off to?'

He stopped where a winding path ran between the old spoil heaps.

'There's a good seat over here.'

'Come here, it's softer.'

I followed him through the bumpy area beside the path until he stopped in a small hollow. He stretched out on the grass and waited for me to join him. I looked down at his smiling face. He wanted to kiss me, of course, but surely we could just sort things out properly first.

'Come here, then.'

I sat down on the grass beside him. Immediately, he flung his arms around me, pushed me back on the short grass and pressed his tongue deep into my mouth. I turned my head away and struggled to sit up, but he rolled over on top of me and went on kissing me. Whether it was the tobacco sodden kisses, or the way he pinned me down, or the piece of stone sticking into the back of my left shoulder, I don't know, but I pushed as hard as I could against his chest. He drew back for a moment, surprised, sure I couldn't mean it, and then reached for the top button of my blouse.

'No. George, please . . . let go of me.'

I scrambled to my feet, breathless and angry, pulled my skirt back down over my thighs and hitched up the shoulder strap of my bra.

'Look, George, if we can't have a sensible conversation, I'm going back to the house,' I said, looking down at him where he lay still sprawled on the grass.

'What's wrong, Elizabeth? Is it the time of the month?' he asked, his tone conciliatory.

In medical terms, it was 'the time of the month'. I'd been bleeding since Saturday and I had backache. But what had that to do with anything? He always behaved as if the menstrual cycle, all twenty-eight days of it, was the complete explanation of any problem he might be having with a woman. As far as he was concerned, failure to comply with his wishes was just another symptom, like fluid retention or stomach cramp.

'No, it isn't,' I lied, without the slightest compunction. 'I'm perfectly well and in possession of my right mind, I just want to get things straightened out for tomorrow.'

'But that's what we were doing,' he said petulantly. 'I must say you don't exactly seem pleased to see me. I get up at some ungodly hour, drive all the way down with no proper directions, and you're not even here to meet me. I don't think that's much of a welcome.'

'It might have been warmer if you'd had a little more consideration for my situation here.'

'Consideration?' he retorted, his Adam's apple bobbing furiously. 'I don't think it's much consideration when you go gallivantin' off with your fine friend Mr Actually Geoffrey and leave Dicky and I hangin' around till you honour us with your presence. I don't think your mother would think that very considerate.'

It might have been the reference to Geoffrey, or to my mother, or the sarcasm of 'honouring him with my presence', I really don't know which, but I felt something snap inside me. I looked at him. How could I ever have imagined I loved him? The books had got it wrong again. It was not that this man wanted one thing and one thing only. It was much worse than that, this man wanted nothing of the person I really was.

What he was looking for was a mixture of parts he could put together, a do-it-yourself kit for someone amenable, available not merely for sex, but for all the other ego-boosting activities females alone can perform. There was no doubt that was what he had always wanted. It had always been perfectly obvious. How could I have failed to see it till this moment?

I struggled with the signet ring on my right hand, the one he had asked me to wear before he went to England. I pulled and tugged at it, twisting it fiercely in both directions, but it wouldn't budge. I could see processions of fictional heroines flinging their rings in the faces of their rejected suitors but I was far too desperate for the irony to amuse me. I put my finger in my mouth to ease the pain and remembered that's what you're supposed to do. When moistened it slipped off quite easily. I held it out to him.

'I'm sorry, George. I won't be coming with you tonight, or tomorrow either.'

My cheeks were flaming and there was a tremble in my voice. He ignored the ring, so I bent down, put it on a flat stone, stepped out of the hollow and went back to the path.

'What do you mean?' he shouted.

'What I said. I'm staying here,' I called over my shoulder.

He scrambled to his feet, grabbed the ring, ran after me and caught at my hand.

'Elizabeth, don't be silly. You can't stay here. You don't

mean it. Be reasonable, Elizabeth. You're tired.'

'Yes, I am. I'm tired of being expected to do whatever you want. I'm tired of being told I'm unreasonable, whenever I object to anything, and I'm tired of having my menstrual cycle used as an excuse to ignore any feelings I might express. Yes, I am tired of all of it. Leave me alone.'

I was walking briskly now and he'd had to run to keep up with me. As I paused briefly to swing myself over a stone wall, he jumped over ahead of me and stood blocking my path. He scowled down at me.

'You think I'm a fool, don't you? I saw you making eyes at Mr Actually Geoffrey. And running off after him. That's it, isn't it?'

I stared at him. He had mimicked Geoffrey's accent quite grotesquely, twisting his own face into a parody of Geoffrey's hesitant manner.

'No, it isn't,' I said firmly, as I walked past him. 'Will you please keep your voice down. The sound carries a long way in this still air.'

Then he mimicked me.

'Oh yes, schoolmarm,' he went on. 'Full of wisdom you are. You'll make a good mate for Frightfully Actually Geoffrey. If he can manage it, that is.'

I came to the last gate on the lowest field. Usually I climb over it, because it's all tied up with binder twine. But I felt so shaky I didn't trust myself not to wobble on the top bar. I began to undo the knots. They weren't difficult, there were just a lot of them and I had to concentrate. I was aware of every fibre as I traced them to the point where I could loosen them. As the last knot fell away, I pushed the gate open and went through. There was no need to tie it up again for the cows were in the top field. I walked on, George continuing his commentary at my heels.

'You'll regret this, Elizabeth.'

I wondered in a leisurely way if I would. I looked back at him, his face covered with sprouting black stubble. That was it, he must be growing a beard. Like Dicky. Dicky said all the best people were wearing beards. No, I didn't think I'd regret it.

'You'll feel better tomorrow, Elizabeth. It's the strain of being apart all these months.'

His tone had changed and softened, but his voice sounded as if it were a long way away. He might as well be reciting the Shorter Catechism.

As we stepped onto the road, Dicky sounded the horn. It was one of those exceedingly loud ones like the Austrians use for hunting. He had turned the car round and I could see he was drumming his fingers on the steering wheel and watching us in his rear-view mirror.

'I'll come for you in the morning about nine. Make sure you're ready now, there's a good girl, and we'll forget all about it. We both said things we didn't mean. We just need time to be alone together.'

He kissed my cheek. I waved as they drove off. Prince appeared from the stackyard and I bent down to stroke him. 'I'm not going, Prince. Definitely not.'

Prince waved his tail enthusiastically. I knew he would agree with me. But I really must sit down. Or lie down. Yes, that was it. Lie down. There was no one in the kitchen, so I pressed the latch on my bedroom door, kicked off my sandals and climbed onto the bed. Tears began to stream down my face, spilling onto the cool starched pillowcase. I wept and wept, quite unable to stop myself, until quite suddenly the tears stopped of their own accord. I sat on the edge of the bed and removed the last of my mascara with a tissue.

No, not grief. It was certainly not that. Relief, rather. I felt like a small creature who has scrambled out from under a stone and now feels safe enough to sit in the sunshine. I lay down again on my back and watched the pattern of reflections on the ceiling. Outside, the sun would be dipping over the islands, the hush of evening already spreading across the land as the shadows lengthened and the day's work came to an end. My day's work was not yet finished, but when it was, I knew there would be both comfort and rest.

Chapter 14

When I heard Mary come back into the kitchen and begin her evening round I knew it was time to get moving. I swung myself off the bed, smoothed out the dint my body had made in the fat, pink eiderdown and reached for my handbag. I took out my diary, glanced at it and then carefully emptied both my wallet and my purse on the bed.

The diary was easy. Apart from a neat, black entry saying 'Freshers' Hop', to which I would not now be going, the ruled pages between today and the beginning of term had no mark upon them. Nothing to stop me there.

The money was more difficult. I unfolded the crumpled notes, stacked up the half-crowns and shillings and made little mounds of the remaining silver and copper. Feely's taxi fare, single tickets to Limerick, Dublin and Belfast. Teapot money for this week. Stamps. Blue exercise books.

I began moving piles and parcels of money as if I were playing some solitary game. Some things I had to guess at, but after I'd moved to one side all the expenses I could think of, there were still some notes and a few piles of silver. I added them up, then divided them equally, placing the coins in a row on a thin base of pound notes, two small armies facing each other across a deep pink valley.

I smiled to myself, remembering my old money box, a

small, shiny black and red replica of the large battered cash box in the shop. My box had a tiny key which I loved. I never thought of using it but kept it carefully among my special things, safe in its tiny cellophane envelope. As a child, I often played with my money box, tipping out the coins, the worn pennies and halfpennies, the gold-coloured threepenny bits, the silver sixpences, the shillings, the occasional large half-crown. 'A right old miser you'll be one day, always counting your money,' my mother said when she saw me, absorbed in what I was doing.

How wrong it is to judge other people by your own way of seeing. In those childhood days with few toys, coins were kings and queens, children or grown-ups, ships or armies. With my pennies I could make towers or fairy rings, with threepenny bits I built eight-sided castles. The stories I invented came back to me as I spread out the remains of my summer's earnings. Today, I was inventing a new story about my future, moving the pieces and asking myself, 'What if I do this?' or 'How could I manage that?' But what I was doing was no fantasy. Today's story was critical to my future, it had to be firmly anchored in reality.

I fingered the grubby notes and counted the coins again. It might just be possible, but there was no margin for emergencies. Except that, of course, there was. I opened the single drawer in the washstand and took out three fat letters in strong white envelopes, the splendid epistles Ben had written me. He'd asked so many questions that I'd numbered them to make it easier to find the bits I needed each time I wrote. There in number one was the neatly folded fiver he'd sent the moment I'd let him know where I was.

I spread it out. Now what I wanted to do was not only possible, but easy. Dear Ben. I stared unseeing at the patterns I'd made. Ben had urged me to stay longer if I could, because he thought it was what I needed to do. He knows how indecisive I can be, how I confuse myself when what I want is what I want for myself, so he had written to encourage me.

In that particular letter he'd said he thought he understood my problem, because of what he'd found out quite recently about his mother. She was the youngest daughter of a village rector in County Antrim. As a little girl she was taught to repeat every day, 'God first, others next, self last.' He thinks that's why still she can never do what she wants and why there's been all this problem with getting her to see specialists about her poor health.

I felt sad when I thought about Ben's mother. She's someone I've always liked but she's never been very well and recently has been quite poorly. That, of course, was why Ben hadn't gone off to England with George and the rest. He told me he'd been so glad he hadn't gone. He'd been sure that what her own doctor dismissed as 'menopausal symptoms' was far more serious, probably some weakness in the kidney area. Now, at last, a specialist had diagnosed the problem. Ben had been right and she was now in hospital awaiting surgery. Of all this he had written, knowing I'd want to hear and assuming I'd understand his detailed medical explanations.

I collected up the money, shook the coins back into my purse and put the notes away. I returned Ben's fiver to his letter, put it back in the drawer and sighed. I'd set out to make one decision about my future and I'd ended up making another one as well.

Never, never again, would I get mixed up with a man who didn't treat me as Ben did, as an equal. Even if I should fancy myself 'in love', as I'd already managed to do, I promised myself I would never again be anyone's 'girlfriend', not as George and his kind understood the word.

No, take me or leave me, I said to myself. Should I remain 'on the shelf', risk becoming 'an old maid', never shed the label of 'spinster', words and phrases my mother used freely with bitter disparagement, it would be a far better fate than spending the rest of my life propping up some male ego. When I wrote to Ben he'd understand when I told him I wouldn't be seeing George any more. It occurred to me as I closed my handbag and hung it over the back of my chair that Ben had guessed something wasn't right between us quite some time ago.

Mary turned to me the moment she heard the latch on my bedroom door. She was still wearing her best blouse and Sunday skirt but they were now enveloped in her familiar spotted overall. As she made up the fire, a strand of grey hair hung down over her eyes, and she looked tired in a way I had not seen before.

'Had ye a headache, astore?'

'I had indeed, but it's better now. Did you wonder where I'd disappeared to?'

'Ah no, I saw you come in. I was beyond in the haggard. The brown hen's laying away again, bad luck to her.'

As she filled her basin with potatoes, I fetched my favourite knife and sat down at the kitchen table beside her. I wondered how much she had seen or heard of George's departure, but I could be sure she'd not mention it if I didn't. Besides, I'd much more important things on my mind.

'Mary, I wanted to ask you a favour.'

'Shure ask away. You know you've only to ask.'

'Do you think, Mary, you and Paddy could put up with me for a bit longer? Till Saturday fortnight, maybe?'

She put her knife down and stretched out her hands on the table, a smile spreading across her face.

'Ah, shure good. An' you know ye needn't ask. Couldn't ye stay till Christmas, if ye'd a mind to. Indeed, it's heartsore I was you thought to leave us so sudden and so unexpected.'

The smile faded as she spoke the words 'sudden and unexpected'. I knew she was thinking of George and would go on worrying if I didn't put her mind at rest.

'I . . . told George I wasn't going back with him, that I wanted to stay on, but he . . . didn't really seem to grasp what I meant. He says he'll be back in the morning.'

'Will I tell him yer out?'

Her reply was so brisk and so uncharacteristic I burst out laughing. She began to laugh herself and in the moments that followed some great dark cloud simply dissolved. With it went all my anxiety about getting ready to go, trying to finish what I still needed to write up, having to leave without any goodbyes to the people who had helped me and, worst of all, without seeing Patrick again. I thought of all my anxiety over Dicky and what he might be going to say next, and trying to keep my temper with both of them over the so-called 'directions'.

It was all gone. Just as a passing squall leaves the air fresh and bright, so the darkness of their coming had moved away and left me feeling elated, ecstatic, my mind so clear I could hardly believe it. I knew now why I was staying. For the moment though, I felt so overjoyed and excited I could find no words to express exactly how I felt.

'Mary, I'm going to be doing an awful lot of writing. Will I not be in your way?'

'Not a bit of it. And shure you'll not write all the time. Won't you want to be out visiting your friends, too. I think there'll be some glad to hear you are staying.'

She considered the eyes of her potato studiously, but it was quite clear who she meant.

'Yes,' I admitted, 'but there'll be others angry with me for changing my mind.'

'And why wouldn't you change your mind? Aren't you well able to make up your own mind now, Elizabeth, and you twenty-one? Shure who's to give orders to you now, tell me that?'

I could think of several people who'd not have the slightest compunction about giving me orders, whether I was twenty-one or ninety-one. I might be free of George, but I still had my mother and a regiment of assorted relatives behind her who'd feel just as free to comment on my decisions as she did. But even the thought of the battles that lay ahead could not suppress the bubble of excitement that had floated up to the surface of my mind.

'Maybe I'm being selfish, Mary. Some may be pleased that I'm staying, but others will say I'm selfish.'

'Well, Others will just have to think again, won't they?'

I had to smile to myself. Some was Patrick, and Others was George. Like Humpty-Dumpty, the words meant what Mary wanted them to mean. She knew I'd understand.

Sitting there, peeling potatoes, it was all I could do not to get up and dance around the kitchen singing. Here, where I had come, a stranger in the place, I'd been accepted as the person I really was. It hadn't happened to me since those far off days of early childhood which had been prompting my waking hours and inhabiting my dreams since the moment I arrived. The longer I could live and work in this place I had come to love, the harder it would be for circumstances to overwhelm me once I was back. However bad things became, I would never forget what it had meant to be accepted. I would never let anyone or anything take that knowledge away from me again.

Chapter 15

Whether it was by chance, or whether it was deliberate, I shall never know, but Mary woke me later than usual the next morning. Paddy had already gone to take the Lisara churns to the creamery and Mary was making up the hens' feed as I sat eating my breakfast. Somewhere in the far distance I heard the echoes of Dicky's flugelhorn. At the sound of it, my stomach turned over and I put down my egg-spoon.

'Ah, now eat your egg, astore, and don't worry yourself about him,' said Mary, coming to the table and pouring another cup of tea for me. 'He'll not annoy you, I'm thinkin', and he'll be soon gone. I'll away to the hens and then start on the butter in the dairy.'

The dairy was as close to the kitchen as anyone could get without actually coming in. Reassured by the firmness in her tone, I took a deep breath and went back to my egg.

'I just hate unpleasantness so much, Mary. I didn't realise what a nasty side he had till yesterday. He likes to get his own way.'

'Oh he would, he would that. You tell him you're staying an' he'll just have to sit on an egg less.'

I hadn't heard that expression for years. It made me laugh and feel better, but my ease was short-lived. The flugelhorn rang out again much closer at hand. Mary picked up the heavy bucket and hurried off. When the horn gave forth again it was directly outside the cottage.

A wave of fury swept over me as I heard the terrified squawks of the hens gathered by the gate waiting to be fed. Only Dicky Sinclair could be so appallingly rude. I sat where I was, but my hand was trembling as I drank my tea. I had no intention whatever of responding to Dicky's horn. It sounded again.

This time I just couldn't keep still. I went to the window and peered out just as I'd seen Mary do so often. But it was no use. The car was so low slung I couldn't see it below the hydrangea. I stood on, undecided. I was just about to sit down again when I heard a door bang. George's head bobbed up above the flourishing pink flowerheads as he got out and walked along the road to the gate. As he'd emerged from the driver's side, presumably it was he and not Dicky who'd used the horn.

I sat down hastily only an instant before he appeared in the doorway. He was wearing a discoloured Aran sweater over his previous outfit and he still hadn't shaved.

'Hallo, George,' I said as calmly as I could manage. 'Would you like a cup of tea?'

'I say, aren't you ready yet? It's after nine, you know.'

His tone was half-reproachful, half-teasing, as if he had made up his mind that bygones were bygones and he was magnanimous enough to overlook a few hasty words.

'Where are your things? I'll put them in the car while you finish off.'

I continued to munch my piece of wheaten bread in silence. I shall never forget that piece of wheaten. It was the end of the cake and it had caught just a bit too much heat, so it was hard and crusty. Usually Prince benefits from such pieces, but today was not a usual day. I chewed it patiently before I dared swallow. All the time, George watched, waiting for some sign that everything was about to return to normal.

'George, I did make the situation clear yesterday.'

Amazed at how calm I was feeling, I became suddenly aware of myself sitting at the table, continuing with my breakfast as if I were a character in a play. I felt sure there was a script somewhere around to which I could refer in moments of doubt: 'George moves centre right and stands awkwardly looking at Elizabeth'; 'Elizabeth continues to eat wheaten bread and drink tea'; 'Elizabeth speaks quietly but firmly'.

'I'm not coming with you. I'm staying to finish my work.'

'But you must have finished by now. Bill Bates only spent a couple of days down at Larne when he did container services. You've been here for weeks. And what about me? How do you think I feel coming all this way to bring you home and then you say you're not coming?'

I could have told him that his coming had been entirely his own idea. Including the nice little place in Limerick with our own room. But I thought better of it.

'How much longer do you need anyway?'

'I'm planning to stay another fortnight.'

'A fortnight?' he exploded, all final traces of amiability blown away. 'But term begins in another week or so. What about Freshers' Week?'

'What about it?'

The dregs of my tea were stone cold and full of leaves, but I continued to drink in tiny sips. Having something to hold helped to keep my hands from trembling.

'But we always do the Jazz Club stand and go to the Freshers' Hop. You can't just stay here and let everyone down. What do you expect me to do, if you're not back?'

I glanced at my empty cup and suddenly remembered what Mary had said when she'd studied my fortune, 'Aye, 'tis darkish at the top, but please God, lighter further down.' She'd said something, too, about a ring and a man I'd turned my back against, but I couldn't remember what. I removed a large black leaf from the inside rim and pushed my cup and saucer away.

'George, I don't expect anything. Nothing at all. That is why I returned your ring. I'm sure there are lots of people who would be delighted to go to the Freshers' Hop with you. But I won't be going. Nor to Limerick, or Wicklow, or Belfast, or the Jazz Club, or the Hop, or to anything else.'

'You mean it's over? You're dropping me. Just like that, after all this time?'

A shot rang out in the distance and I jumped. My hands were shaking now, so I clasped them in my lap below the table where he couldn't see them. I was so agitated it didn't dawn on me until there were several more shots that it wasn't gunfire. It was Geoffrey. If the Morris managed the hill, he'd be here any minute now.

George was standing glaring furiously down at me. He was so close I could see a ladder in one of the panels of cable in his sweater and the brown rim of the cigarette burn which had set it going. Well, I wasn't going to be mending it for him.

I stood up. 'Look, George, I'm sorry you're upset, but there's no use arguing. I've made up my mind. Mary will be back in a minute, she's just feeding the hens.'

My voice was full of anxiety and one look at him told me there wasn't the slightest chance he'd take the hint about Mary, but I had to say something.

He had no intention whatever of moving and my legs were beginning to shake so I had to sit down again. Then he started to go on at me. I was feeling so shaky I hardly heard the words, but I didn't need to. The intonation pattern was enough. That tone and rhythm was only too familiar and it always meant the same thing. He may not actually have said 'after all I've done for you', but the implication was there.

'What's everyone going to say if I go back without you? All you think of is yourself . . .'

As his voice rose higher, his face got redder. Then the flugelhorn sounded twice in quick succession and he craned his neck past me to peer out of the window. When he turned back towards me, his face was livid.

'So that's it, is it? Dicky was right. I should have listened to him last night and not come back here at all. You think I'm a fool, don't you? Well, we'll see who's a fool,' he added menacingly, as he turned on his heel and walked out.

Geoffrey stood aside to let him pass. The car door banged, the engine revved loudly and the car roared off.

'I . . . say . . . Elizabeth . . . I'm . . . most terribly . . . sorry. I didn't mean . . . to butt in . . .'

I took my hands down from my face and looked at him through my streaming eyes. I wanted to say something friendly, but I couldn't speak. I put my hands to my head which felt as if it would burst.

'What's wrong . . . Elizabeth . . . c . . . c . . . can I fetch Mary? I say . . . don't cry.'

Geoffrey's stutter was worse than I'd ever heard it before, his appeal full of utter distress. I took the crumpled object he offered me, mopped my face and blew my nose. His hanky smelt of oil.

'I'm sorry,' I said weakly, 'I'm not crying, it's just my eyes water when I'm upset. I'll stop in a minute.'

Looking up at him, his pale face full of concern, I knew I liked Geoffrey far more than I'd ever liked George and yet I'd managed to convince myself I was in love with him.

'You didn't butt in, Geoffrey, you timed it beautifully. He'd never have gone so quickly if you hadn't arrived.'

I leaned my head back to ease my aching neck and put my hands up again to my throbbing head.

'Here, let me help.'

Before I realised what was happening, Geoffrey had stepped behind my chair and put his hands on my shoulders. He pushed his thumbs firmly into the neck muscles and moved them backwards and forwards.

'Ooowww.'

'Sorry, but it will ease in a minute. Lean forward.'

I was so surprised that I did as I was told. In a few minutes the headache did begin to ease and his thumbs began to work less vigorously. His hands were warm and comforting and under his touch I felt myself relax.

'Is the headache any easier?'

'Yes, it's not blowing my head off any more.'

'You can lock your neck like this climbing a vertical face,' he explained. 'My brother often has trouble with his. If the neck muscles are tight, it can give you an awful head. Lean back again.'

I did as I was told, closed my eyes and let the weariness and relief sweep over me. Geoffrey said something, but his hands were over my ears so I couldn't make out what it was. Suddenly, he took his hands away and I opened my eyes. Outside a car was revving impatiently and there in the doorway George stood glaring at us.

For a moment, as he strode towards us, I thought he was going to strike me, but he merely flung a plastic carrier bag into my lap.

'Your mother thought you might want these for the party,' he said bitterly, looking from Geoffrey to me and then back again. With a final glare, he turned on his heel, strode across the room and almost collided with Mary in the doorway.

Ignoring her completely, he looked round and addressed us again, his voice thick with sarcasm.

'Meantime, until you see her again, I do hope you both enjoy the rest of your time together.'

Mary looked out after him and we heard the Spitfire roar off up the road. 'Boys a dear, d'ye think they're gone for good this time?'

I looked down at the carrier bag on my knee. Its contents were sliding gently down onto the stone floor, my best wool dress, a lace-trimmed slip and a pair of pyjamas my mother had bought in Cleaver's sale.

I thought of George's nice little place in Limerick where nobody knew us, where we would have a room of our own, and of my mother sending me clean pyjamas, red and white striped with a blue rabbit on the pocket.

'Mary, do you think it's too early for another cup of tea? I didn't quite get the goodness of that last one.'

Chapter 16

With my own plans changing at regular intervals, it wasn't surprising I'd got confused about Geoffrey's. As we sat drinking tea with Mary it emerged he wasn't going to Dingle till tomorrow. Today, he was planning to take photographs of the houses in Lisara and their immediate surroundings.

'Would you think of coming with me, Elizabeth,' he asked awkwardly. 'If you could possibly spare the time it really would help. Everybody would know I wasn't from the Revenue or the Land Commission.'

'Ah shure, go, astore. Go and keep Geoffrey company. Won't it do you good to go and see your friends and you so nearly gone,' urged Mary, before I had thought about what I was going to do next. 'And do you both come about one for a bite of lunch, for Paddy's at Carey's and I'm all on my lonesome.'

So we set off to tramp the lanes and paths of Lisara, on a fresh, sunny morning which blew away all thoughts of the ghastly beginning to the day.

Geoffrey was surprisingly easy with the people we met. Although he still said very little, the way he listened did encourage people to talk. I told him he made me think of Professor McDonagh, that he had the same directness of manner and the gentleness.

'You know, Geoffrey, the first night we went to the pub with the storytellers I called him "Professor McDonagh" and he just passed me over a glass of orange and said "Sure Frank will do very nicely." '

Geoffrey seemed pleased. He was looking forward to their meeting. Then he began to talk about McDonagh's work. He really did know a lot about it and as he talked I could see why he found it all so exciting.

By the time we came back to Mary, hungry for lunch and full of news we'd carefully collected for her, I had promised Geoffrey copies of the stories in my notebooks and he'd offered to get me photocopies of some of the work he had already done. We had also managed to photograph half the houses in Lisara while carrying on our conversation.

I hadn't realised what a skilled photographer Geoffrey was. When he produced an elderly Leica with interchangeable lenses I watched carefully, only having a fixed lens camera myself, but it was not until late in the afternoon I finally plucked up my courage and asked him if I might have a look.

'Try it,' he said, as he handed it across.

George had had a new camera for his twenty-first and every time I touched it, he lectured me on how it worked, behaved as if I were about to drop it, and retrieved it at the first possible opportunity. Geoffrey didn't say a word as I screwed in the first of the long lenses.

'Goodness. It does make a difference, doesn't it? I thought long lenses were only for photographing things you couldn't get near to.'

I framed a distant view with waving grasses in a nearby hedgebank, then filled the frame with a handful of wild-flowers.

'Take any pictures you want, please. I've got lots of free

film. My brother-in-law's a professional, he keeps me over-date stuff. It's almost always all right. He does my printing too, so I can easily send you anything you want.

I sat down on a stone wall, swung the barrel of the lens out to sea and focused on the islands lying quiet in the warm sun of early afternoon.

'So you have a sister as well as a brother?'

'Yes, but she's older than me. Married with twin boys. I was the third child, you see, the sticking-plaster child.'

'What d'you mean, the sticking-plaster child?'

'The one who holds a failing marriage together.'

'And did it?'

'No.'

I couldn't think what to say. So many things fell into place. I had learnt more about him in the last five minutes than in the last five days.

He found what he was looking for and passed it across to me. 'Here, try this. You might prefer the wide angle.'

I changed lenses and looked again. The islands were totally different now, spread across the horizon. Much more sea in relation to island. Interesting, but not right at all. Not the way I had come to know them since that wonderful moment when they appeared beyond the window of Michael Feely's taxi.

'What age were you when it broke up?'

'Ten.'

'Was it awful for you?'

'No, not the break-up. It was before that, the rows, the endless rows. I thought it was my fault. Apparently children do think that, but I only found out years later.'

'Yes, isn't it sad? There must be so many things people only find out years later, when the harm's been done.'

I was thinking of George and when I looked back at him it

was obvious he knew that perfectly well.

'Were you planning to marry him?'

I nodded sheepishly. Already the whole affair seemed remote, something long past, a totally ridiculous aberration, like believing in Santa Claus after you've grown up.

'Yes, next year, after graduation. With all the other student Happy-ever-afters.'

'But what about your post-graduate studies? Had you been able to organise that to fit in with his work?'

'It had never entered my head,' I blurted out.

'But you must carry on what you're doing, Elizabeth. You enjoy it so much, and you're so good in the field. Why ever haven't you thought about it?'

'I don't know. Money, I suppose. My family aren't well off. They'll be glad when I'm off their hands.'

'But there are scholarships, and grants. That's how I manage. I get nothing from my parents. My sister and brother-in-law are very kind, I stay with them often, but with the boys at school they have no money either. I've had to do it myself. And you're very practical. You could manage if you wanted to.'

I swung the lens towards him. Taken unawares, he laughed as I pressed the shutter. I hoped the picture would print as I had seen it, one of those moments when Geoffrey looked happy, and a moment I too was unlikely to forget.

Whatever happened after graduation next year, I now saw my future from a new angle. Although I had never even considered going on with my work, something had clicked into place with the same decisive snap as the Leica's shutter.

We sat on the wall for a long time, talking about our lives and the strange pattern of decisions which had brought both of us to this western shore. The afternoon continued warm and sunny, the small clouds formed and dissolved, a slight breeze stirred the heads of yellow ragwort and scattered the rusty brown fruits of the seeding dockens.

'When did Mary say supper would be?'

'Seven,' I replied automatically, my mind still moving over questions of mythology and belief.

'Have you been to the Cliffs of Moher yet?'

'No, no I haven't.'

'Well then, we must go, even if we don't find the hoof print of the fairy horse.'

We drove south along the coast and turned up a rough track to an area of uneven ground fenced round with a few strands of barbed wire. The Morris was the only car there. To our left the mass of the cliff was deep in shadow, the gulls whirling below us tiny white specks against the dark layers of rock. To the right, the land rose even higher. Bathed in sunlight, the steep, grassy slope above the cliff edge was topped by a stone tower. I looked down at the pounding water and shivered. Even today, with an almost flat calm, the swell plucked at the soft shales, wearing them away even as we watched.

Involuntarily, I took a step back, though we were nowhere near the sagging strands of barbed wire, our only protection from the three hundred foot drop.

Geoffrey turned to face me. 'Do heights trouble you?'

'Sometimes. But it's not just the height. I think it's the darkness and the chill.'

'Shall we climb up to the tower? It's in sunlight. And we can see the whole coastline from up there.'

I nodded and made my way quickly towards the thread of path that headed up to O'Brien's Tower. I had such an urge to get away from the chill shadows that I was breathless when I got to the top. We sat down on the short grass by the worn stone base, the whole of the coast to the south spread out beyond us as he had promised.

'Sorry about that,' I said, as he settled himself beside me. 'I just had a funny feeling, very creepy and nasty, and I can't explain it.'

'There are places can make you feel like that. In some the aura is so strong that almost everyone feels something; others, the power is much less and only the more sensitive are able to tune in to it. I would think you were a sensitive. You pick up such a lot in the visible world, I'd be surprised if you weren't picking things up from the Other World as well.'

I looked at him in amazement. For someone who seemed so sensible and rational what he'd just said was extraordinarily strange and fanciful. And yet, I felt again he had said something of great importance to me.

The whole idea of picking up auras from an Other World seemed quite bizarre if I thought about it in practical, sensible terms. But part of me wasn't practical and sensible at all. I'd always recognised powerful feelings I couldn't name, or label, or explain. Perhaps that was why I was so fascinated by the old stories, by myth and legend and the long tradition which had kept them alive in this remote corner of the world.

'I wonder if that is why I had to come to the west,' I said thoughtfully. 'I felt I just had to come.'

' "All life is a voyage of discovery. The most important bits are the bits you do without maps." That's what my Welsh grandmother says, and she's well on her way to being a Wise Woman. You'd like her. You must meet her one day,' he added as he opened his camera bag and took out the Leica. 'You owe me a picture.'

'Geoffrey, I hate being photographed.'

He looked disappointed and put the camera down. Then he picked it up again.

'Could you manage a figure in a landscape? Moira Rhu

looking out for her fairy lover on his magic steed?'

I laughed, and went and stood on a grassy mound with my eyes shaded, gazing out towards the islands. I wished I had long, dark hair flowing in the breeze and a woven cloak streaming from my shoulders. I heard the click, turned and grinned at him.

'Got it?'

I heard a second click.

'I have now,' he confessed, as I went back down the slope to join him. 'You're not cross, are you?'

I was not in the least bit cross. A day begun in heartache and tears was ending in warmth and friendship. Horizons were opening for me as wide and welcoming as the sky now yellowing towards sunset beyond my beloved islands.

It was time to go back to the cottage, to supper, to Mary and Paddy, and an evening by the fire. But we would meet again now, Geoffrey and I. We would meet when he travelled north from Dingle on his way to Donegal. Then we would meet again, somewhere, sometime, that only the future would reveal.

Chapter 17

According to Paddy, the old cliff road along the coast had been used as late as the 1940s, but after that it began to collapse into the sea. Each winter produced new rockfalls and by the 1950s no one used it at all. Now, ten years later, the broad, well-beaten track used for as long as anyone could remember, was almost invisible. To follow its line along the coast, I'd had to take to the adjacent fields, and only where it turned inland towards Ballyvore had I been able to measure its original width between the tumbled and overgrown stone walls.

Late last evening after Geoffrey left us, I'd got Paddy to help me make a sketch map of where the road used to run. From where I now stood it was clear the seaward wall had gone. Now, the landward wall was only a few yards from the cliff edge. So, here at the boundary of Paddy's land, the loss could have been thirty feet in twenty years. So much for the slow wearing away of land surfaces quoted by the text books.

I set aside my clipboard, dropped to the ground, and wriggled forward to the cliff edge. Here, where there had been a recent fall there were no telltale cracks, the edge was firm for the time being. I peered over and felt the cool touch of the updraught on my face. Below me, gulls circled in a leisurely way, some silhouetted against the dark shadow at the foot of the cliffs, others wheeling and diving over the turquoise water which surged against the streaming rocks.

Yesterday, I had felt a kind of panic at the cliffs at Moher, deep in shadow. Today, though these cliffs were every bit as high, I felt no unease at all. Was it just the difference of place, or was the difference in me? I wondered if I had shed some old anxiety.

I lay leaning on my arms, aware of the tiny plants under my fingers and the blissful warmth of the sun penetrating the light fabric of my blouse. I'd hated being on cliffs with George. No matter how far we kept from the frightening drop, I still felt uneasy, as if the actual edge itself had some enormous power to draw me away from my chosen path. But this afternoon I'd been working back and forth quite happily within feet of the edge and now I lay looking down into the water three hundred feet below.

Some old fear had gone. Paddy would call it 'a mystery', something to be accepted whether you understood it or not. As he'd said last night, after telling one of his long and complex tales, 'Shure the tales are full of wisdom and just by listenin' the wisdom comes to us, but it is a mystery how it happens. It is not for us to ask understandin', we must just give thanks for the gift.'

I had been given so many gifts since I'd come to Lisara. I raised my head and looked out at the islands, where the white walls of the cottages were once more visible in the clear light. I ran my eye east along the horizon until it reached the northern shore of the great bay where I had walked with Patrick, nine days ago, on the sweeping curve of the beach at Drennan. I could see the gleam of the Hills of Burren in the slight heat haze, but though I knew exactly where Drennan lay, the beach itself was invisible in the dazzling light.

There were so many things in your life you couldn't see, or touch, or prove, however sure you felt that they existed. Like Paddy's 'mysteries', you simply had to take it on trust that they did. And sometimes, it wasn't easy. When I was back in Belfast, I knew I would have to trust that the islands had not disappeared, that the tiny flowers between my fingers would go on growing and blooming; and that the friends I'd made would not forget me.

At the thought of Belfast, I shivered. I could imagine myself looking out from the top of a double decker bus, the sun setting behind the dark bulk of the gasworks, the trees in Ormeau Park leafless and dripping and the street lights reflected in the slate-coloured waters of the Lagan as I crossed the bridge. Going home. Home from the university to the flat above the shop, its rooms dim and empty and chill, till I pressed the switches on the lights and the electric fires set in the closed-up fireplaces.

'Sufficient unto the day is the greyness thereof,' I said to myself, as I glanced at my watch. Almost four. Mary would expect me for a cup of tea. Later, Patrick would call if he was back in time. All day I had been trying not to think about him. I wanted to see him so much that my longing made me fearful. What if I had imagined he felt more for me than he did? If he had not kissed me, the day we spent together would seem no more than a pleasant outing with a lively companion. But his kissing me changed everything.

I wriggled my way back from the edge, rolled over and sat up. With the brilliance of the sea still in my eyes, all I could make out for a moment was a solid black figure sitting on some mossy stones beside the fallen wall. I thought I was seeing things.

'Patrick,' I cried. 'How long have you been there?'

'Not very long,' he replied, getting to his feet. 'You were

so damned near that edge I wasn't going to risk saying anything.'

He held out his hands for mine and grasped them tightly when I went to him. I wondered if he would kiss me. We were standing close to each other and he was gazing down at me with that same look of tenderness and longing I had tried to evade all through the day we had spent together. But he just smiled broadly and ran his eye over me.

'Well, you seem to be all in one piece.'

There was a curious quality in his voice as if he was enormously relieved, but didn't dare show it.

'More or less,' I replied, aware that my blouse had parted company with my trousers while I wriggled around. 'Did you expect me to be damaged?' I asked lightly.

'Not exactly,' he replied steadily. 'But a man can't be too sure if he goes off and leaves a lovely young woman alone among the rough, rug-headed kerns of the west.'

I laughed at the idea of Sean O'Struithan, or Michael Flannigan, or the bachelors of Ballyvore, playing the part of rug-headed kerns and spiriting me off. Then I remembered how nearly I had been spirited off. If I'd gone with George, I'd be on my way to Dicky's party in Wicklow right now, after the promised night in Limerick.

'How did you know I was down here?'

We sat together on a small grassy patch, our backs against the low hump of the landward wall.

'Paddy,' he said simply. 'He was standing at the gate as I drove up. I came direct, as you see. I was afraid you might be about to leave . . . or worse.'

The uneasy glance he gave me told me 'or worse' had been very much in his mind. The thought of the note I'd have had to write came back to me and the way the tears would prick whenever I tried to imagine what I'd say. Three days ago, the very idea of it had been bad enough, but now it was quite unbearable.

'I nearly was gone . . . on Wednesday.'

'So I heard,' he replied, looking grave. 'But it seems the Red Branch from the north were unsuccessful in their attempts to carry off the lovely Elizabeth.'

He was smiling and he'd caught Paddy's accent and manner so exactly I wondered if he was quoting him.

'He didn't say that, did he? You make it sound like the Cattle Raid of Cooley.'

'Well, he didn't use those actual words, I admit. But he did inject the tale with, shall we say, a little poetic licence.'

'And how did this heroic tale end? You didn't by any chance have a giant Welshman in the denouement?'

'No,' he replied, stopping to consider. 'I think there was a bit more to come, but Mary appeared and hastened the proceedings. She told me where you were and Paddy was not allowed to finish his story, which is a pity in one way. It was shaping up nicely.'

'Remind me to tell you the authorised version sometime.'

As I spoke, I was suddenly aware we were sitting close to each other in a grassy hollow well out of sight of the watchful eyes of Lisara. But for that handclasp on meeting, he had not attempted to touch me, he had just looked at me closely to make sure I was well. All that had happened between us so far was a little friendly talk and my offer to tell him what had really happened in his absence, and yet I knew something far more intimate was going on between us than in those unhappy moments up in the quarry, when George demonstrated the depth of his feeling by sticking his tongue in my mouth.

'But you stayed, didn't you?'

'Yes, I stayed.'

I wondered if I had stayed because of him. Or because of me. Or because of my work. And then to my surprise, I remembered Geoffrey quoting his grandmother, not twenty-four hours ago: 'All life is a voyage of discovery. The most important bits you do without maps.'

'How long have you got?'

'A whole fortnight.'

He seemed pleased. I thought he was about to say something, but then I saw him check himself and I had a moment of blind panic. He sat twiddling a grass stem round his fingers and it seemed an age before he spoke.

'I can be free a good deal in the next fortnight if I want to. Charles is better and the season is nearly over. Would you like to come exploring with me?'

He waved a hand towards the horizon, the hazy hills in the distance and the invisible beach at Drennan.

'Your wish will be my command,' he added, taking my hand and bowing over it.

I nodded and did not take my hand away. 'I should like that very much. I've got such a lot to tell you. And lots more questions.'

'Yes, I thought you might have. I did indeed,' he added, as he helped me to my feet. 'Mary's expecting us for tea.'

He picked up my jacket and clipboard and waited while I rewound the ball of string and the tape measure I'd been using. We climbed the remains of the old wall and walked a yard or two apart as we went up the fields and came under the watchful eye of Lisara. I was sure something was resolved between us, but what it might be I did not know.

Chapter 18

Patrick's study was at the front of the small Georgian house where his family had lived for four generations. Its tall windows faced north and west across a small, parklike area dotted with trees and grazed by sheep. Beyond the curving driveway the main road ran invisible for a quarter of a mile or more shaded by woodland, trees planted by Patrick's great-grandfather when he inherited the Clare estate, came south to live, and grew homesick for the wooded islands of Fermanagh, where he was born.

Where the trees, now touched by autumn colour, gave way to pasture, the road was plain to be seen, rising over a low hill, skirting lush meadows full of buttercups and turning suddenly southwards to the town. I scanned its empty length, hoping for the gleam of sunlight on metal which would tell me Patrick was on his way back. So far, there was no sign of him. With Moyra and Charles in Dublin this weekend, it might well be a problem at the hotel or in the bar delaying him.

I moved away from the window and went back to my interrupted study of his bookcases. I've always found people never come when you watch for them, however much you will them to appear, but as soon as you stop watching they are sure to arrive. After such a long, happy day together, it was a pity he'd had to go out in the first place.

I'd been pleased enough to chat to Mrs Brannigan in the kitchen, have a bath and change my clothes, though even then the smell of the roast lamb was making me hungry. But as time passed and he still wasn't back, I grew restless, fidgeting anxiously, acutely aware of how long he'd been gone.

I paused in front of the mantelpiece and observed myself in the mirror which formed part of the carved overmantel. My face glowed pink through my light make-up. It looked as if I'd caught the sun but when I looked more closely it was not just my face which was radiating such a vibrant sense of well-being. Everything about me seemed brighter, sharper, more clearly defined than usual.

I straightened my neckline and smoothed the skirt of my best dress, the one George had thrown at me just over a week ago when he departed from my life. Mrs Brannigan said it suited me real well. But then, as Patrick would say, she was biased. She had taken to me at our very first meeting and made me so welcome I'd begun to wonder if she too were hoping for a match, like Mary and Bridget, and Mr Feely.

Well, if she was, she would be disappointed could she have followed Patrick and me on our travels this week past. We'd driven far and wide, had walked and talked, picnicked and dined together, had explored Limerick and Galway, and visited the most remote coasts and shores, all without a word suggesting even the possibility of marriage. Not only had we not spoken of marriage, but we had not even kissed again, though we had been alone often enough. It had surprised me a little, but it didn't trouble me. We were so easy in each other's company and I was in so little doubt about his love, I hardly gave it a thought. When I did, I felt that Patrick would return to where we had left things, that evening at Drennan, in his own good time.

I turned away from the hearth, the fire laid carefully with paper and fir cones, and walked over to Patrick's desk, old and worn, well-ordered and well-loved. I thought of the desk in the stockroom where we had first talked together. From its very first moments, my relationship with Patrick had been quite different from any other I'd ever had.

When I first found myself 'going out with boys', the whole issue seemed to come down to one thing, did you or didn't you kiss. Later on, the issue shifted to whether or not you went to bed. Looked at from where I stood now, I could see no difference between the earliest and the most recent of all those relationships. All had been carried on between 'boy-friend' and 'girlfriend': somewhere, somehow, the critical issue of its being this individual girl or boy, this individual man or woman, had got quite left out. However I might try to describe my relationship with Patrick, of one thing I was quite sure, I was no 'girlfriend'. I was always and only Elizabeth. Whether or not we kissed, made love, or married, in his eyes I would always be Elizabeth, not a somebody put together to meet his needs and expectations.

I went back to the window and watched a few small yellowed leaves fall from a weeping birch near the house. Everything had gone very still. It was not the ominous stillness you feel before a storm, rather it was a pause, a point of rest between the last of the day and the dewfall of evening. Shadows were lengthening across the grass and somewhere close by a blackbird was protesting. As I watched, I saw the leaves begin to sway on the delicate, mobile branches of the birch, the larger pink and gold leaves of the chestnut trembled, fluttered, began to move more positively. The evening breeze gathered strength. As I watched it ripple across the fields of pasture, far away, on the grey ribbon of road, a glint of movement caught my eye. I was sure it was Patrick.

★ ★ ★

'Go on,' Patrick said, as we heard Mrs Brannigan bang the front door behind her. 'You were telling me about the Hopi.'

'Was I? It must be the wine. Do you really want to hear about the Hopi?'

'What you mean is that you're not sure you aren't boring me. Well, you're not.'

I always thought candlelight was supposed to soften the features and add a romantic glow. Well, that wasn't true either. As the dusk expanded, he had lit the candles. In their sharp light, his face was stronger, more defined. Even when he laughed, as he did now, there was an angularity, a harshness I had almost forgotten. I remembered how after our very first meeting I had gone home to Mary and said how lonely it must be for him to be so old and not married.

I watched him now as he took away our dinner plates and brought us the generous portions of apple pie Mrs Brannigan had left ready on the sideboard.

'Well, I do go on rather,' I confessed. 'You shouldn't encourage me.'

'I happen to enjoy listening to you, for a variety of reasons. Now, go on. Or I won't give you any coffee.'

'Where was I then?'

'You were just making a distinction about a wave.'

'Yes. I was saying that if you see a wave as best described by the word "slosh" then you see something different from a person who would describe it as "wave".'

I went on to try and explain how the language you speak shapes the way you see the world. He folded his napkin, leaned back in his chair and watched me. I still found the way he did this rather disconcerting. I could never be sure he wasn't seeing things about me I didn't want him to see. Not so much because I wanted to keep them hidden, but because I didn't know what they were myself.

'Mmm . . . interesting. I can see why the idea appeals to you, but I can't see the link with Paddy and Mary.'

I had to laugh, for at that moment, I couldn't see it myself. As I sat trying to put together again what I'd set out to say, I became aware of myself, sitting in a pool of candlelight, surrounded by the darkened rooms of the old house, and the wide spaces of the shadowy countryside beyond the undrawn curtains, under the dark eyes of a man who could see things in me I couldn't see for myself.

'I think I've decided that words mean so much more than any dictionary says they mean. What we say and how we say it is such an important part of us. In a way it shapes us. The reason I can understand Paddy and Mary so well is not that I can guess what their words mean, I can guess at what they want them to mean. So you need to be able to understand people before you try to understand what they are saying. And that doesn't sound very logical, does it?'

'Perhaps not. But you may have a very sound intuition. Often you can't get at what you really want to say, till you've ruled out what doesn't seem relevant.'

'Like knowing what you don't want being halfway to knowing what you do want?'

'Yes. Exactly. Who was it said that?'

'You, actually,' I replied, laughing.

'Did I? Well, it's certainly not original. When did I say that?'

'Long time ago, the day you took me to the Burren. You showed me a plant that doesn't like lime. Remember?'

I was going to say 'and then we went and walked on the beach at Drennan,' but I stopped myself.

'Do you like cognac?'

'I don't know,' I replied, turning round to him. 'I've never had any.'

'Your frankness, my love, is quite disarming,' he said lightly as he polished two enormous brandy goblets.

'If those are for the cognac, I'll have to have some. I couldn't bear to miss drinking out of one of those.'

'I thought you'd like them. There are only two left, I'm afraid. They're rather old, from my mother's family. Shall we take our coffee to the sitting room or have it here?'

I hesitated. There was something about the large, formal sitting room that made me uneasy, although, like the rest of the house, it had some lovely old furniture. In the daytime, with the French windows open to the south-facing garden, and bowls of flowers everywhere, it was fresh and pleasant, but at night, even with a bright fire, I found it gloomy and rather oppressive.

'Or we could take it up to the study if you like,' he offered. 'That's what I usually do when I'm on my own.'

'Yes,' I agreed immediately. 'Let's do that.'

'Can you take the tray, if I have the perc? Then I can turn lights on as we go.'

I followed him into the hall and heard the click of a switch.

'Damn. Bulb must have gone.'

He looked across at me in the dim light filtering through the fanlight above the front door. A large clock ticked at the foot of the stairs and the wind rustling the leaves of a chestnut on the edge of the drive made a sound like the sea. I was aware of the press of darkness all around me. Suddenly, I felt so lost, so desolate, once more a stranger in a strange place. Everything normal and homely and everyday had been swept away. I was marooned in a life so different from my own that I had forgotten how to speak, or to walk, or to do any of the ordinary things of life.

How long I stood, unable to make any move, I don't really

know. I only remember walking carefully upstairs and treading cautiously on the rugs spread over the polished floor outside the study. Patrick followed behind and pushed the door open for me.

'Good Lord, look at that.'

My hands were still shaking as I put the tray down. The room was so full of silvery light there was no need for a lamp. Beyond the window where I had stood so long, awaiting his homecoming, a full moon was rising over the low hill to the west of the stand of trees. The grass was as white as if there'd been a frost.

We stood side by side at the window, watching the enormous pale disc rise clear of the gentle curve of the hill. I was so sharply aware of Patrick beside me, the empty room behind me. Moonlight was supposed to be so romantic. And surely being alone in an empty house with the man you love was supposed to make you excited and happy. A scene like this at the Curzon Cinema would have the violins in a frenzy. But when it happened to you in reality, it wasn't like that at all. Perhaps, long ago, I might have expected it to be, but I had learnt to be wary of what other people expected. It was so very likely to turn out differently for me. Faced with the moonlight, all I felt was small and alone, the bright world out beyond the window a cold, unwelcoming desert. I was grateful when Patrick moved away.

'Coffee,' he said briskly, as he switched on lamps and stepped back again to draw the curtains.

I poured the coffee while he lit the fire. As the flames leapt up and the fir cones crackled, I smelt the perfume of woodland in autumn. He crouched patiently by the flickering flames, waiting for the right moment to add dark squares of turf. In the light of the fire, his face looked drawn. I wondered if he too saw the world as bleak and hostile.

He brushed turf dust from his fingers and took the cup I held out to him. We sat in silence, staring at the leaping flames. Gradually, as I watched, I began to feel easy again. I leaned back in my chair and looked round the room. The glow of lamplight and firelight were just as I had imagined them. Secure, mellow and inviting.

'Do you like it then?' he asked, as I sniffed my cognac.

'When one doesn't know what to expect, it's difficult to decide, isn't it?'

He nodded and moved forward to open up the fire. It blazed and sparked, and I caught the acrid tang of turf, a smell I love so much. Perhaps because it always brought back memories of Uncle Albert and the only truly happy part of my childhood. Once again, unbidden, came the thought that next Saturday night I would be back in Belfast, far away from turf fires and lamplit studies and this man who had come to mean so much to me.

'Elizabeth?'

His voice broke softly across my thoughts, his eyes were full of concern.

'What was it, Elizabeth? For a moment you looked so incredibly sad.'

'I was thinking of Belfast ... of going back ... of not being here.'

I looked hard at the play of flames reflecting in the polished wood. I couldn't talk about going back and go on meeting his eyes.

'You're fond of my study, aren't you?'

'Yes,' I said, dropping my eyes to my coffee, because I could not trust them not to fill with tears. 'I don't think I've ever known a room I liked half as much as this.'

'And I have never known a woman I have loved half as much as you.'

I looked up, startled to hear him say at last what I'd known for a long time, and yet immediately reassured by the way he'd said it.

'And in the story books, it would all end happily ever after, wouldn't it?' he went on, watching my face closely.

'With moonlight and gypsy violins, of course.'

'Naturally.'

The tension between us relaxed momentarily. I was amazed by the calmness of my own voice, just as I had been that awful morning when I had said no to George. I felt anything but calm. Elated, because he had finally said he loved me, but anxious also, because I didn't know what that love might mean for me. What would happen if I were to confess how I felt about him? What indeed did I feel? All I could do was stare into the fire and keep silent.

'I meant to say earlier that I liked your dress.'

I glanced up, surprised. It was such a conventional remark, it would have seemed awkwardly out of place had it not been for the particular way he said it.

'Thank you.'

'It makes you look yourself, Elizabeth,' he continued, more assuredly. 'A lovely but vulnerable young woman. Which is a good thing indeed, my love. If you looked less young or less vulnerable, I might only do what I've wanted to do since that evening on the beach at Drennan. I'd ask you to marry me.'

'Marry me?' I repeated the words as if they were in a foreign language.

'Yes. It's something people agree to do, if they're convinced they love each other,' he said thoughtfully. 'Though that's a difficult enough little word at the best of times and marriage isn't always the best answer, even if they do.'

'But you think I'm too young anyway,' I said, feeling a

hurt that did not seem quite reasonable.

'Yes, but not in the way you mean,' he said, shaking his head and leaning forward in his chair to take my hands in his.

'Some things I know about, Elizabeth, not because I'm wiser than you, but only because I have had more years to observe, more time to reflect on all the things that have happened to me. If I asked you to marry me and you were to agree, I'd have taken away your freedom, your opportunities, your chance to decide what sort of a life you really want for yourself. I can offer you one life, one love, but it is only one of many possibilities, some of which you might never guess at at this moment. It might not be the one you would choose, if you considered those other possibilities. I want you to have real choice.'

'And what if I were to choose the life you offered me?'

At that moment, I felt such love and tenderness for him I'd have married him then and there, even though I had yet to admit to myself that I loved him.

'If that . . . well . . .'

He hesitated and moved his chair closer to mine.

'Elizabeth, if you love someone, love the person, and not just the idea of being in love with them, you want what is best for them. Trust me, my love. I'll be here next summer, and the one after that, and the one after that. What you cannot know is how loving you has changed my life. You've brought back a joy I thought had gone for ever. It would be a poor return, if I took away your freedom just when you've found it for the first time. Does that make sense?'

The tension eased. So like him to use a phrase that was part of our private language. I smiled at him and nodded silently. I had thought for one moment he was telling me he knew best, but the look in his eyes told me it was far more complex than that. What he was saying was clear enough, and yet I found it hard to accept that he was prepared to set aside his own wishes for the sake of mine.

'I want you to choose, Elizabeth, but I won't be going away until you do.'

'But what if you fall in love with someone else?'

'Then I would have to come and tell you, just as you would have to tell me if you see a future that has no place for me. What is important is what we have now.'

'And in the meantime? Between now and the future, what then?'

'Whatever makes you happy, my love,' he replied. 'Your wish will be my command.'

He bowed formally over my hand as he had on the cliffs at Lisara when he had asked me to go exploring with him. There was a touch of irony in his voice and a hint of laughter in his eyes as I smiled across at him.

I stood up suddenly and walked to the fireplace, aware of the tension in my body and the fact that I had been listening so hard I had barely been breathing. One foot had gone to sleep. I laughed and told him so.

My eyes flickered round the room I had come to love and came to rest upon the man who sat watching me. He had given me so much already. I felt poised, as if I stood at the entrance to some other world. Once again, just like that evening on the beach at Drennan, I had a real choice. Patrick had offered me his love and I could accept him as friend, lover, or husband. I understood at last that feeling of relief the first time he'd held me in his arms, the relief at having choice, knowing I was free to make whatever decision was right for me.

I knew now that I did love him. Indeed I was sure I had loved him for some little time. What I also knew was that he had taken away the anxiety I had had that I didn't really know what love was.

Chapter 19

The Limerick bus was vibrating noisily as I climbed up the steep steps and settled myself beside a window, misty on the inside and streaked with raindrops.

'Right-oh, Mick.'

The conductor reappeared from stowing my suitcases and parked his sandwiches on the dashboard. With a final judder we moved slowly forward.

I waved to Michael Feely, who had insisted on staying to see me off, but he was busy waving to someone at the back of the bus he probably thought was me. He had been consistent in his confusions right to the end.

'Now, Mr Feely, you must tell me how much I owe you.'

'Ah, sure, we'll say ten shillings.'

'But what about my lunch and the journey out on the day I arrived?'

'Ah, sure that's all included. Amn't I glad to be of service. I'm lookin' forward to yer book and indeed I'll be glad to assist you when you return for good.'

I settled back in my seat and let the relief pour over me. I hadn't wanted to leave, the goodbyes had been hard and painful, but at least now they were over. The bus gathered speed, the driveway to Patrick's house flashed by so quickly I caught only a glimpse through the pouring rain and the droplets on my window. No matter. I was as unlikely to forget that house as I was to forget Patrick.

He had offered to drive me to Limerick or to Dublin, but I had said no. I could not bear the thought of parting in some public place, so we had said our goodbye last night in his study. I had chosen to leave Lisara as I had come, with the aid of Michael Feely.

I smiled to myself as the sodden green fields streamed past, the damp autumn leaves by the roadside whirling in the turbulence of our passing. Michael Feely had been a memorable part of my time in Lisara. During our last two weeks together, Patrick and I simply assumed that no matter where we went, he would be there to see us go or observe us coming back. I should have guessed he would assume I'd be coming back for good.

Mary and Paddy would enjoy the Feely story when I wrote and told them. The green fields misted again as I thought of them standing together at the gate. Two big tears plopped onto my jacket to join the large spots of rain already there. Leaving them had been almost as hard as parting from Patrick. Paddy had stood at the door watching for Feely's taxi a good hour before he was expected, while Mary wandered round the kitchen distractedly as she made a packed lunch for me. She was in tears when I put my arms round her. Then Paddy clutched me to his stubbly chin and I nearly cried myself. It was all I could do to promise that it wouldn't be long till I was back and go on waving all the way down the hill.

I took out my hanky to mop myself up, but it was dirty from wiping the window of the bus, so I tried the other pocket, found a freshly ironed one and then remembered it held a sprig of heather from one of the flowering tubs in Sean O'Struithan's courtyard. So many souvenirs, I thought, as I transferred the precious fragment to my diary before I wiped my eyes.

Michael Flannigan had made me a set of rush crosses and Mary-at-the-foot-of-the-hill had worked me a sampler with all the stitches used by the local knitters. Patrick had guessed I'd be taking home far more than I'd brought and insisted on buying me a trim, blue weekend case as well as the books he'd found for me in the best bookshop in Limerick.

Tucked away for safety among my clothes, I had a cross from the rafters, a piece of shale from the quarry, a maiden-hair fern wrapped in damp paper inside a plastic bag, and a card with an image of the Virgin and a prayer for the relief of women's pains that Mary had taken from her Bible to give to me. As the miles passed, I was grateful to have these things about me, for I began to grow anxious I might lose hold of some of the really important things, the souvenirs in my mind, if I didn't have some small tangible things to prompt me.

Despite flooding on the roads and stops at rain-soaked villages, the Limerick bus arrived in good time for the Dublin train. As it steamed its way across the map of Ireland, I felt as if the journey were a thousand miles, so different was the world to which I was returning. We moved steadily from west to east, from what Sean called 'the white cabins of de Valera's dream' to the bustling pavements of Dublin.

The taxi man was so friendly that I sat in front with him as he drove me across the city. We talked about the weather as strangers do and I told him how good it had been on the west coast. Dry enough here in Dublin, he said, but not so pleasant. The traffic was heavy and as we crept slowly away from the station I recognised the bridge I had walked across five weeks ago on a Saturday at the end of summer.

'Isn't this Wolfe Tone Quay?'

'That's right, miss. D'ye know the city then?'

'No, I'm afraid not. Not yet, anyhow. But I do know Wolfe Tone Quay.'

It was on my third visit to Sean that he had shown me all his photographs and told me of the long struggle for Catholic Rights. Wolfe Tone had lived and worked in Belfast, a Protestant campaigning for Catholic Rights. No wonder I'd never heard of him before.

'That's the Four Courts, miss.'

Five weeks ago, the Four Courts meant nothing to me. No more than if someone had said 'That's the new library,' or 'That's the childrens' hospital.' Now those two simple words meant struggle and death, passion and courage, dreams and harsh reality. They stood for a struggle that had shaped the lives of so many, a struggle far from over.

We arrived at the station with time to spare. I sat drinking coffee, the tiny pasteboard ticket ready in my jacket pocket, and wondered what it must have felt like to be Sean, at twenty-one, aware that the country he loved was not truly his. It was not whether what he had done was right or wrong that concerned me, for I didn't think I could judge such a matter. What I wanted to know was what I would do if I found myself in the same situation.

Would I struggle for what I believed to be true? Would I risk my life, or the lives of those I loved? Or would I feel that life itself was more important than any political system? I came to no conclusion, except to recognise how the thought of conflict of any kind, personal, national, or international, always made me anxious. One day I would have to face that fear. I just hoped it wouldn't be for a very long time yet.

As I walked along the platform, I remembered I had said no to George. It was hardly an act of heroism, but given all my fears, it was an achievement of a sort. It was something to set against my fear that I had no courage at all to face conflict of any kind.

'Porty-down. Porty-down.' I opened my eyes with a jerk and felt my paperback slide off my knee onto the carriage floor.

'All change for Dungannon, Cookstown . . .'

A voice with a familiar accent reeled off a litany of well-known names as the stationmaster strode past the window and disappeared along the dimly lit platform. I picked up my book, smoothed a crumpled corner and peered out at the unexceptional features of a station I knew well, though the last time I'd been here was with the school hockey team.

I was amazed I could have fallen asleep. Perhaps it was the smooth running of the new diesel car we had been transferred to at the border, or perhaps it was the quiet dusk settling over the empty countryside as we came up through the low hills north of Dundalk. I'd been asleep for nearly an hour.

Three people climbed into the carriage, two women and a man. Immediately we were on our way again. Only a bare half hour remained before we were due to pull in at the Great Northern. Was it my imagination or were we travelling faster than at any time during the day? After all these hours of travel, I was still reluctant to arrive.

The man settled to read his newspaper, but the two women launched into a vigorous conversation, so loud it was impossible to shut out.

'I have it on good authority . . . there's no knowing, you know. As I says "there's no smoke without fire" . . . I'm telling you . . . you can't be too careful.'

I didn't need to look to see the knowledgeable nods, the guarded glances, the signals accompanying their words. How could you fail to understand what was being said, when the

winks and nods flowed so freely? It was not the topic which
was so familiar, though I guessed easily enough what that
might be, it was the tone, that unlovely, self-righteous way of
speaking that will tolerate no different view.

'Tell them you had salmon mayonnaise for your supper
last night with a Catholic, the man you love and may one day
marry.'

The thought came as if someone had spoken it and I
glanced quickly out of the window in case either of them
should see my startled look. But they were too absorbed in
rerunning their well-worn discontents.

The man now rearranged his newspaper noisily and moved
to the sports page, leaving the front page headline stretched
out in front of me like a banner. 'No Catholics vote unani-
mous on new estate.' With headlines like that was it any
surprise that the graffiti already scrawled in biro above the
comfortable new seats said 'No surrender' and 'Remember
1690'.

'You're back, Elizabeth. Now you really know you're
back,' I said to myself. You may have changed in five weeks,
but one thing is sure, they haven't. Look around, observe
them, these three good, staunch Protestants. What would they
say if they knew? Could they allow the man you love any
possible good quality if you told them he was a Catholic?
What does it matter if he doesn't attend Mass, has a strong
dislike for most of the priesthood, and eats fish on Friday out
of courtesy to his housekeeper? What does it matter what he
thinks? It's the label that matters.

We roared past a huge mill, its neon lights winking in the
darkness, advertising itself as world-famous. It belonged to
Dicky's father. Round it the tiny houses clustered, back to
back, red brick boxes full of loyal workers. Beyond the mill
estate, the lights were strung out along the main road from

Lisburn to Belfast, linking other newer estates and factories, until once again the road was obscured by the backs of more red brick houses. We slowed down.

At the kitchen sink of one of them, I saw a man shaving, his face half-covered in soap. In the reflected light from the passing carriages I could see that the window where he stood lay between the legs of a rearing white horse. King Billy was on his way to the Boyne, by way of the Lisburn road.

I had almost finished my book, a battered paperback Sean had given me. Only seven pages left. As I put in my bookmark, I noticed a paragraph had been underlined. A long time ago, for the ink was very faded.

Away then, it is time to go. A voice spoke softly to Stephen's lonely heart, bidding him go and telling him his friendship was coming to an end. Yes, he would go. He could not strive against another. He knew his part.

I closed the book, put it back in my blue suitcase and zipped up my jacket. That was what Sean had had to do. He had left Ireland because in the end, like Stephen, he could not strive against another. He had had to be free of the burden of his culture and the assumptions it made about what it was to be a true son of Ireland.

And what about a true daughter of Ulster, I asked myself, as the brakes squealed and I swung down my suitcases. The train jerked to a standstill, but I was out and halfway along the platform before my travelling companions had even appeared.

Beyond the station entrance with its tall, weathered columns, I could see the lights of shops reflected in broad puddles. Buses were splashing through them as they pulled in to collect the fortunate few from the long lines of would-be

passengers. My arms were sore with carrying and manoeu-
vring cases all day and I looked longingly across at the line
of taxis. The thought tempted me, for I still had a little money
left, but I decided against. Homecoming would be difficult
enough. Arriving by taxi would give the opportunity for one
more charge of extravagance.

I walked faster to avoid the small boys who offered to
carry my cases to the bus, tried to sell me a newspaper, or
asked me if I had a sixpence for a bar of chocolate. I had
almost reached the shallow steps leading down into Great
Victoria Street when one of the more persistent voices hailed
me for the second time.

'Carry yer case, miss.'

The accent was authentic, but something about the style of
delivery didn't seem quite right. I lowered my cases wearily,
turned round and found myself staring at a familiar blue
anorak.

'Carry yer cases. Only six dee. Money back if yer not
satisfied,' he continued, with a broad grin.

'Ben! What on earth are you doing here?'

'Oh, just passing. Just passing,' he said, with studied
vagueness, as he picked them up and set off. 'I've ordered a
special bus that actually has seats in it. Be here in about half
an hour. Just gives us time for a coffee in the Connoisseur.
All right?'

'All right,' I agreed breathlessly as I tried to keep up with
his long strides.

As we crossed the busy road and made for the coffee bar, I
was sure I'd never been so glad to see Ben in all my life.

Chapter 20

From our usual seats on top of the bus Ben and I looked down into the shop as we approached. It was still open. Above the fluorescent glare of its plate-glass windows, those of the flat were dark, unlit rectangles, though it was not far off nine o'clock.

'Lizzie, there's no one there, they wouldn't even notice me carrying them. I'd be gone in two ticks.'

'No, Ben, honestly.'

I had made up my mind before we left the coffee bar that the last small piece of this journey I had to do on my own. He'd protested, muttered about how heavy my cases were and how pale I looked, but, knowing I meant what I said, he'd nodded. Yes, he said, he did understand, he just didn't like it. He'd stay on the bus for the extra stop which left him beyond the end of his own avenue provided I'd come for a walk tomorrow.

'Curzon Cinema.'

The conductor's voice echoed from below as the bus slowed down at the busy pedestrian crossing before the stop itself.

'Don't forget tomorrow, Lizzie,' he said, as I got to my feet, a flicker of anxiety in his green eyes. 'Sunnyside Bridge at three.'

'I'll be there,' I said hastily, as we jerked to a halt. 'Thanks for tonight, Ben, you saved my life ... again,' I added, squeezing his shoulder, as I slid past him and hurried down the aisle.

I unloaded my cases one last time, crossed the road and walked towards the shop. Behind the counter, my father stood, stooping slightly, straightening as he turned to lift cigarettes down from the shelves behind his head. I put my cases down to wave to him through the plate glass, but he didn't see me, so I went round the back, climbed the outside stair and fumbled for my keys at the top, my arms aching after hauling my cases up behind me. Pushing them ahead of me into the small dark hallway, I reached for the light switch and closed the door with my foot.

At the end of the narrow passageway, in the front room that overlooks the road itself, my mother was rummaging through the top drawer of the sideboard, so preoccupied with her search she hadn't heard me come in.

'Hallo, Mum,' I said, coming down the hall.

'You're a stranger.' She glanced up at me, startled. 'Your father said you might have come home sooner,' she added, as she continued her search.

'I did explain why I stayed on, Mum. In my letter.'

She turned to face me, a paper pattern in her hand. 'You've the queer tan. Was the weather good?'

The complete incredulity in her voice reminded me that there could be nothing good about the south, not even the weather.

'We're not closed yet. I only came up to get a pattern for Mrs Purdy. I've left your father up to his eyes. I don't know where they get the money from,' she added, from long habit.

I said nothing and began to take my jacket off.

'The water's not on. You didn't say what time you'd be here at.'

'I didn't know which train I'd be able to get. The buses don't always connect.'

'It might be hot from this morning. I've not been out of the shop all day to use any,' she complained, as she moved towards the stairs.

In a moment she was gone. Weariness flooded over me. I turned back into the passage, took the cases to my room, shut the door behind me and sat on the bed. It smelt of paint. The lampshade still sat on top of the wardrobe, leaving a naked bulb to cast its harsh light over the heavy furniture and the bright, leaf-covered wallpaper. The window was wide open to let out the smell and the room felt chill and dank.

I put my jacket back on again, shut the window and switched on the electric fire. The element sparked and made a funny smell. I sat and watched it begin to glow. It sparked again and I remembered the sparks from the turf fire in Patrick's study. A whole world away. I knew it would be awful coming back and it was. Every bit as bad as I had expected it to be. I blinked the tears out of my eyes.

The room was innocent of any mark I'd ever made upon it. My maps, photographs and postcards that had once cheered the faded wallpaper were unlikely to have survived. My mother was no more a respecter of possessions than of persons.

I stirred myself and opened the blue suitcase, took out my green file and the exercise books I'd written, hour upon hour, at Mary and Paddy's table. Below them lay the books Patrick had bought for me on our day in Limerick, shiny and new, volumes of poetry and folklore, botany and archaeology. I looked at them and stroked their covers, smelling their newness.

The sight of my books and papers comforted me, but it was a momentary comfort. Unless I stacked them at the bottom of the wardrobe with my shoes, I had nowhere at all to put them. No desk, no bookshelf, no broad window ledge. Sadly, I fitted them carefully back into the case and slid it under the bed.

Tears of weariness and frustration rolled down my cheeks and splashed onto my jacket. I put my hand to my pocket for a hanky and found the grubby scrap I'd used to wipe the window of the bus in the Square in Lisdoonvarna. I sat twisting it in my fingers and let the tears roll, too weary to stop myself, until I heard voices in the hallway.

'Elizabeth, where are ye? Are ye still in the bathroom?'

The familiar ring of irritability and impatience struck me like a blow. It had to be faced and faced right now. She'd called me a stranger when I came into the flat and she was right. Far more acutely than ever before, I felt I was indeed a stranger in the place. I wiped my eyes hastily on my sleeve, took off my jacket and stepped out into the hall to say hallo to my father.

Saturday night supper is always bacon and egg. I laid the table, cut the bread and made a pot of tea, as I always do, while my mother cooked. We had hardly picked up our knives and forks when she began to berate me.

'I hear it's all off with George Johnston and you've a great new boyfriend,' she said, as she sawed fiercely at her bacon. 'If it's not a rude question, what did George do on you?'

She didn't wait for any reply.

'I would have thought, Elizabeth, you weren't too badly off atall to get a nice, clean, decent boy like George, without running after this English guy with the long hair and the stammer. What were ye thinkin' about atall?'

Nothing I said had the slightest effect on her. She'd made

up her mind from George's report and I only just managed to keep my temper. When she finally tramped off to the kitchen in disgust, all I could think of was that if Geoffrey, my supposed new boyfriend, reliably British, Protestant, and car-owning, all plus points on my mother's score card, was to cause such fury, what on earth would it be like if she knew about Patrick.

To add to my misery that evening, there was the way my father behaved. He went on with his supper in silence while she harangued me. Then, when he'd finished eating, he simply tipped out the day's takings on the table and started counting, even though she was still in full flight, as if the whole business was nothing to do with him. And I suppose in a way it wasn't. He was only doing what he'd always done, the way he saw it daughters were a woman's affair and a man had better not meddle if he wanted a quiet life.

I went to bed as soon as I decently could and cried myself to sleep. If it hadn't been for the thought of telling Ben all about it the next day, I doubt if I'd have slept a wink. But I actually slept well and felt better next morning. I stayed in my room working on my notes and trying to think out exactly what I'd say to Ben about my relationship with Patrick.

Ben had his mother's car when he met me at Sunnyside Bridge, so we drove to the Giant's Ring, a great earthwork to the south of Belfast. Flickers of sunshine glinted through the heavy massed clouds as we climbed its steep bank. At the top, we stood catching our breath and looking down at the huge circular space spread out before us. We slithered down the inner face together and tramped towards the remains of a megalithic tomb at the centre point. Despite the fact that it was a Sunday afternoon, we were the only two people in the midst of the huge grassy space. I'd just made up my mind to speak about Patrick, when Ben spoke first.

'Well then, Lizzie, here's a real test for you. Football stadium, cathedral or cattle market? What can you tell me about the life and loves, rites and rituals, work and worship, of your average megalith builder?'

'Not a lot,' I said, laughing. 'Not my period.'

'No, nor mine. But I'd like to know more, wouldn't you?'

We examined the huge stones that made up the tomb. Their surfaces were so encrusted with lichens, white and pale grey, bright mustardy-yellow and deep red, that we couldn't see an inch of bare rock, never mind identify what kind of rock it might be, so we turned to the landscape around us and tried to identify other landmarks.

'Would it have looked like this when it was built?' he asked, waving an arm round the great circle.

His face was pale in the chill breeze, the skin tight around the eyes, his fair hair tousled. There was a tenseness about him that was quite new. When he smiled or passed on bits of news, it was the old, familiar Ben – lively, relaxed, completely in possession of himself. But when he stood as he did now, looking to the far horizon, scanning the surrounding high ground, preoccupied, absorbed, there was definitely something I'd not met before and could give no name to.

'The bank might have looked the way it does now, but the surroundings might be different. The climate's changed but I can never remember how the sequence of warm bits and wet bits goes, after the last Ice Age.'

'Like me and small bones. I'm fine on the big ones, it's when we get down to the little fellows I'm in trouble.'

He sighed and I wondered if he was thinking of all the hours he'd have to spend in the coming year memorising every small detail of the human anatomy. So much of his future rested upon his doing well in his MD exams.

'Lizzie, there are some public lectures at the Ulster Museum on Wednesdays this term. "From Prehistoric to Iron Age". Would you come?'

Something in the way he spoke, the way he didn't look at me, made me feel I couldn't say no, even if I'd wanted to, which I most certainly didn't.

'Yes, I'd like to. What time?'

'Six o'clock. I thought we could go and have a bite to eat afterwards. Nothing posh, Chalet d'Or or Queen's Espresso. My treat, I've been doing Saturday nights at the Rosetta.'

'Ben, you've just reminded me. I've something to give you,' I said hastily, as I dug my purse out of my jacket pocket, took out the five pound note he'd sent me in Clare and held it out to him. To my amazement I saw his face fall. He looked terribly upset.

'Ben, what is it?'

'I thought you'd used that to help you stay.'

'But I did, Ben,' I protested. 'I couldn't have risked staying on what I'd got. I was just lucky. Feely undercharged me and the Dublin single wasn't as bad as I thought. Even at that, I've only got five and tenpence left.'

'Five and tenpence won't last long,' he said abruptly.

'True, Ben, true. But my grant cheque's come through.'

I had never seen Ben look so sad. It was quite unlike him to be upset, especially over money. He stood looking at me, his hands stuck resolutely in his pockets, ignoring the offending fiver.

'Now, come on, Ben, tell me what's wrong. This isn't like you. What have I said, or not said? Come on, tell me.'

The sky had grown overcast, spots of rain began to fall.

'Come on, Lizzie, we'll get soaked,' he said, striding off.

I pushed the fiver back into my purse and hurried after him, but he arrived at the car well ahead of me. As I scrambled in, the rain began in earnest.

'Ben, will you tell me why you're upset? Please.'

His face softened slightly, but he said nothing. I waited. And went on waiting as the rain sheeted down around us.

'I don't know why I'm upset, but I am. Sorry.'

'Oh Ben, you don't think I'm rejecting what you offered, do you? I've just brought it back so we can do something together. It will buy lots of teas, if they aren't too posh.'

'Are you sure?'

'Sure of what?'

'That you want lots of not very posh teas with me?'

'Yes, of course I am,' I said firmly. 'Now, here, take it and keep it for us and tell me about the Brigadier. I forgot to ask you about him last night.'

To my surprise, he closed his hand round mine, leaned forward and kissed me for the first time, very gently, on the lips.

Chapter 21

The autumn term was even busier than I'd expected. As well as an endless stream of essays to write, I was drafting my thesis and it gave me a bad time. I just couldn't keep inside the prescribed length. Twice my tutor sent me away to cut out huge sections and synthesize others. I felt that everything I did involved unhappy compromises. Even the splendid black and white prints I'd had from Geoffrey, exactly the illustrations I needed, created problems with binding and made it far more expensive than I'd expected.

I could cope with this sort of problem and with the misery of a particularly wet autumn, but living with the atmosphere at home was a quite different matter. I spent as little time there as I could, escaped to my room when I had nowhere else to go and thought about Patrick continuously. Eventually I had to discipline myself and put him out of mind when I was at lectures, or working in the library, but as soon as I relaxed even a little, walking between seminars and practicals, riding on buses or heating baked beans for my tea, I thought of him compulsively.

At night, lying in bed, I imagined his arms around me, and thought about what it would be like making love to him, but when I fell asleep my dreams would be full of obstacles and difficulties, and I'd wake up frustrated and desolate.

The worst of it was, there was no one I could talk to about Patrick. I daren't tell Adrienne or any of my friends at Queen's, because such interesting news was sure to travel outwards, reaching girls I'd been at school with, some of whose mothers were customers at the shop. The only person I could rely on was Ben, but somehow after that first afternoon when I'd not managed to tell him as I'd planned, it now seemed more and more difficult to introduce the subject easily and naturally.

Patrick's letters arrived regularly. In his first one, he apologised for being out of practice with a pen, but I was so delighted to hear from him I hardly noticed the formality of his style. His accounts of assessing his uncle's pedigree herd for breeding purposes and planning a new series of land drains were written with a wry humour that always made me smile.

His letters were long and I read them avidly, enjoying his descriptions of people he'd met and places he'd visited. He always included news of the people I knew, particularly Mary and Paddy, and he often added messages from Mrs Brannigan, or Kathleen from the shop, and even John Carlyle, the blacksmith, who always asked after me. Often, he enclosed newspaper cuttings from the *Clare Champion* and book reviews from the *Irish Times*.

With Patrick and our time together occupying so much of my thoughts, it came as a real shock when it dawned on me that the excitement I felt at finding a letter in the familiar spiky hand had ebbed away in the time it took to read it. It happened so regularly and left me feeling so sad, that I could not ignore it. Each time a letter came, I set out hopefully but ended up puzzled and depressed by my disappointment. I told myself philosophically it was nothing more than the obvious: a letter was a poor substitute for a real, live Patrick.

But, progressively, I wasn't able to convince myself.

Beyond an occasional 'my dear', he never used any terms of affection and all his letters ended simply: 'with love'. At first this didn't trouble me, for I accepted it as part of the rather formal style. After all, what else should I expect from someone whose feelings were so rigidly controlled. Would I rather he wrote the sort of passionate and meaningless nonsense I'd had from George?

Weeks turned to months and still he never confessed to missing me, never once referred to the happiness of our times together, and made no mention of our meeting. I began to think more often of the dark shadows which had so often crossed his face. I had dispersed those shadows with my questions and stories, but I had no idea how deep set they were and what effect they might have on him, now I was so far away.

After the early weeks of October, most of his letters were posted in Dublin. His great-uncle, the one whose death had almost defeated our relationship, had made him his executor, so he was forced to visit Dublin regularly. First, he stayed at a hotel, but, as the need for visits grew more frequent, cousins in Rathfarnham invited him to use their house. Each time I saw the Dublin postmark, I hoped he might suggest coming to Belfast, but November ended with sleety snow and the posting of the Christmas cards to our Canadian relatives and still he did not suggest that he might come.

There was one helpful outcome of his regular visits to Dublin, however. After I'd received a transcript of some stories from Professor McDonagh's office on St Stephen's Green, my mother decided that anything from Dublin was something to do with my work. As that was a subject of no interest whatever to her, my letters from Patrick arrived without comment to be parked behind the living room clock until I could carry them off eagerly to my room.

It was a short note arriving in early December and not the hoped for letter from Patrick, that set events in my life moving again.

'Yer Uncle Joe is not one bit well,' my mother announced shortly, when she tore open the flimsy envelope. 'Jimmy says they've let him out of hospital at his own wish.' She compressed her lips. 'If anything happens we'll have to shut the shop. An' it couldn't be a worse time with trade so good.'

Uncle Joe was the brother closest in age to my father, a slight, frail-looking man, who said little and seldom smiled. Apart from his passion for growing giant dahlias, I had never been able to find any interest or activity which gave him the slightest pleasure in life, even the running of his very successful dairy farm. When the news came of his death and my mother insisted I go to Keady with them for the funeral, I was completely taken aback.

'It's not as if I even knew him very well,' I confessed to Ben, as we came out of the library, where we'd been working together all evening. 'The service isn't till three and then there'll be a bun fight. I'll not be back for our lecture and it's the last one as well.'

'Can't be helped,' he said easily. 'Actually, there's something else I'd like you to come to. Perhaps it would make up for missing our lecture.'

'What's that then?'

'Medical Formal.'

'But Ben, you never go to Formals? You've always said you hated wearing a penguin suit . . .'

'But you'll come, Lizzie, won't you?'

'Yes, I'd love to.'

Sitting in the back of the van on the way to Keady in company with a large cardboard box of groceries for Aunt

Lily, two umbrellas and my mother's hat, I thought about Ben and the Medical Formal and the sort of comments my going would inevitably provoke. I still hadn't managed to tell Ben about Patrick. Since that first walk at the Giant's Ring when I'd missed my chance, I'd been waiting for the right moment, but the right moment just didn't seem to turn up. By now, so much time had passed, I wasn't sure what it was I had to tell him anyway.

If I confessed that I loved Patrick he might feel I'd only been going out with him because I was lonely. That certainly wasn't the reason. Oh yes, I was lonely, but then so was Ben. For all his circle of friends, he seemed to be happiest in my company. The same was true for me. We felt safe with each other, more confident we could cope with all the strains and stresses of a difficult year because each of us had the other to comfort and encourage them. When I thought about this, often I saw us as we stood that Sunday, at the centre of that great earthwork, two small figures in an immensity of space.

And as often as not, another and very different image would follow it into my mind: the dazzle of sky and sea and the light reflecting from the limestone, the day Patrick and I had gone to the Burren. Standing with him in that very different immensity of space, I had felt I'd never feel lonely again, so long as he were with me.

I stared out at the frosty countryside, the grass crisp with ice crystals, stiff and white, except under the south-facing hedges where it lay, vivid green, beaded with droplets that caught the light and sparkled. Even at midday, the sun was low in the sky, casting long shadows in the empty fields, reflecting back from the surface of the road, spilling down on barns and outhouses, picking out their corrugated roofs and the pale colour of the bales of hay stacked up for winter feed.

Was it possible to feel the same thing with two quite

different people? I sighed to myself. As Patrick had once said, love was a tricky little word at the best of times. I hadn't appreciated then just what a variety of feelings might be involved and how difficult it was to work out what they were.

'To the best of my knowledge that clock in Joe's sitting room is left to our Elizabeth,' my mother pronounced as my father drove down the hill into Armagh, turned along the side of the Mall, crossed the front of the county jail, and made his way through the old horse market to the junction with the Keady road.

'When Albert died, Joe told me that he'd left that clock to Elizabeth, but that Joe was to have it for his lifetime. D'ye hear me, Elizabeth?'

She twisted round in her seat to see what I was doing. Satisfied I was paying attention, she issued her instructions. 'Now if that clock's mentioned you're to say nothing. Just leave it to your father an' me. Just close yer han' on it. Must be worth a right bit.'

'Ach no, Florrie, those clocks were mass-produced in America,' my father replied mildly. 'You'd see one in whatever house you went into when I was a lad. You might get a pound or two from these antique dealers that come round the countryside looking for stuff, but that'd be the height of it.'

'Yer wrong there. Sure look at the work in those wee columns up the side of the face. It's all twisty bits. Nellie used to say it was always the very divil to clean.'

They argued back and forth most of the way to Keady, but perhaps as a tribute to the solemn nature of the occasion, my mother didn't go into a huff, her usual response to any disagreement in which she'd not come off best. As she got out of the van, I reached for her hat and took my chance as I handed it to her.

'Uncle Albert did say I could have his clock, but I thought

he'd forgotten. I'd like to have it whether it's worth anything or not.'

The funeral passed off without event, the graveyard iced with white except where the open grave had spread heavy, clayey soil around its narrow trench. The sun was setting, pink and gold behind the bare trees on the edge of the old burying ground, as we hurried, shivering, back to the farm kitchen where tea was waiting.

The object of disagreement sat silent in the centre of the sitting-room mantelpiece, the room used only for such state occasions. Over the teacups and glasses of whiskey, it provided exactly the topic needed to oil the social wheels and keep the conversation going. Everyone seemed to know something about it, remembered it from Uncle Albert's cottage, had heard his intentions, or Joe's intentions. Stories were told, opinions offered, but agreement was general and surprisingly amicable. The clock had been intended for me.

'Would you not like to keep it, Aunt Lily?' I asked quietly, ignoring my mother's sideways look. 'You might miss it.'

'Ach, not at all, chile dear, I have the keys here for you and a note Joe left to say what Albert's wishes were. Now wait till I get that box the groceries came in and we'll pack it with newspaper for you.'

The drive back to Belfast was slow and unpleasant, the lanes around Keady already filling with drifting snow, the Portadown road gleaming with ice and the junction with the motorway at Lisburn closed, because a lorry had shed its load.

'Ye may put that box under the bed for there's no room for a clock that size on these mantelpieces,' my mother said, as my father dropped us at the back of the shop and drove off to lock up the van in his rented garage. She climbed the outside stairs ahead of me, jabbed on the light and took off her hat.

'I'm not makin' tea at this hour, it's time we were all in our beds.'

I took the hint, carried my box into my bedroom and shut the door gratefully. Fairy Liquid, I read, as I parked it on the bed. Every time I used Fairy Liquid, I thought of Bridget Doherty. It always amazes me how a single phrase can conjure up so many memories: that chilly morning after the dance at the Kincora Ballroom; Bridget's hands, red and chapped from scrubbing and cleaning; our talk at her kitchen table. At our last meeting, I'd told her about George and she'd grinned slyly.

'Sure there's plenty of others better than him – an' one not so far away, I do hear tell.'

I pushed the thought out of mind and found myself abstractedly smoothing out the crumpled sheets of the *Armagh Gazette* the clock had been packed with. 'Nettie Falloon Carnagh's Beauty Queen,' I whispered to myself. 'City Man Gets Top Job in Belfast. Armagh City, that is,' I added. 'Spanish Honeymoon For Lisnadill Couple, Creamery Manager Marries Schoolteacher, Customs Crackdown On Smuggled Heifers.'

What different worlds we all live in. Not the grand differences of continent, or country, or even county. Within a village, a street, within one house, people live in quite different worlds. It was all a question of what was important to you: dahlias or dairy cattle, boxes of Fairy Liquid from the cash and carry, or the Cycles of the Kings in Irish mythology. But how much choice did anyone really have as to what they drew into their lives and what they excluded? Some people, it seemed to me, had very little choice.

I got down on the floor and put the silent clock on the levellest piece I could find. I took the keys from their envelope and opened the other one, addressed to me in Uncle Joe's large shaky script.

To whom it may concern

On the instructions of my brother Albert Stewart of this townland, I, Joseph Stewart, do record his last wishes in respect of the clock formerly to be seen at his residence and now in mine. This clock is to go on my decease to Elizabeth Stewart of Belfast together with its keys and the following message which I do not understand, but record faithfully, my brother being of sound mind till his decease.

Elizabeth, do ye mind the wee key you used to keep in its cellophane bag? Well, here is another wee key. But see you take it out and use it for what it was intended.

Your loving Uncle, Albert.

Tears rolled down my cheeks. I could hear the way he said, 'Do ye mind?' instead of 'Do you remember?' which was what town people said. Who else in all my family would have paid the slightest attention to my little key, once the dearest of my childhood treasures?

I'd run out of hankies, so I had to go to the bathroom and pull off a long piece of toilet roll. I blew my nose, mopped myself up and read the bit about the key again. I wasn't sure I understood it either, whether I was of sound mind or not.

I stared at the clock and began to recall what Uncle Albert had once explained to me.

'Ye see, Elizabeth, in the old days people used to put anything they had of any importance under the clock. It might be a land deed, or the money for the rates, or a letter from Amerikay. But the newer clocks had no space underneath them, they weren't raised up the way the older ones were, so there was nowhere to put anything, till one bright spark comes along and has this great idea. He puts a wee drawer at the back of the clock where ye can't even see it and he puts a lock on it. An' he advertises it as a Security Clock and sells thousands.'

I turned the clock round to face me. The drawer was the full width of the base and about an inch deep. The wood was dark with smoke from the fire, but the tiny keyhole was perfectly visible. I picked up the keys. There were the two brass ones I had seen him use every Saturday night to adjust the time to the wireless and wind it for the week. And then there was a very small one, smaller than my key that I had never used.

It took only a moment to do as I had been bidden. I turned the key in the lock. It clicked round without sticking. Gently, I eased open the drawer. A thick wodge of creased paper filled it. Only it wasn't paper. When I unfolded the neat pack he had folded to fit the drawer exactly, I found it was made up of old five pound notes just like the note the Brigadier had given to Ben and me. I started to count and began to cry again. One hundred. Two hundred. Three hundred. I sat back on my heels, the tears pouring unheeded down my cheeks. Dear Uncle Albert had left me his entire life savings.

Chapter 22

After the initial shock, I was faced with the problem of what to do about Uncle Albert's money. If I told my parents I could be quite sure my mother would expect her share. At the very least, she would insist I now 'pay for my keep' after three years of 'having to be kept'. However I might try to explain the workings of the means test and its effect on my scholarship, she had never accepted that my father received an allowance for my board and lodging. If it didn't arrive in cash, it didn't exist.

I considered approaching my father but decided there was little point. Outside the shop, he so seldom made decisions about anything that he'd only pass it up the line to my mother. In the end, I went to the bank and put all the money, except for ten pounds, into a deposit account. When I discovered that my shiny, new pass book with its single entry fitted the drawer at the back of my clock, I was quite delighted. It seemed so appropriate for me to tuck the little book away, turn the key on it, and slide the clock back under the bed, my secret safe from prying eyes.

I spent a long time planning what I should buy and send as thank you presents to all my friends in Lisara. Mary and Paddy came top of my list and I began to fill a small box with little treats for them.

'So why do you want a dispensary label, Lizzie?' Ben asked, laughing.

'For Paddy's medicine. I've got him a half-bottle of Powers and I want a proper doctor's scribble that you can only just make out, saying "Take as required or as prescribed by your physician." '

'All right, I'll see what I can do when I'm up at the Royal tomorrow,' he agreed, as we parked our files and settled ourselves with coffee in the students' union. 'What about Mary?'

'Fine red wool scarf and matching gloves. She loves bright colours but she always buys black. And real coffee. It will pack nicely round the whiskey.'

'And Sean?'

'Photo of his cottage with the flower tubs in bloom. Two enlargements, so he can send one to his brother.'

'Geoffrey?'

'Second-hand copy of *The Cycles of the Kings*, by Myles Dillon. I had an incredible bit of luck: it's out of print but I found it in Smithfield for two shillings.'

He continued to go through every one of the names of all the people I'd written about, asking what I'd worked out for each of them.

'You have been busy, haven't you? Hasn't your mother been asking questions?'

'No. She's far too bound up in her own affairs. It is Christmas, you see, and the only good thing about Christmas in the Stewart establishment is that she wouldn't notice if I dropped dead.'

'Don't do that, Lizzie?'

'Do what?'

'Drop dead. I'd miss you so. Besides, you'd make a rotten angel.'

'And why would I make a rotten angel, Ben Milligan?'

'You'd never be able to keep your harp in tune. Will you come to the carol service at St Jude's? Guaranteed no sermon.'

'Yes, if you'll tell me what you'd like for your present. You helped me too, in lots of ways.'

'You, mostly.'

'What?'

'For my present. And my future. You. That's what I'd really like.'

He said it so easily and lightly, so completely the direct and forthcoming Ben I'd always known, I was amazed to find myself blushing. I was grateful when a crowd of agriculture students at the next table rose en masse and filled the air with noise, and the space around us with duffel-coated figures. I just managed to mutter something inane about not giving him handkerchiefs or socks before I left him to go to my tutorial.

Halfway up the stairs to the department it suddenly hit me that Ben hadn't mentioned Patrick when he'd taken me through the list of the friends from Clare for whom I'd bought presents. Once again I berated myself for not telling him about Patrick the very moment I got back. Half a dozen times I'd made up my mind to do it and not been able to manage it. But far worse, I'd not even been able to mention Patrick in ordinary conversation. I was sure Ben sensed something wasn't quite right.

It would explain why I would suddenly be aware of him drawing back sometimes, when we were at our happiest and easiest, even avoiding contact, kissing me briefly only when we parted.

I felt sad, sad and anxious. I couldn't see what I was going to do. All at once, finding a suitable Christmas present for Patrick had become a major undertaking with very little joy in it, while giving Ben what he most wanted raised issues I simply couldn't begin to resolve.

Later that day, I sent off the first parcels and packets. By the end of the week, they had all gone. I had collected my thesis from the binders and handed in my term essay. There was nothing left now but to resign myself to the Christmas vacation and the unavoidable festivities of the season.

Christmas week was grim. Far from being white, the rain sheeted down and produced a landscape made up of washes of grey, dark brown and black. Looking out of my bedroom window each morning over dripping backyards and minute squares of sodden grass, I tried to tell myself that things would improve as the year turned. But I wasn't convinced.

The ordeal of the gathering at Short Strand, where my mother and her sisters convened to demolish the obligatory turkey on Christmas Day, made Uncle Joe's funeral seem like a rather jolly outing. Somewhat to my surprise I got through without the usual depression and took to working in my room when not required for family duty, a baize-covered card table wedged between the electric fire and the edge of the bed on which I had to sit. My own legs and the legs of the table got scorched regularly, but the alternative was to freeze. I had long ago abandoned the impossible task of trying to write while wrapped in an eiderdown.

The post was disrupted after Christmas, but even allowing for that, the gap in Patrick's letters had grown wider. When the next fat letter arrived on a bleak New Year's morning, I carried it off to my room at once, but didn't open it immediately. I sat down again at my card table and arranged my notes and coloured paper markers into neat piles until there was a clear space for the white envelope to sit in their midst.

The patterns I'd produced brought back that last evening of Geoffrey's when we'd persuaded Mary to read the cards for us. With her usual disclaimer that she was no good at it, she'd dealt out the battered rectangles in circles and squares, calling each pattern by a different name. The Wheel of Fortune. The Marriage Bed. The Hand of Friendship. I had listened closely, anxious to hear anything that might point to a future with Patrick, the one future that seemed at all relevant to me, despite all the difficulties it would involve.

But there was nothing in what Mary said that I could connect directly with Patrick, however I might try to interpret the ambiguities of what she said.

'I would have great success in all my enterprises. I would cross water with a fair man who stood in the best of loving hearts to me. I would stand out in front of people and I would often have something sharp in my right hand.'

She shuffled a second time and said she would make up my marriage bed. I watched, fascinated, as she laid the cards face downwards. Two each, at the top and bottom of the bed. Two at each side. Two cards within, myself and my lover. Two more she added for the bedcovers. And these she wove deftly between the others to make a solid shape.

'Come on, astore, pick a card till we turn you over.'

I drew a card from the fan shape she offered me. It was the Queen of Hearts. A good card, I thought, from what I'd learnt so far. But Mary seemed indifferent to it, being for the moment wholly preoccupied with the interwoven construction in front of her. Then she did take it and turned it over.

'Oh boys a dear, aren't you the lucky one? Aren't all the cards light, but for two and those are two old people. You'll have joy and long life with a fair man. You'll shed tears in sorrow, but never in bitterness. Tears of weariness, but never of hardship. Tears of longing, but never of regret.'

As her words echoed again in my mind, I closed my eyes on my bedroom and let myself go back to the cottage, feeling its warmth, imagining the smell of the turf, the sharp tang of Paddy's tobacco.

Geoffrey had watched Mary too, as absorbed as I was. When she turned over his marriage bed however, the cards were all dark and fell apart. She'd blamed the stiffness of her fingers and tried a second time. The same thing happened again.

'Ah sure you must watch the carpenter that makes your bed, Geoffrey. Don't be sleeping on one of those put-u-ups for as sure as eggs is eggs it'll let you down.'

We had laughed easily, but a chill had stolen across my mind and I was grateful when she began to deal again.

'Choose a card, one each, and exchange it. Now put your left hand over the card you've exchanged and I'll deal the Hand of Friendship for the two of you.'

I saw her smile and I was so thankful.

'Ah sure good. Don't I see letters and packets between you, even when oceans divide you. You'll be spending a fortune on stamps, I'm thinking, for there'll always be one of you a journey away.'

I put out my hand and touched the white envelope with its Dublin postmark, my name written in black ink. To my surprise, I heard Mary's voice, as clearly as if she were beside me. 'Aye, 'tis darkish at the top, but lighter further down. 'Twill all work out with the help o' God.'

Neither that letter nor the ones that followed through the snowy weeks of January and February brought any resolution to my growing unease. He had spent Christmas at Rathfarnham, he had written, with the cousins he'd mentioned when he took up his duties as executor. He penned lively sketches of the three young sons of the household for me, Andrew, Patrick and Declan, the eldest training to be a pilot with KLM, the second reading history at the University of Cork, and the youngest, at University College, Dublin, given to radical political pronouncements that completely unnerved his quiet, artistic mother. There was also news of Mary and Paddy, of storm damage and flooding in Roadford, where the tiny river, already swollen with winter rain, was inundated by exceptionally high tides. But he still did not refer back to the summer or say that he missed me.

When subsequent fat letters did arrive, invariably they contained newspaper photographs he thought might be useful for my file. But once, he would have said 'the Green File', and refer to it affectionately as if it had a life of its own. Then, he'd come back from Limerick with pads of punched paper, handed them to me, and said, laughing, 'Green File fodder.' Now there was no more lightness in what he wrote than there was in the slushy streets, where each day's thaw was enough to make the pavements dirty and slippery but never went on for long enough to dispose of the remnants of the previous week's snow.

'Let's have a weekend in Bermuda,' said Ben, as we passed the travel agent's in Royal Avenue on our way to the bookshop one morning early in February.

He looked at me hopefully, but I didn't even smile.

'Lizzie, what's wrong? Is the work getting you down? Or is it your mother?'

I shook my head silently. I really didn't know why I felt so depressed. Patrick had to be part of it, of course, but I sensed that it was much more than that.

'Oh just the grey and the cold, I suppose. I'll be better in the spring.'

'Is it me, Lizzie. Are you fed up with me?'

'No, I am not,' I objected fiercely. 'If it weren't for you I think I'd go mad.'

'Thank goodness for that. My penguin suit is nearly ready

and it's only two weeks now to the Medical Formal. That's something to look forward to, isn't it?'

'Oh yes, it is indeed,' I said quickly, making a huge effort to be cheerful. 'And February will be nearly over by then. I think January and February ought to be abolished.'

There was no way I could tell Ben that the Medical Formal he was looking forward to so much, was just one more problem for me.

Chapter 23

A few nights before the Medical Formal I folded up my card table, turned off the electric fire and took my one and only long dress from the wardrobe. I unwrapped it from its dust sheet, a layer of filmy tulle over silky white fabric. Hardly the height of fashion with its halter neck and low back, but I had always liked it. I slid it over my head, zipped it up and wriggled experimentally. Tighter on the bust and looser on the waist than when I'd last worn it, but it did still fit.

Made by a local dressmaker for the Sixth Form dance four years ago, this dress had seen service throughout my relationship with George. He had inherited his father's dinner jacket and as he liked nothing better than dressing up, we'd been to every ball in the university calendar.

But memories of Formals with George were not what was making me anxious over the Medical Formal. George and my life as his girlfriend seemed very far away now. Not only did he avoid me when chance brought us together in the same place, the union, or the library, or the bank, but he'd actually stopped speaking to Ben, after he'd seen us coming out of the library together one day. No, it wasn't the past that bothered me at all, it was the vicious and hurtful remarks I knew I would have to cope with here in the present because Ben was not at all what my mother had in mind for me.

My mother had known Ben and his family as long as I had, and on the face of it, he seemed to fit in with her list of requirements for a 'nice, respectable, young man'. He lived in the 'best' area of the Ormeau Road in a large, pleasant house. His father was a senior civil servant, his mother, a well-known soprano who had taught singing since her retirement. He had a much older brother and sister, both graduates, one married and living in England, the other a lecturer in Magee College, Londonderry. In another family, such a description would bring her strong approval but for some reason whenever the Milligans were mentioned in the shop, or by relatives who knew them, she had always announced that they were 'a very respectable family' with precisely that tightness of her face and aspect of brow which made it clear she didn't like them.

But what was even worse than her unreasonable hostility to Ben's family was her unshiftable conviction that medical students were a bad lot. For years now she had treated them with the same violent distaste she reserved for foreigners, Catholics, coloured people and what she called The English.

When I'd confessed this problem to Ben himself, he'd suggested her reaction might stem from *Doctor in the House*, the film itself, or perhaps just the posters displayed outside the Curzon when it was showing. He'd tried to be light about it, but, sadly, I couldn't raise a smile even to please him. Since my return from Clare either her prejudices and her comments had become more virulent, particularly on our Catholic neighbours, or my ability to ignore them had radically decreased. Now, the thought of her bitter and unreasoned comments when she heard I was going to the Medical Formal with Ben, was more than I could bear.

I shivered and took off the dress, wrapped it up and put it away. It was one thing meeting at Sunnyside Bridge when we were going for a walk, or getting off the bus at our respective stops to avoid being seen from the shop, but I could hardly slip down the back stairs in a full length dress.

As I put on my pyjamas and got into bed, tears sprang into my eyes. It was one more problem to add to all the others weighing me down. I had tried so hard to be sensible, to be patient, to get on with my work, to enjoy what I could, but suddenly it seemed as if the burden of the list of things I couldn't do had become quite intolerable. So many things I could not say, places I could not go, decisions I was in no position to make. It was not simply working so hard for Finals and the confinement of living at home, it was more than that. Every time I tried to think something through I found myself going round in circles. And every circle always led back to what was to happen between me and Patrick.

Before I went to sleep that night I made up my mind that if he didn't suggest a meeting by the end of March I would write and tell him I was coming to Dublin to see Professor McDonagh. I'd ask him when he'd next be in Dublin and where we could meet.

A few days later, I bought myself some new earrings, a woolly wrap and a pair of long gloves, all in the same shade of deep midnight blue. It made me think of the four sisters in *Little Women*, swapping bows and bits of fabric to brighten up dresses they'd been wearing season after season. Like them, it was the best I could do. Ben was looking forward to his first Medical Formal and I wasn't going to let him down.

Something so totally unexpected happened three days before, however, that it drove all thoughts of dressing up and dancing right out of my mind.

The weather had turned bitterly cold again. When my alarm went off at seven on that Tuesday morning and I nipped out of bed to put the electric fire on, I could see my

breath rise in a cloud. The window was so thickly encrusted
with icy patterns I could catch no glimpse of the prospect
beyond as I dived back into bed and snuggled down for a
blissful fifteen minutes before the bathroom was free.

Only moments later, there was a loud crash, the room
shook and I heard the noise of a deluge of falling, shattering
glass. The bedroom door flew open, the electric fire crackled
and went out, and a shower of plaster fell from the ceiling. I
leapt out of bed, grabbed my dressing gown and peered
through the open door. The air in the passageway was full of
choking dust and beyond its end I could just make out a vast
patch of unfamiliar daylight. I heard my mother's voice shout
'Willy, where are ye', just as my father, his face half-soaped,
appeared from the bathroom behind me, dragging his dressing gown round him.

I reached the open door of their bedroom ahead of him, in
time to see the double bed tilt backwards and downwards
towards a gaping hole in the bedroom wall where once the
window had been. I made a grab at it as it slowly began to
slide.

'Get out, Mum, quick,' I shouted, as I felt the floor vibrate
beneath my feet.

'Give us yer han', Willy, for dear sakes,' she cried, ignoring me.

But he was too slow. Another chunk of floor fell away, a
stream of plaster descended on the pillow beside her and the
bed tilted further, jerking loose my grip upon it. I tried to
catch hold of it again but it had gathered momentum and was
already out of reach. I watched helplessly as the bed, complete with my mother in curlers and chenille nightdress, still
protesting, slid rapidly downhill and came to rest on the back
of a long vehicle which was blocking half the road outside.

The floor tilted beneath my feet again and my father and I

had just got back into the passageway when another slice of the bedroom floor collapsed. As we made for the back stairs, lumps of plaster from both ceiling and walls fell around us like giant snowflakes, water trickled out from under the bathroom door and through the choking fume of dust came the unmistakable smell of gas.

The icy cold hit me like a blow as we left the flat and ran round to the front of the shop, or what was left of it. My mother was being helped out of bed by two men who'd been on their way to work. I stood shivering as I watched her descend the load of concrete girders on which the bed had come to rest. She was quite unhurt and was stepping down from girder to girder as if she were coming down a grand staircase. At the edge of the vehicle she paused until someone produced a kitchen chair to enable her to make the last step down to the ground.

A heavy coat dropped round my shoulders and I felt myself propelled towards the police car which had just arrived and now sat empty with its lights flashing.

'In you go, miss. Stay there like a good girl till the ambulance comes.'

I sat shuddering so violently I wondered if my teeth might damage themselves. I pushed my arms into the huge, police great-coat and wrapped its surplus bulk round me, then wiped the misted window nearest to me to see what was going on.

The street was full of people. I wondered wherever they could possible have come from at only five past seven in the morning. Still more people were arriving all the time. Two policemen were setting up diversion signs, others had roped off the area around the shop. It was only when the Fire Brigade arrived I finally figured out what had happened. The long articulated lorry with its load of concrete girders had skidded into the shop, demolishing most of it. Part of the flat was being held up by the cab, the back of it was skewed across the road reducing traffic to one lane.

My mind was working very slowly. I couldn't puzzle out why the Fire Brigade had come when there was no fire. Then the penny dropped and I gasped out, 'Oh no. No. Please let him be all right.' Somewhere under the debris, the driver of the lorry must still be in his cab. Tears trickled down my cheeks and I began to sob as if my heart would break.

How long I sat and cried in the back of the police car I don't know, but when the burly officer came back to collect me, I found my legs were shivering so much I couldn't stand up properly. He half-carried me to an ambulance, where a young man in shirtsleeves sat chatting to one of the team.

'You all right, miss?' he asked, as the man in uniform helped me out of the policeman's coat and wrapped me in red blankets.

'I'm fine, thank you,' I said, annoyed by the shake in my voice and the tears which streamed silently down my cheeks. 'Have they got the driver out yet?'

'Yeah, that's me. Right as rain. Sorry 'bout the way I dropped in on you. Old gent walked out in front of me, must 'ave been pure ice in the gutter. Next thing I knew, I was lookin' out at boxes of cornflakes.'

I giggled and drew my blankets round me as the doors banged shut and we drove off. For some ridiculous reason I felt quite sure that as long as he was safe everything else was going to be all right.

So much happened that day of the accident, I still can't remember whether it was my own idea or someone else's that I ask the Student Accommodation Officer to find me some-where to stay. Not only was the woman in question warmly sympathetic when I explained my situation, she also moved very fast. By late morning I had a bed for the night in a hostel and an appointment the following afternoon to see a room at the women's hall of residence.

I climbed the broad steps and rang the bell. I heard it echo round the lofty spaces that lay beyond the glass panes of the inner doors. A maid admitted me, small and square, dressed in black, a white cap positioned so erratically it almost obscured one eye, parked me in a waiting room, and waddled off to fetch the lady housekeeper.

'I'm afraid it's one of our smaller rooms, my dear,' the elderly Scots woman began, as I walked beside her up the impressive staircase and across the broad, polished landing on the first floor. 'But it is very bright. We always put our overseas students on the south side. It seems the least we can do for them in our dreadful climate.'

She threw open a door and we stepped into a room bathed in sunlight. I looked around me. The room was at least three times the size of the bedroom I'd revisited the previous afternoon in the company of a curly-headed young fireman with an axe tucked into his belt and a whistle dangling from his top pocket.

It felt rather empty. The floorboards were polished and there were large expanses of bare wall, but beyond the single bed, quite pleasantly disguised to look like a couch, I found there was a wardrobe, a dressing chest, and an armchair. More important still, there was not only a bureau but a table by the window, a corner cupboard and two large bookcases in the deep alcoves on either side of the closed up fireplace. I could hardly believe my luck.

'We're due for decorating on this corridor this summer, so we do turn a blind eye to sellotape, but I'm sure I needn't tell you that we take a very dim view of biro marks, or any other kind of mark, on the walls.'

I moved to the window. Beneath us on the sunlit terrace, stone steps led down to lawns bordered on one side by a rose garden. Beyond the green slopes, at the edge of a shrubbery that spread across a small valley, a few delicate sprays of pink blossom had appeared on an early-flowering tree.

'It's a lovely room,' I said, as I turned away.

My guide had dropped a sixpence into a meter and was bent over the electric fire, checking that it was working properly.

'The central heating is the same age as the building, I'm afraid. Like the rest of us, it gets less efficient as it grows older, but these electric fires are quite effective. Miss Kumar always worked up here, though the library downstairs is always beautifully warm and reliably quiet.'

She talked on in a friendly, ruminative way. She told me how poor Miss Kumar had had to return unexpectedly to Kenya because of family troubles. She went on to give me a brief history of the hall and an interesting sketch of the two formidable ladies who had endowed it. She insisted on showing me the kitchen used by students on this corridor and then took me downstairs to her own sitting room. I listened politely to all she said, made noises in the right places and tried to conceal my growing delight.

Even if the efficient lady at Student Accommodation couldn't persuade the Education Committee to pay my fees right away, I could certainly afford to pay them myself for the time being. One look at that table in the window and the sunshine falling on the garden had told me all I really needed to know about my very first room of my own.

'When would it be possible for me to move in?'

'Whenever you wish. Officially, you ought to have an interview with the Warden, who isn't available this afternoon, but I think in the circumstances . . . Yes, I don't think we have any problem there. Shall we expect you for dinner at six-thirty? We do dress for dinner, but if you haven't been able to retrieve your clothes it will be quite understood. Those photographs in the *Belfast Telegraph* were really most dramatic. The Warden was so concerned when we heard about you from Mrs Wilson at Queen's. I take it your parents are quite comfortable with your neighbour?'

I assured her that they were and explained that it would be mid-evening before I had transport available to bring my things. As I wished her goodbye I had to smile to myself. What was my mother going to make of dressing for dinner? I positively skipped down the steps from the red brick building and tripped along the curving drive to the bus stop on the main road as if I had a following wind behind me.

I was out. Out. Out. A young man in shirtsleeves had smashed open my home and disrupted my life. Yes, I could see that it might have had a quite different effect, I could understand Ben's anxiety, and the enquiries of relatives and friends, the concern of the Warden at the pictures in the *Telegraph*, but I couldn't hide from myself the fact that Tuesday morning's disaster was rapidly transforming itself into a most wonderful opportunity, every aspect of which I fully intended to exploit.

Chapter 24

Within a day of my moving into my room I'd managed to make it look very different. I unpacked the books from the blue suitcase and the assorted cardboard boxes that had lived for so long under my bed, installed Uncle Albert's clock on the broad mantelpiece and spent a whole evening mounting my collection of photographs and postcards on sheets of cartridge paper. They filled the large bare spaces on the walls with images of the people and places that I loved.

The bookshelves were still very empty, even when I'd unpacked all my books and files, so I used them to display a few treasured possessions like my pottery horse, the decorated teapot Mary had given me from the dresser at the cottage, and my only surviving teddy-bear. Ben's mother had given me a Donegal-woven rug and I used it to drape the worn armchair. Ben himself had bought me a bunch of daffodils. All I could find to put them in was an empty coffee jar, but they looked so bright and welcoming sitting on my table in the pale sunlight that no one would have noticed they hadn't got a proper vase.

I slept late after the Medical Formal, which we enjoyed enormously, and spent most of that Saturday with Ben, going for a walk in the afternoon and having supper with his parents in the evening. It was a really happy day. Next morning, comforted by my room and the unexpected delights of the last two days, I gathered myself, sat down at my table in the window and wrote to Patrick.

I wasn't very successful. Nothing I wanted to say seemed to fit together very well. There was a missing piece somewhere, I couldn't seem to get a hold of. I produced several quite different letters, all of which ended up in the wastepaper basket. Finally, I wrote a short note telling him what had happened on the Ormeau Road and where I was to be found. As I wrote his Lisdoonvarna address on the envelope, it occurred to me he might be in Rathfarnham, so I wrote another note, just in case, and went out and posted them both.

I had a reply from Rathfarnham by return. I was surprised by his promptness, but even more surprised that he suggested we meet for lunch in Belfast the following week. He named a day, a time, and a place and asked me to let him know at Rathfarnham if it would fit in with my lectures. If not, he'd come on the nearest possible day that suited me, or on the following Saturday.

The Wednesday he named presented no difficulties as far as lectures were concerned, rather, my problem was trying to work out why he had suddenly suggested a meeting. I could see that things might seem easier now I was no longer living at home, but if it was merely a question of meeting for lunch, surely we could have managed that any time in the last five months. So why now?

Perhaps my tension was more obvious than I realised as the week passed, or it may have been Ben was on the lookout for any signs of delayed shock. Whatever the reason, the day before my meeting with Patrick, he suggested we drive to the coast the next afternoon. The weather had turned mild and as his mother never taught on a Wednesday afternoon, she'd offered him the car. She'd actually said she thought a spot of sea air would do us good.

Panic swept over me as he laid out his plan. I'd rehearsed what I would say if he suggested something that clashed with Patrick's coming, but at the moment he spoke all I'd planned went right out of my head.

'I've got to go into town on Wednesday, Ben. Sorry.'

My voice sounded peculiar and I knew he couldn't help but notice.

'Shopping?'

'Er . . . no. No, actually I . . . I've to meet someone for lunch. Professor McDonagh,' I added hastily. 'He's just passing through. We could meet in the evening if you like.'

I felt a rush of colour to my face. I hate telling lies at the best of times and I couldn't bear the thought of lying to Ben. There was a strange look about him which I couldn't read. I just didn't know whether he believed me or not. I wasn't even sure I wanted him to believe me, but once I'd started I had to carry it through. I said I'd meet him in the union as soon as dinner was over on Wednesday evening.

I had to leave him then rather abruptly for a lecture in the department. I hurried off feeling miserable and upset, dashed up the stairs as the clock struck the hour, glanced at the Fourth Year notice board as I hurried past and had to stop when I saw a note pinned up with my name on it. I grabbed it and unfolded it as soon as I found a seat. 'Elizabeth Stewart – The professor would like to see you in his study immediately after his lecture.'

Another wave of panic hit me as I tried in vain to concentrate on the diffusion of agriculture in the ancient Near East. By the end of the professor's lecture I felt so dreadful I had to go downstairs to the loos and drink a glass of water before I could face returning to the first floor and knocking on his door.

He was standing by the window lighting his pipe when I went in, brows furrowed with concentration. My thesis lay on his desk in its expensive, shiny binding. Pushing it to one side and reaching for a large ashtray, he smiled and told me to sit down. It dawned on me the irritability he was displaying might relate to the lighting of his pipe.

'I understand you've had some difficulty with your thesis, Miss Stewart?'

My heart sank. It was my thesis after all.

'Yes, I'm afraid I found it difficult to say all I had to say in the space available.'

To my amazement, he laughed. He said it was rather better to be faced with that problem than spinning out a few half-baked ideas and precious little evidence to cover the pages necessary. Then he tilted his chair, chewed the end of his pipe and said abruptly: 'I met Frank McDonagh in Cork last weekend. Nice man. Knew his work, but not him. You seem to have made an impression there. How did you do that?'

I told him about the two days' work in Lisara, the stories we'd listened to, and how I'd noticed similarities with fragments I'd heard as a child in the border areas of Armagh. He listened carefully, nodding, but what he said next took me completely by surprise.

'Of course, we've precious little here in the way of research grants, and naturally a certain amount hangs on your Finals, but we ought to start thinking what you do next. The English universities have more in the way of grants, particularly Oxford and Cambridge, but there's money about if you can produce a subject that looks good on paper. Once you've been accepted, you can then go and do what you actually want to do. Would you be interested?'

I left his study half an hour later with a list of references, the names of possible fund-awarding bodies and details of the temporary jobs available at the new Ulster Folk Museum where I could do something interesting on a reasonable salary while I worked out a detailed research proposal. I was so excited I immediately thought of trying to find Ben to share my good news. Then I remembered how awkwardly we'd parted and decided I had better stick to the plan we'd made.

Getting through the next twenty-four hours till it was time to go into town for my lunch with Patrick was almost unbearable. I tried desperately to work, but ended up doing my washing and ironing to help me get through the hours and not waste them completely. I had a long, leisurely bath before bed and then spent half the night tossing and turning. Or so it seemed. Next morning was even worse. I don't have many clothes, but for the first time in my life, I changed three times before I finally made up my mind what I was going to wear.

In the end, I chose a checked skirt with a plain wool sweater, a dark jacket, high heels and a pretty silky scarf. I surveyed my efforts in the long mirror of my wardrobe hoping that I looked poised and in command of myself, but the figure who solemnly returned my gaze, though very neat, was far from poised. I had to admit it looked decidedly uneasy.

I knew the hotel in Royal Avenue, but I'd never been beyond the plate-glass doors before. My high heels sank into the thick carpet and I tried not to blink in the battery of spotlights which had been carefully positioned to reflect from the tall, highly decorated mirrors. I walked towards the reception desk, my eye upon the heavily made-up woman who stood there smiling automatically, and rather too brightly, at the business-men who paused to collect their keys or pick up long envelopes with travel reservations.

Before I reached her with my carefully practised request for Mr Delargy, a hand touched my arm and Patrick stood at my side.

'My goodness, you are looking well. No ill-effects at all from your adventures?'

'No, not at all. I'm fine.'

I had been through this moment a hundred times. I had done my best to imagine my possible reactions as some preparation for the event itself. Now the moment had come and gone. We were walking through to the bar to have a sherry and I had no idea at all how I felt.

Certainly, Patrick was no different from the man I met in Lisdoonvarna six long months ago. Smiling, courteous, easy to talk to, interested in whatever I had to say, it was as if we had never been apart. Then it struck me that perhaps we'd never really been together.

Lunch was very good. After all the agitations of the morning I discovered how very hungry I was. We enjoyed the food and we enjoyed our conversation, as we had enjoyed meals and talk together in Limerick and Galway and in Patrick's own home. I almost began to wonder what the problem was with the letters, when he was so clearly the same person I had known in the summer.

Time was passing and I was perfectly aware he had no plans to stay overnight. I could not bring myself to ask him why he had suggested we meet, but I could have spared myself that particular anxiety. The waiter left us our coffee, he poured mine, handed it to me and looked at me very directly.

'There is something I must say to you, Elizabeth. You know that, don't you?'

'Yes, of course.'

All the old anxieties returned with a rush. I sat trying to

behave normally, though my mind was in a state of complete turmoil.

'You know, this has been a very strange year for me. Full of experiences I could never have guessed at, if you'd asked me. And most of them nice.'

He paused and smiled at me and for the first time I felt something of the old intimacy that had been between us.

'When you came into my life, you showed me just how sad and empty it had become. Because of you, I came to see how much I needed a companion, someone to share my life with. Love is a very important thing, a great gift, but companionship is very precious too. I've decided, Elizabeth, that I want to marry.'

For a moment I could say absolutely nothing. I felt stunned, distressed, overwhelmed. I couldn't possibly make up my mind to marry him. Not now. Not ever perhaps, however much I might believe I loved him. But before I could say anything, he took my hand and went on speaking.

'Perhaps you've guessed something was changing over the winter, for you are so sensitive to what goes on between people. You know I've been staying regularly in Rathfarnham, in my cousin's house. What you didn't know is that Alexander was killed in a car crash five years ago. Rosemary has been coping on her own ever since.'

Already, I could see what was coming, but I said nothing, wanting to hear him say what he had to say.

'Rosemary and I have known each other for many, many years. She was an only child so her mother sent her to spend her holidays with our family in Clare. Rosemary's older than I am and when she went and married Alexander at eighteen I was furious because she had just started teaching me to sketch,' he went on, laughing easily. 'We've always got on well, but it's only in these last months I've realised how much we could give each other. The difference in age doesn't seem to matter very much as one gets older.'

Suddenly, it all fitted into place. The increasingly frequent visits to Rathfarnham, the long letters to me full of cuttings, and news, and interest in my activities, but nothing which touched on what we'd had together. All my unease that there was something wrong had been justified, that something precious was closing, coming to an end, dying. Not my love for him, or even perhaps his love for me, but the possibility of making a life together. Patrick and I could not make a life together because he had his life already made. It was a life Rosemary knew well and could share. But I couldn't. To me it was distant, remote from anything I knew or would choose for myself. Besides, I wanted a life made with someone I loved, a life worked out a bit at a time, changing and shaping as we changed, not a life I could step into ready-made like a garment, just needing a small adjustment here or there to make it fit perfectly.

Tears came trickling down my cheeks. I didn't tell him they were tears of relief but I said how very happy I was for him. That I always cried at weddings. After a moment, he smiled. It must have been clear by then that I was taking it well. I saw the relief flow over him as I blew my nose and poured us both more coffee.

'When will you be married, Patrick?'

'Very soon. We hope to go to America to visit relatives immediately after. You can guess I'll need to be back before the summer season and there will be a lot of work to do on my house.'

I drank my coffee gratefully, amazed that I could look at him quite steadily, the man who had once held me in his arms and wanted to ask me to marry him. Suddenly, it felt as if I was standing a long, long way away, watching two people having lunch in a hotel dining room. Two people who had once intersected for a moment in time, touched each other, changed each other, and were now moving past and away to lead lives so different, soon it would be hard to imagine how they had ever once intersected.

Chapter 25

Dinner that evening was interminable. The moment it ended I grabbed my coat, hurried down the steps outside and sprinted to the bus stop. I paused only a moment to see if there might be one coming, but there wasn't, so I kept going, walking so fast I got a stitch in my side. I arrived breathless at the door of the union just after seven-thirty.

I stepped inside and scanned the few figures drinking coffee at this quiet time between late suppers and mid-evening breaks from work in the library. There was no sign of Ben. I stood poised, undecided. If I went to meet him from the Ormeau Road bus I might miss him, but the thought of waiting a moment longer was more than I could bear.

I turned to go out again so hastily I nearly fell over him in the doorway. For a moment, I hardly recognised him, he looked so pale and tired. There were dark smudges under his eyes and a droop to his shoulders that was quite unlike him.

'Ben, are you all right?'

'Yes, yes, I'm fine.'

'It's not your mother ill again, is it?'

'No, she's grand. She's not looked back since the op,' he muttered, evading my gaze.

Whatever was upsetting Ben, the echoing emptiness of the

union wasn't going to help. We needed somewhere a lot more private.

'Ben, I've been to the bank. Let's go to the Lilac Room. My treat.'

We headed for the coffee bar without another word, parked ourselves in the furthest corner and ordered cappuccinos.

'Look, Ben. I told you a lie yesterday and it really upset me, but I couldn't explain then. Can I tell you about it now?'

He nodded, but still wouldn't look at me. I had never seen him so utterly dejected. The only thing to do was get on with it, so I told him all about Patrick, how he wanted to ask me to marry him, and how he'd felt I had to have time to choose the life I wanted.

'And he gave you six months?'

'No, there wasn't a time limit. I didn't know I was going to see him today until I had his letter last week.'

'And you're going to marry him?'

'No, of course I'm not. He's going to marry his cousin's widow, a woman called Rosemary, with three sons.'

'But he can't marry her if *you* love him.'

'Why not?'

He looked at me in amazement. He was still very pale, but a little colour was now creeping back into his face.

'Ben dear, one thing Patrick did teach me is that though you can love someone, truly love them, that isn't always a good reason for marrying them. It depends on whether you want to make a life with them and what the chances are that you'll be able to manage it if you do.'

'I want to make a life with you, Lizzie,' he said firmly, looking me straight in the eyes at last.

Said in that plain, unvarnished way of his I knew he meant it.

'Ben,' I began, laughing, 'am I to take that as a proposal or a proposition?'

He smiled at last. The whole set of his body changed and the light came back into his eyes.

'I thought I'd had it,' he confessed, 'that you were going to marry him and I'd never see you again. I couldn't bear that, Lizzie.'

'But, Ben, neither could I.'

Two weeks later, we did have our afternoon out. It was a breezy March day with glints of sun and we walked on the beach at Brown's Bay until our faces were frozen. Then we sat in the car drinking tea from a thermos, looking out at the grey-green mass of the Irish Sea, watching the ferries plough their way back and forth to Stranraer.

'D'you think we'll cross water, Ben?'

'Could do. But there's my year in the Royal next year. After that I'm free to go anywhere that'll take me. There's a big hospital in Oxford called the Radcliffe. I could try that.'

'But would you be happy in Oxford if I can get a grant?'

'I'd be happy anywhere so long as you're there.'

We sat silent, watching the gulls skim the white-capped water and a man throwing a stick for a black Labrador puppy.

'I wish we could live together,' he said suddenly.

'So do I.'

'Probably all right if we got to Oxford. Not much chance in Belfast though, unless we got married.'

'You don't sound very enthusiastic about the idea,' I protested.

'Oh Lizzie, come off it. Just think what your dear mother would say if I turn up on the doorstep next week to ask your dad for your hand in marriage. It's the stuff of comedy.

A medical student. Penniless. With a year before I earn anything.'

'Well, we could try an experiment and let me ask your mother for your hand in marriage. If I get that job with the Folk Museum, I'd have a salary. And there's always Uncle Albert to bail us out.'

'So you think it's a good idea?'

'Worth considering.'

'Marriage without prejudice?'

'What d'you mean, "without prejudice"?'

'I mean not letting the whole business get in our way, like so many of the people we know. If we decide to get married let's be clear it's to make our life easier, not to satisfy other people's conventions or expectations. I don't need a wife, Lizzie, and you don't need a husband. We just want to be with each other.'

He took my plastic mug, parked it on the dashboard and drew me into his arms. It was some time before we came up for air and were able to go on with our conversation.

'If we do decide to get married and we have a bun fight afterwards, let's invite the Brigadier,' I said lightly.

'Only one problem.'

'What?'

'He's an Air Commodore.'

I wound my arms around him. 'Let's invite him anyway.'

Chapter 26

Flat 2b
Marlbrough Park North
Belfast,
25 July, 1961.

My dear Mary and Paddy,

It was lovely to get your letter and to know you're both well and that the weather's held up for the peat and the thatch. It was great that Larry was able to come over for a few days and help you. I loved your stories, Mary, about his little boy 'helping'. I wonder what he'll tell his nursery teacher when he goes back to school in Manchester?

You asked for my news. Well, there's a lot of it. I can't quite believe how much has happened in such a short time, but the biggest news of all is that we are getting married on August 10th, which is Ben's birthday. He says that way he won't be able to forget our wedding anniversary!

My mother, as you know, was not pleased when Ben and I got engaged, but my father has been very generous. A few weeks ago he got a big cheque from the insurance people for the damage to the shop and flat and he gave me the money for a second-hand car on condition I didn't tell her.

I wonder if you can guess what's coming next?

We've been lent a cottage in the Mournes for a week's honeymoon, but we have a second week before my job with the Folk Museum begins. I want to bring Ben down to meet you and all the people I told him about last year when I was with you.

We don't want to make extra work for you, Mary, we could stay in a bed-and-breakfast, but I know you'll tell me what suits you best. Ben is a great hand at peeling spuds. I don't think you'd feel you had a stranger in the place.

I wish so much you could be at our wedding, but I know it's not possible. I'll keep you some cake and bring the photos with me when we come. Did I tell you Geoffrey will be in Dublin in August and is coming up to be our photographer? I'm sure he'll come to Clare while we're with you. Maybe we can persuade you to take the cards out again for us all. You've been right about most things so far!

There's more to tell, but I must stop now. As you see I've moved into the flat we've found and there's such a lot to do. I'm supposed to be stripping walls this morning while Ben's in town buying paint so I'll tell you the rest when I see you.

All my love,
Elizabeth.

I put my letter in its envelope, wrote the address and parked it on the mantelpiece. Brilliant sunlight streamed into the empty room making patches of brightness on the yellowed wallpaper and the bare floorboards. I went to the window and looked out. Above the heavy canopy of the chestnuts that lined the avenue, the edge of the Antrim hills cut a sharp line across the vivid sky. From the overgrown shrubbery below me the song of a blackbird soared effortlessly above the muffled noise of traffic on the nearby Lisburn Road.

As I turned back to the empty room, seeing it transformed, fresh and bright, full of the things we had found for it, Uncle Albert's clock on the mantelpiece, Ben's bookcases in the alcoves, I heard the doorbell. As it echoed up the deep stairwell of the old Victorian villa, I counted. Three rings.

'It is. It is. He's early,' I said out loud, as I ran downstairs to open the door.

Mare's Milk

Barbara Esstman

Spring 1947: Nora Mahler's son, Simon, died aged only seventeen in a fall from a mare that he and his mother had loved almost as another child. And with his death the family falls into an abyss of grief from which it seems they may never emerge.

Neal, Simon's father, destroys the animal that killed his son, although it is the one creature that could have helped his distraught wife heal herself, and leaves the farm that has been home to Nora's family for generations, taking their only surviving child with him. Nora, trapped in a fog of despair, is unable to stop him.

She must find again the strength of spirit that twenty years earlier drew her to Ozzie Kline, a farmhand from the wrong side of the tracks, her first love and the man she should have married; the man who may now be able to show her the way home . . .

0 7472 5595 4

HEADLINE

Cloud Mountain

Aimee Liu

In California of 1906, where it is a crime for them even to touch, Hope Newfield and Leong Po-yo fall desperately in love. Defying every taboo, this independent American woman and the aristocratic young Chinese man from Wuchang decide to marry. But in the coming years, as they move from San Francisco to China and start to raise a family, their love is tested by prejudice, by revolution, by conflicting loyalties and by their own drastically different traditions.

Inspired by the true story of Aimee Liu's grandparents, CLOUD MOUNTAIN is set against the vast panorama of turn-of-the-century America, China's brutal Warlord era, and the two World Wars – a moving and unforgettable love story.

'Riveting, romantic and readable' *Independent*

'This powerful saga that stretches continents and spans generations is impressive' *Belfast Telegraph*

0 7472 5852 X

HEADLINE